Meet the crew . . .

NATHAN "NATE" FORD ("The Mastermind"): Former insurance fraud investigator who leads the team and calls the shots.

SOPHIE DEVEREAUX ("The Grifter"): British wannabe actress. Onstage, she's no award-winner, but running a con, she makes brilliant use of her skills with character and accents to manipulate the marks.

ALEC HARDISON ("The Hacker"): The crew's computer specialist, hacker, and all-around techno-geek who handles communications and info gathering.

ELIOT SPENCER ("The Hitter"): Ex-soldier, martial artist, and hard case who takes care of team security.

PARKER ("The Thief"): Master thief, cat burglar, pickpocket, and safecracker with a dark past. If it has a lock, she can open it.

The Leverage Novels

THE CON JOB
THE ZOO JOB
THE BESTSELLER JOB

LEVERAGE

THE BESTSELLER JOB

GREG COX

BERKLEY BOULEVARD BOOKS, NEW YORK

THE BERKLEY PUBLISHING GROUP
Published by the Penguin Group
Penguin Group (USA) Inc.
375 Hudson Street, New York, New York 10014, USA

USA I Canada I UK I Ireland I Australia I New Zealand I India I South Africa I China

Penguin Books Ltd., Registered Offices: 80 Strand, London WC2R 0RL, England
For more information about the Penguin Group, visit penguin.com.

THE BESTSELLER JOB

A Berkley Boulevard Book / published by arrangement with
Leverage Holdings, Inc., and Greg Cox

Berkley Boulevard Books are published by The Berkley Publishing Group.
Berkley Boulevard and its logo are registered trademarks of Penguin Group (USA) Inc.
For information, address: The Berkley Publishing Group
a division of Penguin Group (USA) Inc.
375 Hudson Street, New York 10014

ISBN: 978-0-425-25385-4

PUBLISHING HISTORY
Berkley Boulevard mass-market edition / May 2013

PRINTED IN THE UNITED STATES OF AMERICA

10 9 8 7 6 5 4 3 2

Interior text design by Laura K. Corless.
Cover design by Jason Gill.

MANHATTAN

Gavin Lee's wrist hurt.

After autographing books all night at his favorite midtown bookstore, until his signature devolved into an indecipherable scrawl, he never wanted to sign anything again—or at least not until the big book tour started next week. The line for his autograph had stretched all the way out to the sidewalk and he had felt obliged to keep on signing until closing time. Who knew so many people still read books these days? He had even signed the backs of a few ebook readers.

Still, he couldn't complain. At this point, *Assassins Never Forget* had been climbing the bestseller lists for weeks now and only seemed to be gaining in popularity. Not bad for a first novel by a relatively obscure photojournalist. A poster in the store window proudly displayed

Gavin's author photo, showing a trim, thirtysomething young man with short blond hair and some decorative stubble. He shook his head in disbelief, still not used to seeing his photo everywhere. To be honest, it was more than he—or Denise—had ever anticipated.

Which reminded him . . .

Standing on the sidewalk in front of the store, after all the well-wishers and bookstore staff had finally dispersed, he fished his phone from his pocket and dialed his girlfriend. She picked up right away.

"Gavin?"

"Hi there," he said. "Just wanted to let you know that I'm running a little late."

"The signing a big success?" she asked.

"A mob scene." He looked forward to telling her all about it. "You should've seen it."

"Uh-uh," she demurred. Shy of crowds, she seldom attended his public appearances. "I'll take your word for it."

"It's a trip, I admit. All those people, so excited about the book . . . and hungry for a piece of the author."

"Better you than me," she insisted. "You heading home now?"

"You bet." He glanced at his watch and saw that it was already well past eleven. Their apartment was several blocks away on Bank Street. With any luck, he'd be home before long.

"You going to catch a cab?" she asked.

"Nah. It's a nice night. I think I'll walk."

"Well, be careful. Watch your back."

He smiled at her concern. Like he had never walked home late at night before. "Will do. Should I swing by an all-night market and pick up something? You need any-thing?"

"Just you," she said, her voice adopting a sultry tease. "Assuming your adoring public left me anything."

"Never fear. I saved all the best parts for you." He imagined her waiting for him in their cozy one-bedroom apartment and felt warm despite the crisp night air. "Just hold that thought."

"I will," she promised. "And, Gavin, I'm serious. Be careful, okay?"

He heard the genuine worry in her voice. He knew better than to dismiss it.

"Always. See you soon, sweetie."

Putting his phone away, he took a moment to orient himself. The store was on West Twenty-third Street, about a dozen blocks north of the Village. He took off down the sidewalk.

Traffic cruised past him on Eighth Avenue. For a second, he considered the taxi option again, but decided against it. It felt good to stretch his legs after sitting behind a shrinking stack of hardcovers all night. The cool spring night was a pleasant change from the hot, overcrowded bookshop. He hummed quietly to himself as he made his way down the street. A slight limp, left over from that ambush in Somalia, barely slowed him down, although his days of dashing about war zones were probably over.

Good thing I have this "bestselling author" thing to fall back on, he thought. *Wonder when we're going to start seeing some serious royalties.*

It was a weeknight, so the sidewalks, if not totally deserted, were hardly crammed with pedestrians. Even the traffic was sparse this time of night. A cool breeze stirred up the litter in the gutters. Horns honked a couple blocks over. A siren blared in the distance. Years of navigating dicey neighborhoods all over the globe, along with his promise to Denise, kept him alert to his surroundings. He knew she wasn't wrong to be worried. They were playing a dangerous game.

What if it blows up in our faces—literally?

He heard footsteps behind him, keeping pace with his own. A glance back over his shoulder revealed a stocky-looking bruiser whose face was shadowed by the brim of a baseball cap. He loped after Gavin, keeping his gaze turned toward the pavement. His hands were buried in the pockets of a rumpled windbreaker. For all Gavin knew, one or both of those hands was clutching a weapon.

A chill ran down the back of Gavin's neck. The title of the book he had been signing all night flashed through his brain:

Assassins Never Forget.

He was probably just being paranoid, but why take chances? He quickened his pace, hoping to put a little more distance between himself and his (inadvertent?) tail. A taxi was sounding better and better, but now that he actually wanted one, he looked in vain for an unoccupied cab. Darkened storefronts, guarded by iron bars and pull-down metal shutters, offered little in the way of shelter should he need to get off the street in a hurry. He searched his own pockets for something to defend himself with, just in case, but found only his favorite Sharpie.

Great, he thought sarcastically. Whoever said the pen was mightier than the sword had obviously never been stalked down a lonely city street by a guy who looked like he could go nine rounds with Bigfoot. *Next time I arrange for an escort home.*

If there was a next time . . .

He risked another backward glance. If anything, the other guy appeared to be gaining on him. Gavin glanced around; all of a sudden they had the sidewalk all to themselves. He considered cutting across to Seventh, which was likely to be more heavily populated at this hour, but would his pursuer let him get that far? Gavin mentally calculated the distance to home.

Only five or six more blocks to go.

An intersection beckoned up ahead. The crosswalk signal was already flashing, but if he hurried he might be able to make it before the light changed—and leave the other guy on the wrong side of DON'T WALK. If nothing else, he could find out just how determined the hulking stranger was to keep up with him. Surging forward, he reached the curb and looked both ways to make sure nobody was running the light. A black stretch limo was idling to the right. The driver signaled him to go ahead.

Thanks, buddy, Gavin thought sincerely. *You have no idea.*

A heavy tread approached from behind, sounding even closer than before. Gavin stepped out in front of the limo— which hit the gas at the worst possible moment. Its engine roared.

The limo hit Gavin head-on. His body went flying into the street.

His wrist stopped hurting.

|||||| ONE ||||||

BOSTON

"'Overblown'? 'Self-indulgent'? 'Sublimely awful'?" Sophie Devereaux stared indignantly at the screen of the laptop, which rested atop their usual table at McRory's Bar and Grill. A posh English accent added class to her outrage. She turned toward Nate Ford, who was sitting next to her, nursing his second scotch, even though it was barely lunchtime. "Can you believe these reviews?"

He tried to pivot the laptop away from her. "Just some random opinions on the Internet," he said, dismissing them. "You shouldn't even bother with them. What do those people know?"

"But it's not fair, Nate. I put my heart and soul into that show, you know that. How many actresses can play Cleopatra, Joan of Arc, Madame Curie, *and* Mata Hari in one night?" A classically beautiful brunette, stylishly attired in a striped Jersey-knit sweater and slacks, she spun the screen back toward her. "And yet some snarky hack at *Boston Theater Buzz* says that my one-woman show had, quote, one so-called actress too many." She sighed theatrically. "Small wonder the show closed after only a single night, after hatchet jobs like that!"

"It's a crime," he agreed, none too convincingly. Unruly hair and a rumpled sport jacket belied his razor-sharp mind. A careworn face hinted at his tragic past, which included a dead child and a failed marriage—in that order. Shrewd brown eyes glanced at his watch. "So what's keeping our prospective new client?"

Sophie ignored his transparent attempt to change the subject. She turned toward the third member of their party. "What do you think, Eliot? Tell me the truth. Was my performance truly 'more cheesy than aged Havarti'?"

Damn, Eliot Spencer thought. His perpetual scowl deepened. A mane of long, brown hair framed his surly expression. A scruffy goatee carpeted his chin. He was dressed more casually than either Nate or Sophie, in a flannel shirt and jeans. A weathered windbreaker was draped over the back of his chair. *I was hoping to stay out of this.*

Post-traumatic flashbacks of being trapped in a stuffy hole-in-the-wall theater while Sophie emoted for the ages surfaced from the darkest recesses of his memory, where he had done his best to bury them. That had been a long night; Afghanistan and North Korea had been breezes by comparison. No way was he telling her the truth about her acting. *I'm a hitter, not a sadist.*

"You have a very . . . distinctive . . . style," he said diplomatically. "Not everybody gets it."

"You see!" she said, vindicated. "That's just what I'm saying. So which of my portrayals did you find most convincing? Cleopatra? Saint Joan?"

"Er, I honestly couldn't choose." He concentrated on his calamari, avoiding her eyes. Truth to tell, he hadn't been able to tell the characters apart. "They were all very . . . you."

"But you must have some preference," she pressed. "Please. I'm certainly open to *constructive* criticism."

He looked to Nate for assistance. *Help me out here, man,* he thought, but their ringleader stared pensively into the amber depths of his scotch, apparently content to let Eliot take the heat. *Sorry,* Eliot thought. *That's not how we're playing this.*

"I don't know," he said. "What do you think, Nate?"

Nate shot him a dirty look.

Tough, Eliot thought. *You're the one who's sleeping with her. Sometimes. Maybe.*

He had given up trying to figure out Nate and Sophie's relationship, whatever it was. He figured it was none of his business, as long as it didn't cause trouble on the job. Bad enough that Parker and Hardison were kinda, sorta a couple these days. The last thing this crew needed was boyfriend/girlfriend crap getting in the way of staying in one piece. In his experience, emotions and missions didn't mix. That's why he kept his private life private.

"Yes," she said. "What about you, Nate? You know my work better than anyone."

Nate squirmed uncomfortably in his seat. "Well, I'm biased, of course, but—"

The door to the bar swung open, letting in a gust of cold air and an attractive redhead who looked to be in her midthirties. A scuffed leather jacket, turtleneck sweater, and jeans flattered her slim, athletic figure. A canvas tote bag hung from her grip. Henna tinted her long red hair. Emerald eyes were rimmed with red, as though she had been crying recently. Dark shadows under her eyes suggested that she hadn't been sleeping well. A small brass compass dangled on a chain around her neck.

"Ah, here's our client," Nate announced, sounding more than a little relieved by the timely interruption. "Only a few minutes late."

And none too soon, Eliot thought.

The woman glanced around the bar uncertainly before her gaze lighted on Eliot and the others. She headed toward them. Eliot sat up straighter. He didn't usually do the initial meeting with the client, but this time was different. He should've met this particular woman years ago.

"You must be Eliot," Denise Gallo said. "I recognize you from Gavin's photos."

"Likewise." He stood up and pulled out a chair for her, then introduced her to Nate and Sophie. "I'm sorry I couldn't make the funeral."

They had been running a con in Rajasthan when he'd gotten word that Gavin Lee had died in a hit-and-run accident in Manhattan. With Nate busy fixing a camel race, and the water rights to a crucial oasis at stake, hopping a plane back to the States for the memorial service simply hadn't been an option.

Not even for an old friend.

SEVERAL YEARS AGO:

The terrorist camp was hidden deep in the Sumatran rain forest. A lush green canopy shielded the compound from aerial surveillance. Hanging roots and vines, slowly choking the life from the trees that hosted them, added to the dense foliage sheltering the camouflaged base, which consisted of a large command center surrounded by several smaller outbuildings, including weapons depots and munitions dumps. As was common in Indonesia, the wooden structures were supported by stilts that lifted them ten to twelve feet above the jungle floor. Ladders, which could be withdrawn to deter intruders, provided the only means of access. Spiky vines covered the rooftops. Sentries, armed with black-market AK-47s, patrolled the perimeter.

Bamboo, palms, ferns, and creepers encroached on the camp from all sides. The abundant flora surrounding the camp was a two-edged sword. While it effectively insulated the compound from the outside world, it also made it easier to approach the camp undetected. A moonless night filled the gaps between the trees and underbrush with impenetrable black shadows. Monkeys capered through the overhanging branches, squeaking in the night. Nocturnal predators rustled through the jungle.

Some of them were human.

Eliot Spencer, a fresh-faced young American soldier, lay belly down in the ferns and vines abutting the compound. Cradling a Heckler & Koch MP5 submachine gun, he spied on the terrorist base. His hair was short, his features clean-cut. Green camouflage paint, masking his features, matched his jungle gear, which bore no identifying insignia. Only recently inducted into Special Forces from the regular army, he was primed for action.

His recon team had located the base a few hours ago. After a terse, hushed huddle, it had been decided to clean out the compound now before the terrorists could use it to stage more attacks and bombings on civilian targets and foreign nationals. At this very moment, the rest of the six-man team were taking up positions in preparation for an all-out assault on the central command center. The plan was to go in hard and fast before the rebels even knew what hit them. With any luck, the team would take out the whole nest in a matter of minutes, and maybe even capture vital intel on the guerrillas' plans and support systems. Eliot judged the potential rewards well worth the risk.

Too bad he was stuck babysitting.

Gavin Lee crouched beside Eliot, armed only with a machete and his favorite camera. The young photojournalist had been embedded with the Special Forces team for a couple of weeks now, much to Eliot's annoyance. Sure, Gavin seemed like a stand-up guy, who had endured the rigors of a jungle tour without complaint, but who in their right mind thought sticking a civilian into a military operation was a good idea? Eliot could only imagine what kind of strings had been pulled to get Gavin assigned to their unit in the first place.

"What's happening?" Gavin whispered. He wore an olive-green safari jacket with plenty of pouches for his film. His alert eyes scanned the camp as though he were already

taking pictures with his mind. The moist, tropical heat bathed his face in sweat. "When do the fireworks start?"

Eliot shot him a dirty look. He placed a finger before his lips.

Damn it, *he thought, scowling at the photographer's loose lips.* Remind me never to work with civilians again.

To his credit, Gavin got the message and shut up. He hunkered down into the greenery, keeping his head low. Eliot gestured for him to stay down.

That's more like it, *he thought.* I've got work to do.

A weapons depot rose up on stilts a few yards away. A bored-looking sentry, his rifle slung over his shoulder, stood guard over the tower. The guard munched on a durian, the spiky, foul-smelling fruit that was a staple of the local diet. Eliot could smell the pungent odor from where he was hiding. It made his gorge rise.

The guard finished up his snack and tossed the rind into the bushes, barely missing Eliot. Hefting his gun, he sighed wearily as he resumed his rounds.

Right on schedule, *Eliot thought.*

He waited until the guard had trudged past him before rising up from the brush like a ghost. Slipping out of the jungle, he crept up on the sentry from behind. He had left his rifle behind with Gavin; this exercise required speed and stealth, not firepower. Noise was the enemy.

The sentry didn't hear him coming. Eliot grabbed the guard's gun arm to keep the weapon pointed away from him, then clasped his other hand over the guard's mouth to stifle any cries. Yanking the man's head back exposed his throat to a forearm strike that silenced him long enough for

Eliot to drag him backward onto the ground, where his head hit the earth with a muffled thud. The impact stunned the guard, allowing Eliot to wrench the AK-47 from his grasp. He slammed the butt of the weapon into the man's skull. The sentry went limp.

The whole takedown had taken less than a minute.

So much for that, *Eliot thought.*

Confident that the sentry had been neutralized, Eliot sprinted over to his main objective: the elevated weapons depot. Moving with practiced skill and efficiency, he attached a wad of C4 explosive to the nearest stilt. The timer was set to go off in a matter of minutes, right before his fellow commandos stormed the compound. The result would be one heck of a distraction, not to mention maximum shock and awe.

Least I'm doing something useful, *he thought.* Besides babysitting.

"Eliot! Behind you!"

He spun around to see that a second guard had arrived unexpectedly, possibly to relieve the first. Rifle in hand, he was creeping up on Eliot. It was unclear if he intended to kill or capture the intruder, but he already had the drop on him. The young soldier found himself looking down the barrel of the man's AK-47, even as the timer on the C4 counted down behind him.

This was not good.

A flashbulb went off in the jungle, distracting the sentry. Startled, he swung his gun toward the flash, away from Eliot.

Eliot saw his chance. Snatching his combat knife from its sheath, he hurled it at the sentry's exposed back. The six-inch stainless-steel blade lodged deep between the man's shoulder blades. He fell forward, his rifle firing wildly into the jungle.

Gavin!

Shouts arose from the command center. Eliot didn't need to check his watch to know that the C4 was going off any second now. He scrambled away from the elevated platform, diving for cover. The weapons depot exploded with a deafening boom, lighting up the rebel base and the surrounding rain forest with billowing red flames. Smoking debris rained on the grounds. The shock wave buffeted Eliot. His ears were ringing.

"Gavin!" he shouted over the din. "Gavin?"

All hell broke loose. Explosive charges blew away the stilts supporting the command center, which toppled over onto the ground. Special Forces, almost invisible in their camo gear and night-vision goggles, charged the ruins of the center, opening fire on the disoriented survivors, who scrambled from the wreckage only to be met by grenades, smoke bombs, and automatic weapons fire. Caught by surprise, and battered by the crash and explosions, the disorganized guerrillas were no match for the highly trained soldiers. Lifting his head from the ground, Eliot was glad to see that the good guys already had the terrorists on the ropes.

Mission accomplished.

But what about Gavin? Scrambling to his feet, Eliot plunged into the jungle in search of the reckless photog, who had definitely not kept his head down as instructed. Eliot braced himself for the sight of Gavin's bullet-riddled body.

Some babysitter I am, he thought.

To his relief, he found Gavin alive and well among the bamboo and ferns, frantically snapping photo after photo of the chaos engulfing the terrorist base. Eliot felt like punching him.

"What the hell were you thinking?" he shouted. "I told you to stay put!"

Gavin grinned at him. "You're welcome."

"That's not the point," Eliot said, even though he knew the other man had probably just saved his life. "You trying to get yourself killed?"

"Not going to happen."

Gavin lowered his camera and reached beneath his shirt. He drew out a small metallic object, about the size of a Cracker Jack prize, dangling from a chain around his neck. Looking closer, Eliot saw that it was a miniature compass.

"My lucky charm," Gavin explained. He tucked the compass back beneath his shirt. "Makes sure things always go in the right direction."

Eliot had to admit it. He liked the guy's attitude.

And he owed him one.

"Better hang on to it," he said.

"It's fine," Denise assured him. Her slender fingers toyed with the compass on its chain. "Gavin would've understood. He knew what your life was like." She took off her coat and sat down at the table. "He always spoke highly of you."

"You, too." Guilt stabbed Eliot in the gut. Gavin and

Denise had been together for a couple of years; it wasn't right that he was only just now meeting her for the first time, and under these circumstances. "I always meant to visit you folks. Lord knows Gavin kept inviting me, but . . ."

"I know." Sorrow tinged her voice. "You think you have all the time in the world and then . . ." She choked back a sob. Her eyes welled with tears. "I'm sorry. It's just that, it's still so . . ."

Eliot instinctively placed his hand over hers. "It sucks what happened—and what's still happening."

"Why don't you tell us about it?" Nate suggested. He handed her a tissue. "Eliot told me something about your situation, but I'd like to hear it in your own words."

"Yes," Sophie said. "We all would."

"All right." Denise dabbed at her eyes. She took a moment to compose herself. "It's all about the book. *Assassins Never Forget.* Have you heard of it?"

"Hard to miss," Nate said. "It's a big bestseller, isn't it?"

"More than we ever imagined." She reached into her tote bag and took out a thick hardcover with Gavin's photo on the back. "Months on the *New York Times* list. Book clubs. Audio deals. Foreign translations. Major studios bidding for the movie rights. It would be a dream come true, if not for . . ."

Her voice trailed off.

"Gavin's accident," Nate prompted. "And his brother."

"His no-good, *estranged* brother," she said angrily. "It's ridiculous. Brad bullied Gavin when they were kids, then ditched him after their parents died. They'd hardly spoken for years. But now Brad has swooped in as next of kin to claim Gavin's literary estate."

"Cutting you out of the picture," Nate said.

She displayed her bare left hand. "No ring, no will, no power of attorney." She shook her head. "I suppose that must sound incredibly foolish and irresponsible now, but we had no kids, and before *Assassins* hit it big, not much in the way of assets to worry about. We always meant to get our legal house in order, one of these days, but like I said, we thought we had all the time in the world . . ."

Nate handed her another tissue.

"So now I'm just the girlfriend," she added bitterly. "And Brad, of all people, gets to profit from Gavin's success."

"Even though you had plenty to do with the book as well," Nate said.

"You could say that, I guess."

"Don't be modest," Sophie said. "Eliot told us all about it. You were Gavin's unofficial collaborator, researcher, and editor. You read every draft, offered your input, encouraged him to keep writing . . ."

Denise nodded. "We slaved over that book, together. It was our whole lives."

"And now you're getting screwed by Gavin's loser of a brother," Eliot snarled. He had never met Brad Lee, but he'd heard about him from Gavin. Brad was an ex-con and small-time criminal who was nothing but an embarrassment to his more righteous younger brother. "That's not right. I know how much Gavin loved you. He would have wanted you taken care of."

"It's not just about the money," Denise insisted. "It's about Gavin's legacy, and everything we hoped to accomplish. *Assassins* isn't just a page-turner; it's an exposé, a fictionalized account of true events, meant to shine a light on the shadowy world of covert black-ops activities: arms smuggling, money laundering, illegal assassinations, wire-tappings, break-ins, renditions, etc." Her voice grew more heated; she was clearly passionate on the subject. "Gavin and I intended to use the book to raise public awareness of such abuses. We wanted to donate a majority of the pro-ceeds to human rights groups, but knowing Brad, he's just going to milk the book for all its worth—and maybe even hire some hack to churn out formulaic, action-packed se-quels with no real substance or content."

More tears leaked from her eyes. She placed a loving hand on Gavin's author photo. "We were going to make a difference, Mr. Ford. *Gavin* wanted to make a difference. You can't let Brad take that away."

"I get it," Nate said. "I have to wonder about that hit-and-run accident, though. Is it possible Brad was behind it?"

"His own brother?" Denise winced at the idea. "I don't want to think so, but . . ."

"We can't rule out that possibility," Eliot said, half hop-ing that Brad was responsible for his brother's death. Every time Eliot thought about Gavin being run down at some lonely street corner, he felt like hitting something. Hard and more than once.

Brad Lee might do.

"What about Gavin's agent?" Sophie asked. "Can't he do something?"

Denise shook her head. "He's sympathetic, but Gavin's name is on all the contracts. Legally at least, I'm nobody."

"Not to Gavin you weren't," Eliot said. He might not have seen Gavin in the flesh recently, but they had stayed in touch over the years. He knew how much Denise had meant to his friend. He glared fiercely at his partners. "C'mon, Nate, Sophie. We've got to do this. For Gavin."

"All right," Nate said, convinced. "Let's steal back a book."

Sophie's heart went out to Denise. As an artist herself, she could only imagine what it must feel like to lose a loved one, then see his artistic legacy squandered and corrupted. She wondered what sort of scam Nate had in mind to set things right. The Gypsy Blanket? The Donkey Round-about? Maybe even a variation on the Deaf-Mute Duchess?

That could be fun, she thought. *I haven't run that one in years.*

Sophie was a grifter, one of the best. "Sophie Devereaux" wasn't even her real name, but it suited her for now. Sometimes she almost forgot she had ever been anyone else.

Almost.

While Nate and Eliot picked Denise's brain a bit more, Sophie flipped through the hardcover copy of *Assassins Never Forget.* Not a bad title, she reflected, and sadly accurate in her experience. She'd survived her share of assassination attempts, both before and after she joined Nate's crew, and knew only too well how old enemies had a tendency to come sneaking out of the past when you least expected it. A healthy degree of paranoia was essential in their line of work.

In fact, was it just her imagination or did she suddenly feel as though she was being watched?

Tiny hairs prickled at the back of her neck as she lifted

her eyes from the book to discreetly scan the familiar bar. At first, all she saw were the usual regulars and a smattering of new customers caught up in their own affairs, but then her eyes made contact with those of a solitary stranger spying on her from a table by the front entrance. The man was thin and gangly, with pale skin sorely in need of a little sun. Horn-rim glasses, with lenses thick enough to serve as magnifying glasses, perched upon his nose. An olive-green hoodie partially concealed his face. A full glass of ale sat neglected before him. He looked away furtively, as though embarrassed at being caught peering at her. He thrust a smartphone into his pocket.

Sophie frowned. Granted, she was hardly unaccustomed to male attention, but was this fellow just another random admirer or something rather more ominous? Not wanting to alarm Denise, she kept her concerns to herself as she fished through her bag for her phone. If she could snap a photo of the peeper, Hardison could always run it through one of his comprehensive facial-recognition programs and see if this was anybody they needed to watch out for.

Better safe than sorry, she thought. *Now where the devil is that phone?*

"It was nice to meet you, Ms. Devereaux," Denise said, distracting her. "And thank you all so much for hearing me out."

"Our pleasure," Sophie said, taking her hand. She tried to keep one eye on the peeper, but then Eliot got up and helped Denise on with her coat, momentarily blocking Sophie's view. "And, please, call me Sophie."

"All right." Denise looked anxiously at Nate. "Keep me posted, okay?"

"Don't worry about it," he said. "We'll be in touch."

Eliot escorted her toward the door. Sophie scooted out from behind the table to peek around him, but a gust of cold air hinted that she was already too late.

Sure enough, the peeper was gone, leaving a nearly full glass of ale behind.

Nate noticed her staring at the empty table. "Something wrong?"

"I don't know," she said. "Perhaps."

TWO

BOSTON

"Dead-tree books are history," Alec Hardison insisted. He held up his plastic ebook reader. "See this? Digital is where it's at these days. We're talking the future of fiction, man. Nobody reads old-school paper books anymore."

Eliot shrugged. "I like real books. I like the way they feel."

"You're hopeless, you know that?" Hardison rolled his eyes. He was an energetic young black man dressed casually in a vintage cardigan over a printed black T-shirt. "I do my best to drag you into the twenty-first century, but do you listen to me? Nope, not one bit. If it was up to you, we'd still be lugging around clay tablets!"

A buzzing fly landed on the polished wooden table in front of Eliot. He squashed it with the hardcover Denise had left behind. "Works for me."

The crew had gathered in Nate's apartment above the bar. The spacious living area served as the unofficial head-quarters and briefing room of Leverage Consulting & Associates. Exposed brick walls enclosed the area, while a spiral staircase led to the bedroom upstairs, which Nate had so far managed to keep more or less to himself. The crew was seated at a long bar-shaped table facing an array of state-of-the-art flat-screen monitors. Printed dossiers were spread out on the table in front of everybody. Nate already had the files memorized.

He wandered over to the attached kitchenette and poured himself an Irish whiskey. Briefings were thirsty work.

"It's really quite a gripping thriller," Sophie observed, retrieving the book from the table. She wiped the dead bug off the jacket. "I was reading it last night, and was particularly impressed by the complexity of the heroine. An idealistic young woman, recruited to be an assassin in the War on Terror, who comes to question the morality of her actions. Any actress would love to sink her teeth into the part. I wonder if they're casting for the movie yet."

Nate prayed she wouldn't get her hopes up. Although she hadn't completely given up on her theatrical ambitions, she was a much better grifter than a thespian. The paradox of Sophie Devereaux was that she truly was a brilliant actress, but only when she was running a con. Onstage, it was a whole different story.

"But it's just a *story,* right?" Parker sounded bemused by the notion. The lithe blond cat burglar perched on a stool between Sophie and Hardison, wearing a man's suit vest over a fitted black tank top. Her gamine face bore a puzzled expression. "I don't get stories. What's the point in reading about stuff that never really happened?"

"It's all about exploring the human condition, Parker," Sophie tried to explain. She had taken it upon herself to try to broaden the younger woman's horizons beyond simply crime and cash. "And allowing the free play of imagination and creativity. Transforming the random chaos of real life into works of art so as to illuminate and elevate the spirit."

"Uh-huh," Parker said, still not getting it. Her idea of recreational reading was technical specs for safes and security systems. "Whatever."

Sophie slid the book toward Parker. "Give it a chance. You might be surprised at how easy it is to get caught up in a great story."

Parker eyed the book warily.

"The book may be a work of fiction," Nate observed, "but its portrait of illicit black ops, of covert assassinations and shady arms deals, has the ring of truth." He had stayed up reading the book as well, over a well-aged bottle. A mild hangover throbbed behind his eyes. "Gavin got all the details right."

"Yeah, about that." Hardison skimmed the book on his e-reader. "How'd a globe-trotting cameraman like Gavin learn so much about all this cloak-and-dagger stuff? He wasn't actually a spook, was he?"

"Nah," Eliot said. "Gavin was a straight shooter. He wasn't mixed up in any of that. He was all about reporting the truth, not covering it up."

"Are you sure of that?" Sophie asked. "How well did you truly know him?"

"Well enough," Eliot said. His tone challenged anybody to disagree.

Nate was inclined to trust Eliot's instincts where his friend was concerned, especially when there was already a plausible explanation for the book's verisimilitude.

"According to Denise," Nate explained, "Gavin had an anonymous informant, referred to only as 'Tarantula,' who provided much of the background material for the book. Gavin's version of 'Deep Throat,' basically."

"Deep who?" Parker asked.

"I'll explain later," Hardison promised. "*Don't* google it."

"And Denise has no idea who Tarantula is?" Sophie asked.

Eliot shook his head. "Gavin never told her, he said it was safer that way." He gave his buddy the benefit of the doubt. "He just wanted to protect her."

"How mysterious," Sophie said. "The plot thickens."

"The *real* plot, right?" Parker cautiously cracked open the novel, as though suspecting a trap. "Not the fake story plot?"

"As far as we know, Tarantula is quite real, whoever he or she might be. He was Gavin's window into the shadowy world he and Denise hoped to expose." Nate rejoined them at the table. He decided it was time to get the briefing properly under way. "But Tarantula is not our target. Gavin's brother, Brad, is." Nate nodded at Hardison. "You're up."

Hardison took his customary place in front of the wall screens. The team's resident hacker and techno-wizard, he generally handled the background research on their targets. With pretty much the entire Internet at his disposal, including back doors into dozens of confidential databases, he could dig up dirt on people who thought they were spotless. Gesturing toward the monitors, he clicked the remote in his hand.

Mug shots appeared on the screens, providing front and side views of a middle-aged Caucasian male who fit the profile Denise had provided them. Brad Lee was distinctly piggish in appearance, with a ruddy complexion, sagging jowls, and a receding hairline. Bloodshot eyes peered out from the mug shot. A swollen red nose, lined with bulging veins, advertised a drinking problem. He scowled petulantly at the camera.

Nate glanced over at Gavin's author photo. *Not much of a family resemblance.*

"Meet Brad Lee," Hardison declared. "High school dropout. Two-time loser, with convictions for burglary, grand theft auto, a convenience-store robbery. Pretty low-rent stuff. Currently out on parole—and living large on his dead brother's literary success."

He clicked the remote again and an aerial view of a conspicuously large and ostentatious mansion took over some of the screens, along with a recent real estate listing. The house's garish exterior was a jumble of mismatched architectural styles: Greco-Roman, Tudor, colonial, and New Jersey. Corinthian columns clashed with Gothic turrets, French windows, and random terra cotta roofs. An excess of ornamentation overran the stone-veneer façade. Marble cherubs and nymphs cavorted in a faux-classical fountain in the manicured front yard. An infinity pool, complete with waterslide, sparkled in the back, between the tennis court and putting green. Oversize satellite dishes looked like they could pick up signals from Jupiter and beyond. A Hummer was parked out front.

"Brad just moved into this ridiculously overpriced Mc-Mansion on Long Island. Six thousand square feet, eight bedrooms, ten baths, a home theater with working snack bar, sauna, hot tub, wine cellar, tennis court, and a split-level, four-car garage complete with car elevator. He's currently in the process of tearing up the rose garden and koi pond to put in a dog-racing track."

"How very nouveau riche," Sophie commented. "People with poor taste shouldn't be allowed to have that much money."

Maybe we can do something about that, Nate thought.

"What's the security like?" Parker asked.

"The usual," Hardison said. "Wireless alarms, motion sensors, security cameras, door/window sensors, off-site monitoring, panic button . . ."

Parker snorted in derision. "That's all? Seriously?"

By her standards, anything less than Fort Knox was a joke. And Nate had his doubts about Fort Knox.

"So what do we think?" Hardison asked. "Did Brad knock off his brother?"

"Hard to say," Nate said. He reviewed Brad's file. "Brad's not exactly an upstanding citizen, but there's nothing in his record to indicate that he's particularly violent or dangerous. Even with the convenience-store holdup, he was just driving the getaway car, and claimed that he didn't know what his drinking buddies were up to until they pulled out their guns."

"Do we believe him?" Sophie asked.

"Not necessarily," Nate said, "but I'm not exactly seeing Al Capone here."

"I don't know." Eliot stared intensely at Brad's mug shot. "Killing your own brother. That's pretty cold."

"But millions of dollars in royalties and movie deals is an awful big temptation," Sophie pointed out. "And you don't have to be a criminal mastermind to run somebody down with a car, especially if you already know where they live. Brad could have been tailing Gavin for a while, learning his routines."

"And the book signing Gavin was walking home from the night of the accident had been well publicized," Nate admitted. "*Anybody* could have been lying in wait." Nate looked up at Hardison. "Do the police have anything on the accident?"

"Not really," Hardison said. "The NYPD investigated it as a hit-and-run, but according to the police reports, which I just happened to hack into, they ran seriously short on leads. By now, the case is as cold as last night's pizza." Copies of confidential police files cascaded across the monitors. He refrained from calling up any grisly crime-scene photos, probably out of respect for Eliot's feelings. "But I can do some more digging if you like."

"Do that," Nate said. "In the meantime, we need to get Gavin's literary estate back into Denise's hands."

Righting injustices like this were his crew's raison d'être. For four years now, they had been providing . . . well, leverage for ordinary people who got screwed over by the system. Nate liked to think that his team picked up where the law left off.

"And how do we do that, Nate?" Sophie looked to him to call the play. "What's our angle?"

Nate had been giving this question plenty of thought even before their first meeting with Denise. The trick to any successful con was figuring out what the mark really wanted—and dangling it in front of them. Nate contemplated the lavish mansion on the screen. Spinning wheels clicked into place inside his head.

"Brad's seen what one bestseller can do for his bank account and lifestyle," he told the others. He smiled slyly in anticipation.

"I'm thinking *sequel*."

FRANKFURT

The Frankfurt Book Fair was the biggest in the world. More than seven thousand exhibitors, from all over the world, crammed the seemingly endless exhibition halls. Close to three hundred thousand publishers, editors, agents, authors, publicists, and bibliophiles roamed the crowded aisles, hoping to strike lucrative rights deals—or maybe just catch a glimpse of their favorite writer. Open booths proudly displayed blown-up book jackets and author photos. Junior editors, assistants, and interns handed out catalogs, posters, bookmarks, and other promotional materials, while their bosses huddled over tables, doing business in dozens of different languages. Milling fairgoers carried tote bags weighed down by freebies. The first three days of the fair catered exclusively to publishing professionals, but the event was open to the general public on the weekend, which made the teeming corridors all the more packed.

Nate soaked up the atmosphere as he strolled through the exhibition hall, settling into his role. This wasn't his first time at the trade fair; he had attended Frankfurt several years ago, back when he was still legit, working as an insurance investigator, in order to get to the bottom of a high-profile case of plagiarism. That was before his own company screwed him over—and he found out that he could do more good on the other side of the law. He glanced around the hall. If anything, the fair had only grown more immense and overwhelming since his last visit. The babble of countless conversations competed with the spiels of eager publishing employees trying to entice people into their booths. Lines formed for book signings, readings, and giveaways. A six-foot-tall plush purple Pomeranian, modeled on a popular children's-book character, waved at Nate as it skipped down the aisle.

He didn't wave back.

"Everything set?" he murmured, seemingly to himself. "You reading me?"

"Loud and clear," Hardison answered via the electronic bud nestled in Nate's left ear. Bone conduction transmitted his voice and could pick up Nate's speech as well. The concealed devices allowed the crew to stay in touch during a con. *"We are good to go."*

"All right, then," Nate said, confident that the others were already in position. He approached a large booth at the end of the aisle. Shelves of recent titles, turned face out, adorned the walls of the carpeted booth. Book trailers played upon mounted video screens. Conversation nooks allowed for meetings and deal making. "It's showtime."

He found Brad Lee holding court in the booth set up by

Gavin's American publisher. According to Denise, Sussex House had originally scheduled Gavin himself for this slot, but Brad had graciously volunteered to take his place. A large cardboard mock-up of the book cover advertised his appearance. Nate took his place in line behind a small crowd of interested parties. He guessed that the real author would have drawn a bigger crowd.

"I can't tell you how impressed I was by *Assassins Never Forget*," a stylish Italian woman gushed. "It was like an inspired combination of Stieg Larsson and John le Carré."

"Who?" Brad said. He had cleaned up some from his mug-shot days, having picked up a shave and a better haircut. A new suit looked expensive. A pinkie ring glittered on his right hand. Nicotine stained his pudgy fingers. A world-famous romance novelist walked by, but Brad didn't seem to notice. He didn't strike Nate as much of a reader. Nate wondered if Brad had even bothered to peruse the book that was making him rich.

"Such a tragedy what happened to your brother," the woman continued. "He had a remarkable talent."

"Yeah, yeah, it was a damn shame," Brad said, for no doubt the thousandth time. He made the effort to sigh mournfully. "I'm still broken up about it, you know." He shrugged and tried to peek down the woman's blouse. "But life goes on, I guess."

"Indeed." The woman offered him a business card. "I'm not sure what your schedule is like, but I'd love to talk to you about possibly doing a graphic-novel adaptation of *Assassins*."

"Take a number, sister. I've already got plenty of offers

on the table. Comic books, manga, computer games . . . you name it. Everybody wants a piece of the action." He gave her an appreciative once-over, leering shamelessly. "But, sure, we can talk about it later. Maybe over drinks in my room?"

"Um, I'm kind of booked up tonight," she said, retreating. Nate noted the ring on her finger, even if Brad hadn't . . . or maybe Brad just didn't care. The woman attempted to salvage something from the encounter. "Give me a call if you want to talk business."

"Yeah, right," he said sourly as he watched her walk away. He tore up her business card, littering the floor of the booth. He reached for a glass of ice water, only to find it empty. Twisting around in his chair, he called to one of the assistants working the booth. "Hey, sugar, any chance I can get a real drink around here?"

"There's a decent bar on Level Three," Nate supplied, stepping up to the table. "Let me buy you a beer?"

"Now we're talking!" Brad shoved away from the table and lumbered to his feet. "I'm outta here," he declared. "I'll be back later . . . if I don't get a better offer."

His handlers made no effort to keep him from leaving. Nate guessed that the good folks at Sussex House were having second thoughts about letting Brad meet the public.

"This way," Nate said. "To be honest, I could use a drink myself."

"A man after my own heart." Brad paused in the aisle to look Nate over. "So who are you anyway?"

"Max." Nate held out his hand. "Max Dunfee. Antipodes Press."

"Never heard of you." He shook Nate's hand regardless.

"Really? We're the second-largest, up-and-coming pub-lisher of quality suspense fiction in New Zealand. Maybe you read our most recent bestseller, *The Kiwi Conundrum*?"

"Must have missed that one," Brad said. "But, hey, you're buying, right?"

"Absolutely." They made their way down the aisle. Throngs of avid fairgoers jostled them as they walked. It was a pickpocket's dream; Nate hoped Parker was behaving herself. "I gotta say, Mr. Lee—can I call you Brad?—that your brother's book is really going great guns Down Under. I've been in the business twenty years now and I've never seen anything like it. You're sitting on a gold mine, if you don't mind me saying so."

"Tell me about it. Little brother did me a solid, I'll give him that."

"But what about the girlfriend?"

Brad bristled. "What about her?"

"Hey, don't shoot the messenger," Nate said, throwing up his hands. "I just heard a rumor that she might have some legal claim on the property."

"You heard wrong," Brad insisted. "Just because that chick was shacking up with my bro when he died doesn't mean she's entitled to one thin dime. *I'm* Gavin's next of kin. I own his work free and clear."

"Great. That's all I wanted to know," Nate assured him. "Just wanted to make sure there weren't any messy legal complications before we talked business."

"What sort of business?" Brad asked. They rode an es-calator up to the next level, where a corner beer garden offered weary fairgoers a chance to rest their feet and slake their thirst. Every table was occupied, but they managed to find a couple of seats at the bar. "I think we already have a deal for Australia, or New Zealand, or wherever."

"For the first book, sure," Nate agreed. He ordered a couple of local beers. "But what about a sequel? I don't need to tell you that a lot of people, including Antipodes, would pay good money to find out what happens next. *Assassins* primed the pump. People are going to want more."

"You and everybody else," Brad said. "As it happens, I'm already talking to a couple of experienced writers about, you know, carrying on my brother's vision. I've even had a few ideas about the story myself." He puffed out his chest. "Gavin didn't get all the talent in the family, you know."

"If you say so," Nate said skeptically. "I mean, you could do that, of course. Hire some anonymous hack to churn out a cheap imitation of your brother's work. And, yeah, it would probably sell . . . somewhat." He let his interest flag noticeably. "But can I be honest with you? That sort of manufactured product wouldn't be nearly as valuable as a genuine sequel by the original author. I can tell you now that Antipodes would pay a lot more for a *real* sequel than for some ghostwritten hack job. And so would anybody else."

"Yeah, I've heard that before," Brad admitted. "From other publishers." Their beers arrived and Brad took a deep quaff. "But can't we just say Gavin wrote the new book, too? Who's going to know?"

"Readers. Critics," Nate said. "They can always tell. Trust me on this. Your brother had a singular voice and vision. Trying to fake it would be like trying to counterfeit a brand-new classic by Graham Greene or Eric Ambler."

"Who?"

"Never mind," Nate said. "Are you absolutely sure your brother didn't have some sort of work in progress when he died? Not even a first draft or partial manuscript?"

"Not that I know of." Brad shrugged. "Sorry."

"That's too bad." Nate glanced at his watch. "Crikey, look at the time. I've got an appointment in Hall Five in ten minutes." He gulped down the last of his beer. "Been good talking to you, but I've got to run." He handed Brad a card with a chain of islands embossed on it. "Let's stay in touch anyway. Maybe we can still do *some* kind of deal."

"Yeah, maybe," Brad said. "Thanks for the brew."

Nate left Brad at the bar. He waited until he was safely out of earshot before speaking in a low voice.

"Okay, the hook has been baited. Let's see if he bites." He passed Sophie on his way out. "Your turn."

"Brad? Brad Lee?" Sophie sat down at the bar beside him. She was professionally attired in a tailored blue dress suit and skirt. A pair of retro cat-eye glasses rested on her nose. She'd traded her usual English accent in for something with a hint of Queens. "I must say, you're a hard man to find."

He leaned back to inspect her, obviously liking what he saw. "Who's looking?"

"Veronica Drury. Of Drury and Associates."

"You an agent?"

"Not just any agent." She thrust out a well-manicured hand. "I represent Denise Gallo."

His jowly face hardened. He let her hand hang in the air. "We've got nothing to talk about."

"I beg to differ," she replied. "Unless you're satisfied with just one bestseller."

His eyes narrowed suspiciously. "What do you mean?"

"Suppose, just hypothetically, that my client happened to be in possession of a sequel to *Assassins Never Forget,* completed shortly before your brother's untimely accident?"

Brad's eyes widened, but Sophie could tell he wasn't convinced yet. "So how come I'm just hearing about this now?"

"Well, it's not as though you've been all that receptive to communicating with my client." According to Denise, Brad had barely made an appearance at Gavin's funeral before heading straight to a lawyer to secure his claim on his brother's estate. He had ignored all of Denise's calls or e-mails since. "You can hardly blame her for wanting to secure representation before coming forward with this highly valuable property."

Brad scowled. "Why you? What happened to the old agent?"

"That was *Gavin's* agent, as your lawyer made abundantly clear." She came on strong, like she was holding all the cards. "Denise was smart enough to realize that she needed someone looking out specifically for her interests."

"And that would be you, huh?"

"Bingo." She held out her hand again. "Pleased to meet you."

"Not so fast. Let's say, just for the moment, that this isn't a pile of bull. What exactly does 'your client' want for the book?"

"A fifty-fifty share of the proceeds, plus creative control."

He nearly choked on his beer. "Like hell," he sputtered. "Even if there really is a sequel, and you're not just making this all up, anything Gavin wrote belongs to me now. I don't owe that gold digger anything."

"In theory, perhaps," Sophie conceded. "But all of that is academic if you don't actually have a copy of the text. And possession, need I remind you, is nine tenths of the law."

He glared at her. "And suppose I get a court order demanding the book?"

"What book? Where? Let me assure you that any hypothetical computer files are safely stowed away where you will never find them, court order or no court order. And do you really want to fight this out in the courts for the next several years, when there's a fortune just waiting to be made? The reading public has a lamentably short attention span. Believe me, you want to strike while *Assassins* is still on the bestseller lists, before the Next Big Thing comes along." Her voice took on a more conciliatory tone. "Look, we don't have to go to war here. We all want the same thing: for Gavin's work to reach an eager audience, and for his loved ones to benefit from the fruits of his imagination."

"But I'm his brother! She's not even blood."

"Right," Sophie said, unimpressed. "And which of you would he have trusted with the sequel?"

Sophie and the rest of the team were counting on the fact that Brad had no way of knowing if his estranged brother had been working on a sequel or not, and that Denise was the person most likely to know about any hypothetical works in progress. As with any good con, the narrative had the ring of plausibility. It was not unlike writing a novel, really. The trick was not to ask the reader to suspend his disbelief *too* far.

As Brad mulled things over, she let her gaze drift around the quaintly Teutonic beer garden. She had many fond memories of Frankfurt, which was the financial and business center of Germany. Why, she had once managed to pull off a highly profitable stock swindle a few blocks from here, simply by posing as a naive barmaid from Stuttgart.

Of course, that was before Nate found a more altruistic use for her talents.

Her nostalgic stroll down Memory Lane came to an abrupt halt when she spotted a too-familiar figure lurking near the entrance. The peeper from McRory's snapped a photo of her with his phone while trying unsuccessfully to remain undetected. Sophie's eyes widened slightly. It took effort to keep her shock and dismay out of her expression. What on earth was the lurker doing here, nearly four thousand miles from Boston?

This is not a coincidence, she realized. *This is trouble.*

Unfortunately, there was no way she could confront him now, not without breaking character in front of Brad, so she did the next best thing instead.

"Excuse me for a minute," she told Brad. "I need to check my messages." She stepped away from the bar. "Don't go anywhere."

Turning her back on him, she lowered her voice. "We have a problem," she told the others via the earbud. "That peeper I told you about? The one from McRory's? He's here."

"In Frankfurt?" Nate's voice asked with concern.

"I'm looking right at him," she said, risking another glance at the mystery man in the green hoodie. Their eyes met across the beer garden and he bolted for the exit again. "Hold on. He's on the move."

"I'm on it," Eliot said. *"Leave it to me."*

Sophie watched the lurker retreat. She was tempted to pursue him herself, find out just what he was after, but she wasn't done hooking Brad yet. She would just have to trust that Eliot and the others had her back—as usual.

"Sorry about that," she said, rejoining Brad at the bar. "An agent's work is never done." She put away her phone. "So, are we ready to talk terms yet?"

"I need to think about this," he grumbled.

"Of course," she said reasonably. "In the meantime, here's a little teaser, as a gesture of good faith." She tucked a portable thumb drive into the vest pocket of his suit. "The first three chapters, free of charge."

She figured she had done enough to whet his interest. She got up from the bar and headed for the exit. "We'll be in touch."

By now, of course, the lurker was long gone. She waited until she was safely clear of Brad before checking in anxiously.

"What's happening? Did you get him?"

"Excuse me, sir," the young Russian woman asked in German. Her equally attractive companion giggled beside her. "Can you help us find the lost and found?"

Eliot was patrolling the exhibition halls, disguised as a member of the fair's security staff. A stolen blue uniform helped sell the role. His flowing mane was tied back in a neat ponytail. A bogus headset completed the picture and gave him an excuse for talking to himself. He was on hand in the unlikely event that things got physical, but was keeping his distance from Brad; it wouldn't do for the mark to get a look at him this early in the operation. They didn't want Brad to recognize him later on; once a team member was "burned" on an operation, they couldn't be brought in later as needed. Besides, it wasn't as if Nate or Sophie was likely to need a hitter anytime soon. They were at a book fair, for Pete's sake. How dangerous could it get?

The biggest threat around here was paper cuts.

"You girls lose something?" he asked, maintaining his cover. *Mr. Helpful,* he thought. *That's me.*

"Maybe," the first girl said. A name tag on her vest identified her as SONIA. Her friend was KATYA. They both made Russian publishing look good. She eyed him speculatively. "Or maybe we're just looking to see what can be found."

"Da," Katya said. "This place is *so* big and confusing. Maybe you can show us the way."

Eliot grinned back at the girls, in a way that had served him well with women on all seven continents (including one memorably toasty night in Antarctica). He was on the job, of course, but he figured there were worse ways to pass the time than flirting with a couple of bored Russian bibliophiles. Sonia took hold of his right arm. Katya took his left. He admired their tactics.

He was trying to remember exactly where the lost and found was when Sophie spoke urgently into his ear: *"We've got a problem . . ."*

His boyish grin evaporated. He disengaged himself from his shapely Russian distractions.

"Sorry, ladies. Something's come up." He thrust a folded map of the complex into Sonia's hands. "Good luck finding . . . whatever."

They pouted in disappointment, but he couldn't worry about that now. As he hurried to intercept the fleeing lurker, he wondered what this unwanted complication was all about. Did it have something to do with the con they were running at present, or was it something completely unrelated to Denise and her troubles? The Leverage crew had made more than their share of enemies over the years, and stepped on some very big toes. This wouldn't be the first time that somebody had placed them under surveillance— or worse.

Heading toward the beer garden, which was one level above his current position, he searched the crowd ahead for someone matching Sophie's description of the lurker. His fists clenched in frustration as he fought his way through the slow-moving crowd. There were too many looky-loos dawdling in the aisles and not enough people getting out of his way. The PA system announced a book giveaway two halls over. A famous historian and his entourage paused to sign galleys in the middle of the aisle, causing a traffic jam. Eliot mentally struck the historian's next book from his reading list.

"Security," he grunted. "Coming through."

By the time he neared the escalator, he felt like hitting somebody, which, to be honest, was a fairly common state of affairs for him. Craning his head back, he spotted a likely suspect coming down the crowded escalator. His brain checked off the details of Sophie's description.

Pale. Scrawny. Green hoodie. Thick glasses. Shifty-looking. The four-eyed geek descending the escalator looked like the guy all right. Sweating nervously, he kept looking back over his shoulder, as though he was trying to get away from somebody. He fidgeted impatiently on the moving stairs, hemmed in by people above and below him. In other words, he looked guilty as hell.

"Got him in my sights," Eliot reported.

"Be careful," Nate advised. *"We don't know who this character is, or what he's after."*

"Roger that," Eliot said. The guy on the stairs didn't look too tough, but you never knew. Eliot still had a four-inch scar from a petite East German mercenary he had tangled with in this very city six years ago. She had seemed harmless, too, until she'd slashed a box cutter across his ribs. The embarrassment of being suckered by somebody half his size had hurt worse than the cut.

He wasn't about to make that mistake again.

Eliot positioned himself at the bottom of the escalator, letting the mechanism bring his target to him. He considered the best way to play this. Take the guy aside, still posing as security, and find out what his story was? Maybe escort him to some quiet storage room or service corridor where he could interrogate him with extreme prejudice?

Works for me, he thought. *Nobody spies on my friends and gets away with it.*

Too late he remembered that the lurker had already seen him sharing a table with Sophie at McRory's, back when they were meeting with Denise. The guy's eyes bugged out behind the Coke-bottle lenses of his glasses as he spotted Eliot waiting at the bottom of the escalator. His face went even paler, if that was humanly possible.

"Damn it," Eliot growled. "He's made me."

Sure enough, the guy spun around and starting shoving his way up the down escalator, pushing his way past startled men and women heavily laden with laptops, briefcases, and bulging book bags. Indignant protests in myriad languages greeted the man's frantic exodus as he rushed back the way he'd come. An irate fräulein swatted him with her purse.

Eliot sprang into action. He knew better than to try forcing his way up through the confused bystanders clogging the escalator. His prey already had too much of a head start. Eliot dashed for the up escalator instead, only to find it just as congested. Nobody seemed in a hurry to get out of his way. He felt like a salmon fighting his way upstream.

"Security!" he shouted, in every language he could think of. "Move it!"

It was no use. By the time he squeezed his way past the uncooperative, uncomprehending civilians blocking his way, the lurker had vanished into the mobs crowding the upper level. Eliot scanned the overpopulated exhibition hall, with its endless aisles and displays. It was like trying to find a single sports fan at the Super Bowl. There were bookworms everywhere.

"Parker! Hardison!" he barked. "He rabbited. I lost him."

"I'm looking, I'm looking," Hardison replied. In theory, the team's resident geek was hacked into the fair's umpteen zillion security cameras, but that was a lot to keep track of. The trade-fair complex covered over six hundred thousand

square feet and consisted of at least nine multilevel exhibition halls. They could only hope that that the nameless lurker was still in the same general vicinity, and that the crowds were slowing him down, too. How far could he have gotten yet?

"Hardison?" Eliot asked impatiently.

"Found him!" Hardison said. *"Level One, Aisle G. Looks like he's making a break for the subway entrance outside the far end of the hall."* Eliot ran through the layout of the fairgrounds in his head, wishing he had hung on to that map he'd given the Russian dolls. *"He's heading your way, Parker. It's on you, girl."*

She did not respond immediately.

"Parker?"

Next time, she decided, *Eliot has to wear the dog suit.*

Parker fumed inside the plush Pomeranian costume. She was far from claustrophobic—indeed, she had once crawled through more than two hundred feet of narrow air ducts to lift a pricey Botticelli from Frankfurt's own Städelsches Kunstinstitut—but the cartoon dog suit was stuffy, smelly, and severely cut down on her peripheral vision. She felt like she was trapped inside the world's most disgustingly cute deep-sea diving outfit. For someone who had always survived by being light on her feet, being stuck inside the cumbersome suit made her skin crawl.

And then there were the kids . . .

"Smile for the camera, Gretchen. Don't be scared."

A middle-aged German mom was determined to snap a photo of her nervous *Kinder* with the oversize grape-colored canine, even though little Gretchen seemed distinctly unenthusiastic about the prospect. The mom shoved the reluctant child toward Parker, who posed awkwardly for the camera. She had been alternately attracting and terrifying kids all afternoon.

"Look at the big, funny dog," the mom urged, trying to pry a smile from the tot. She eyed Parker quizzically. "Who are you supposed to be again?"

"Polly, the Perky Purple Pup," Parker said in a less-than-perky monotone. "Bowwow. Arf."

The kid started crying.

Hardison had better not keep any video of this, Parker thought grumpily. A directional sign pointed toward the antiquarian books exhibit a few halls over. Parker wondered if any of the crew would mind if she snuck away long enough to lift a couple of rare first editions, just to soothe her nerves. Heists were her comfort food.

An urgent SOS from Sophie, followed by rapid updates from Eliot and Hardison, squelched any hopes of a little recreational kleptomania. Parker tensed inside the dog suit, wondering who was after them now.

"Parker?" Hardison repeated anxiously.

"I heard you!" she snapped, her voice echoing oddly inside the large hollow dog head. Gretchen bawled at her feet. "I'm kind of in the middle of something here, okay?"

"Well, make like the Flash, girl. We got a runaway peeper to nab."

They had been working together long enough for her to catch the comic-book reference. Hardison was proud of his geekdom.

"Coming!"

She shoved the sobbing kid aside and glanced around for the quickest route to Aisle G. The dog costume was hard to see out of, frustrating her efforts to orient herself. *Screw this,* she thought.

She ripped off Polly's head and threw it onto the floor in front of Gretchen's mom. The little girl screamed in terror.

"Sorry about that," Parker said, dashing away. She hoped little Gretchen wouldn't need too much therapy. *Could be worse. She could be an orphan who learned to steal at an early age . . .*

"Wait!" the agitated mom cried out. "What about my picture?"

That was the least of Parker's worries. She elbowed her way through the crowded aisle, determined not to let the lurker get away. "Talk to me, Hardison! Where is he?"

"Heading down to Level One," he reported. *"You better make tracks, girl. No pun intended."*

"I *never* make tracks!"

She kicked off Polly's oversize back paws and ran barefoot through the hall. The clumsy gloves went next. Her eyes, no longer hidden behind a suffocating mask, scanned the crowd for her target. An escalator led to the ground floor of the building. Reaching the top of the stairs, she spied a suspicious character exiting the bottom of the escalator. Unlike the hundreds of other fairgoers in view, he wasn't pausing to check out the various booths and exhibits. He was making a beeline down the nearest aisle.

"I see him! I think."

"Scrawny guy, moving like a bat out of hell?" Eliot asked.

"That's the one."

"Stay on him, Parker," Nate advised. *"I want to know what he wants with Sophie."*

"You're not the only one," Sophie said. *"Get him, Parker!"*

It sounded as though there was an entire briefing going on in her ear, but that was okay; she was used to that.

"What do you think I'm doing?" she snapped. "Playing fetch?"

The escalator was packed, so she bypassed the moving steps and hopped onto the handrail instead. Whooping in glee, she slid down the steep, shiny rail at top speed while startled pedestrians yanked their hands out of the way. She took a second to enjoy the ride. Next to cold hard cash and, oh, yeah, helping people, adrenaline was one of her favorite things.

Okay, this is fun, she thought. *Maybe this job doesn't completely suck.*

She hit the ground running and took off after the suspicious dude. But her stunt, as exhilarating as it was, had hardly escaped his notice. He froze in shock for a moment, then ran like mad, apparently alarmed by the sight of a fierce-looking blonde in a partial dog costume chasing after him.

Go figure.

She sprinted after him, annoyed at having to blow her cover. Abandoning the crowded aisle, he cut across a large, open booth to the next row over. He knocked over a metal rack, spilling catalogs and flyers onto the carpet. An award-winning Argentinean poet yelped in fright. Parker vaulted over the obstacles strewn in her path. Way too many slow-moving people obstructed her progress. She cursed under her breath. With rare exceptions, she wasn't a big fan of people. She didn't have time to go around them.

So she took another route.

An ersatz marble archway, fashioned to resemble a Greek temple, marked the booth's exit. Getting a running start, Parker leaped for the top of the arch. Her fingers caught hold and she swung up onto the top of the gate, nailing the landing like a gymnast. Seen from her new vantage point, the sprawling trade fair resembled a maze of interconnected booths divided by modular, prefabricated walls. Only the larger exhibits had roofs.

She ran nimbly along the tops of the walls, which were less than four inches in width. Compared to some of the skyscraper ledges she had traversed over the years, this was like a playground balance beam. And, best of all, she had the impromptu walkway all to herself.

All right, she thought. *This is more like it.*

Granted, her elevated detour wasn't exactly inconspicuous. Baffled fairgoers shouted and pointed as she raced atop the booths, shaking the walls. Hardcovers and paperbacks toppled from their shelves. A four-foot gap appeared before her and she jumped it without missing a step. She flew over the heads of the strolling booksellers below.

"Holey moley!" Hardison exclaimed in her ear. *"What the Ringling Brothers do you think you're doing, girl?"*

"You want me to catch this guy or not?" She glimpsed a security camera out of the corner of her eye. "Say, you can scrub all the video footage, right?"

He sighed wearily. *"For you, sure."*

Maybe I should've kept the dog mask, she thought.

Doing her best to ignore the tumult her stunt was generating, she zeroed in on the lurker, whom she was quickly gaining on. He was almost to the far end of the hall, approaching the exit, when she jumped back down onto the floor, directly in front of him. She glared at him.

"That's enough," she said. "End of the road."

He stared at her in fear and confusion. He backed up into an unattended information booth containing brochures on local restaurants, hotels, and attractions. She had him cornered.

"Wh-who are you?"

"Polly, the Perky Purple Pup," she said ominously. "You're coming with me."

"No!" Panic was written all over his pasty face. "Leave me alone! I have every right to be here!"

"Tell it to my friends."

Eliot would have punched him by now, but Parker had her own way of dealing with uncooperative individuals. She retrieved her favorite stun gun from a Velcro pouch on Polly's belly. Twin electrodes waited to spark.

She grinned in anticipation.

She liked Tasering people. Maybe a little too much.

"Stay back!" the lurker shrieked. He looked around frantically, for help or maybe just a way out. But it looked like he was on his own. "You can't do this!"

"Pretty sure I can."

You could practically see the wheels spinning inside his head as he tried to think his way out of this. Inspiration dawned behind a really unflattering pair of glasses.

"Look!" he shouted at the top of his lungs. "It's J. K. Rowling!"

Who? Parker thought.

It was as though he had just offered free samples of the Crown Jewels to all comers. Suddenly everybody at the fair seemed to come charging toward them from all directions. Scores of people poured out of every booth and nearby aisle. A flood of bookish humanity swept over the hall, carrying the lurker away with them. Parker tried to keep him in sight, but there were too many pushy people, all excited about something. Parker shoved back against the turbulent mob. Somebody called her a "Muggle."

"Hardison!" She cupped a hand over her ear to hear him over the chaos. She was tempted to clear a path through the mob with her Taser, but suspected that Nate wouldn't approve. "Give me something!"

"Are you kidding, girl? It's like trying to find Waldo at Woodstock. I can barely spot you in that crush."

She couldn't believe her ears. "You lost him? Seriously?"

"You try keeping track of one dude in the middle of Bookapalooza," he said defensively. *"FYI, your little circus act got the attention of the real security staff. They're on their way and they don't look happy. If I was you, I'd ditch what's left of that doggy costume, pronto."*

"Way ahead of you."

Diving headfirst into an empty information booth, she stripped out of the dog suit, revealing the black slacks and sweater she was wearing underneath. A pair of plain black glasses was tucked safely in a pocket. She slipped them on, and stuffed Polly into a shelf behind the counter, just as the guards arrived on the scene. They were red-faced and out of breath, as though they had run all the way. She stood up inside the booth, which helped to hide her bare feet.

"Excuse me, miss," a guard asked her. "You see a crazy blonde in a purple costume?"

Who you calling crazy? She pointed randomly. "That way." For a tense moment, she was acutely aware of her exposed saffron tresses, only to remember she was in Germany. Blondes were more common than bratwurst. "Some kind of wacky publicity stunt, I guess." She feigned indignation. "The nerve!"

The guard took off on a wild pup chase. Parker calmly adjusted her glasses, put on a pair of slippers, and strolled away from the booth containing the remains of Polly.

Good riddance.

By now, the hordes of disappointed Rowling fans were beginning to disperse, but there was no sign of the lurker. He was in the wind and halfway to wherever by now. Parker frowned. After all that, she figured she deserved a break.

Maybe just one first edition?

FRANKFURT

Hardison had christened his German van "Lilli."

Back in the States, he usually worked out of a tricked-out van nicknamed "Lucille," of which there had been a couple of incarnations. Shipping Lucille 3.0 all the way to Frankfurt had hardly been feasible, however, so he'd needed to acquire and equip a local version for this job. An impressive array of computers, monitors, communications equipment, and other sophisticated electronics was crammed into a silvery-gray Mercedes-Benz Sprinter. A portable refrigerator held several two-liter bottles of orange soda, aka hacking fuel. He munched on a bowl of gummy bears. At the moment, Lilli was parked on the top floor of the trade fair's capacious parking garage. Tinted windows provided a necessary degree of privacy.

"Any sign of him?" Nate asked, leaning over Hardison's shoulder.

"Nope, he's long gone." Hardison sat at his console in front of a half-dozen screens offering multiple views of the exhibition halls and grounds. The rest of the crew were packed into the van behind him, impinging on his personal space. "But I managed to capture a couple of good shots of him before Pottermania broke out." A few deft strokes on the keyboard brought up multiple images of a furtive stranger fleeing across the hall. "That the same guy y'all were chasing?"

"That's him," Eliot confirmed, sounding even surlier than usual. He clearly wasn't happy about the lurker eluding him. "Parker?"

"Looks like him." She peered at the screens. "Unless he's twins . . . or triplets!"

"Let's not jump to that assumption just yet," Nate advised. He turned toward Sophie. "And that's definitely the same guy who was watching us at the bar back in Boston?"

"I think so," she said. "What do you think this is about, Nate? Who is he?"

"No idea," he confessed. "And I don't like not knowing."

Hardison knew the feeling. The last thing they needed was an unknown third party snooping around in the middle of a complicated operation. Question marks meant danger in this racket. "You think we ought to call off this job, just to be safe?"

"No way," Eliot said emphatically. "Denise is counting on us."

"Whoa, man." Hardison threw up his hands defensively. "I know Gavin was your bud, and this job is personal and all, but we've got one great big X factor running around loose. Who knows what Mr. Peepers is up to . . . or who he might be working for. Maybe we need to take a time-out while we figure out if we've got another target on our backs."

"What about your fancy facial-recognition programs?" Eliot challenged him. "Can't they tell us who this joker is?"

"Maybe, if he's in the right databases." Hardison selected the best close-up he could find of the lurker's face and set the program to breaking down its biometric proportions. Green positioning dots isolated the nodal points on his face while sophisticated algorithms compiled a biometric face print based on various measurements, including the distance between the eyes and the width of his nose. Other quantifiable features included the shape of his jawline. "But that could take a while and there's no guarantee that we'll get a hit." He turned away from the screens. "In the meantime, our bespectacled buddy there has the advantage on us."

"I should have Tasered him," Parker grumbled. She toyed with her stun gun in a way that made Hardison more than a little uneasy. "Right away, zap!"

"Well, Nate?" Sophie asked. "What's the verdict? Are we pulling the plug?"

Nate thought it over. The mastermind behind the crew's operations, he usually had the last word, whether the rest of them agreed or not. He took his time before answering.

"No," he said finally. "We're too far in. We back out now

and we'll never get a better chance to fix things for Denise." He swept his gaze over the team, making eye contact with each of them. "We've been under surveillance before—by Latimer, Sterling, and others. That's never stopped us from getting the job done. We'll just have to be on the lookout for any unwelcome surprises . . . and watch each other's backs. Even more than usual."

"Okay, Nate," Hardison said. To be honest, he, too, hated the idea of quitting, especially after all the effort he had put into getting everything set up for this job. "Just wanted to be the voice of reason this time around."

Eliot snorted. "You? That'll be the day."

"Says the guy who likes to take on armed gunmen with his fists." Hardison placed a hand over his heart, as though mortally wounded by his friend's insinuation. "I'll have you know I'm the very soul of prudence when it comes to avoiding unnecessary risks."

"Uh-huh," Eliot said. "And who came up with a phony treasure hunt so complicated that the marks caught on before we could lower the boom? And who had to get rescued from Russian mobsters because you couldn't resist taking credit for Parker's heists?"

Hardison shifted uncomfortably. "Okay, so I got carried away a couple of times . . ."

"A couple?" Eliot said. "Seems to me I recall hauling your butt out of the fire more times than a couple. Remember when—"

"I hacked into that plane's electrical system and kept it from crashing with y'all aboard?" Hardison interrupted. "Why, yes, I do remember that, but no need to thank me. I was just doing what I do best, bro, like that time—"

"Enough of this," Nate said, taking charge. "Let's put our mystery man on the back burner for now and get back to Brad." He glanced at Hardison. "He taken the bait yet?"

"Funny you should ask." Hardison cleared the lurker from the screens and opened another program. "Looks to me like a certain greedy next of kin couldn't wait to check out those sample chapters."

He clicked his mouse and Brad Lee's porcine countenance filled the central screen. Brad was leaning forward, like he was staring right at them. His flabby lips moved as he perused the bogus chapters. A messy hotel room could be glimpsed in the background. He burped loudly.

"Ugh," Sophie said, recoiling. "How exactly are you doing this, Hardison?"

"Pure ingenuity." He welcomed the chance to show off a little. "Not only did I electronically backdate the chapters to make them look as though they were written before Gavin's death, but I also included a worm that's letting me hijack Brad's laptop, including its built-in webcam and mike, without him knowing. From now on, his own hardware is spying on him."

Sophie shook her head. "You can do that?"

"Not just me," he admitted. "This sort of spyware has been around for a few years now. Governments in the Middle East and elsewhere have been using it to monitor and crack down on dissidents."

Sophie shuddered. "Remind me never to undress in front of my laptop again."

"Oh, the laptop's just the beginning," Hardison bragged. "Now that I'm in the back door, I'll have access to his home computer . . . and security system."

That got Parker's attention. "Nice."

Her approval gave his ego a boost. He liked looking good in front of his girl.

"Not that I'd need any help breaking into his place," she added. "Just saying."

"Good job," Nate said, doling out a rare tidbit of praise. As bosses went, he could be a tad distant and withholding. "Now we just have to hope that Brad will buy that those chapters were actually written by Gavin before he died." He glanced over at Eliot. "You think they're good enough?"

Eliot watched Brad read the counterfeit pages.

"They ought to be."

A WEEK AGO:

"You can do this," Eliot said. "You know Gavin's characters and style better than anyone else."

He and Denise were holed up in a hotel room in Boston, knocking out the bogus chapters. She sat before her keyboard, staring anxiously at the blank page on the screen while he pulled up a chair beside her. The remains of a room-service dinner waited to be put out in the hall. A fresh pot of coffee was percolating.

"Are you sure?" she asked.

"Positive. All we need is a couple of dummy chapters, just enough to fool Brad. Not an entire book."

"Well, I appreciate you collaborating with me on this," she said. "I can really use your technical expertise."

"No problem," he said. "Glad to be of assistance."

For better or for worse, he knew more than most about shady dealings in dangerous hot spots. Prior to hooking up with Nate's crew, he had worked as a soldier of fortune and "retrieval specialist" all over the planet, cracking heads and kicking butt everywhere from Myanmar to Syria. He had seen, and taken part in, some pretty brutal stuff over the years. There were times he wished he had never left his hometown.

"You have no idea," she said. "I'm just a semi-employed office temp. Everything I know about spies and assassins I learned from Gavin's book."

Lucky you, *Eliot thought. He barely remembered the innocent young soldier he had once been. There had been a lot of water under the bridge since then, most of it dirty.* "So, you haven't heard from this 'Tarantula' character since Gavin died?"

"Not a peep," she said. "I wouldn't know how to contact him if I wanted to. That's the way Gavin wanted it. Said it was safer that way."

Not for the first time, Eliot wondered who Gavin's shadowy informant was. Maybe the guy who was watching Sophie back at the bar? Or some ruthless black-ops type Eliot might have crossed paths with before?

"Could be just as well," he said. "Maybe Gavin knew what he was doing."

Or perhaps he got himself killed.

He didn't share this latter thought with Denise. She had enough to worry about right now, like getting the chapters finished before the book fair next week. Hardison was waiting to work his computer hoodoo on the files.

"Probably," she agreed. "And the way things are going, I think I'm glad you're helping me and not some anonymous spook." She gave him a grateful smile. "Seriously, I can't thank you enough."

They had been slaving away on the chapters all day now. So far they had worked well together, maybe too much so. As she leaned back in her chair and stretched, he couldn't help admiring her striking features and graceful contours. The lustrous sheen of her red hair gleamed beneath the hotel lights. A tank top and skinny jeans displayed her athletic figure to advantage, but there was more to her than just her obvious good looks. Denise had turned out to be just as smart and appealing as Gavin had said in his letters and emails. She was good company, despite an understandable air of sadness haunting her, and they had clicked right away. He was acutely aware of her physical presence, only a few inches away. If she wasn't his dead friend's girl . . .

Guilt pricked his conscience.

"Hey, anything for Gavin, you know."

"It just feels so strange doing this without him. When I think of all the hours we spent poring over every chapter, the endless edits and revisions . . ." She choked up, unable to finish. "I don't think I could do this alone."

"You don't have to." He reached out to pat her shoulder, but thought better of it. He got up and poured her a fresh cup of coffee instead. "Now, how about we get going on Chapter Two?"

"Okay." She reached over and squeezed his hand.

Three hours later, they had a decent first draft in hand.

He gave it another read while Denise paced expectantly behind him, awaiting his response. "Well?" she asked. "What do you think?"

"Works for me," he said. "You did a really good job of impersonating Gavin's style."

"You think so?" she asked, a bit nervously.

"It's a very distinctive style."

LONG ISLAND

.

"Get on with it, Parker," Nate said.

"In a second," she replied. "Just one more page."

She was hanging upside down from a crystal chandelier twenty feet above the foyer of Brad's opulent Long Island mansion, reading *Assassins Never Forget* on the screen of her phone. It was after midnight and all the lights were off, but she could easily read the text on the illuminated screen. Brad had turned in hours ago, after a long night of Internet porn and gambling, often at the same time.

"Parker," Nate repeated.

"Okay, okay." She bookmarked her page and put the phone away. "This is all Sophie's fault, you know."

If Sophie hadn't urged her to give literature a chance, she would've never gotten hooked on Gavin's book, and needed to know, right this very minute, whether Dmitri was actually a double agent and who had really poisoned the Belgian ambassador . . .

"You can read the rest later," Sophie promised. *"But we're on a timetable here."*

"Fine," Parker said irritably. "I'm on it."

She unclipped a hacksaw from her belt.

The crash woke Brad from a dream in which all three Kardashians were auditioning for a role in the *Assassins* movie. Jolted upright, he gasped out loud in the darkened master bedroom, which was at least twice the size of his old apartment in Poughkeepsie. He fumbled for the light by the bed while he tried to figure out what had just happened.

He listened intently to the sleeping house. In theory, he had all thirty-plus rooms to himself, despite his best efforts to convince those strippers to stay for the weekend. A fierce autumn wind howled outside, but the house itself sounded quiet. Had he only imagined the crash?

A second crash, only slightly smaller than the first, shot that comforting notion to hell. He jumped at the sound of glass or china shattering downstairs.

"What the—"

A beer belly hung over his saggy boxer shorts. He got out of bed and threw on a red silk dressing gown before creeping to the security control panel mounted on the wall. According to the lighted LED display, all the doors and windows were secure, but clearly something had caused a ruckus downstairs. So how come the motion sensors hadn't gone off?

He considered hitting the panic button, but hesitated. He had been having a bit of a private party earlier. Had he put all the booze and blow away before he'd called it a night? Maybe he ought to take a look-see himself before he had a bunch of rent-a-cops traipsing through the place?

Just to avoid any awkward moments.

His parole officer frowned on firearms in the house, so he grabbed the baseball bat he kept under the bed. His heart pounding fast enough to make him wish he had watched his cholesterol, he tiptoed out of the bedroom and snuck down the hall to the top of the grand stairway. He gasped at the sight of the expensive chandelier lying in pieces on the tiled floor of the foyer. Twisted metal and shattered crystal shards littered the marble tiles. A severed chain dangled from the ceiling.

"Jeez!"

His voice echoed in the empty house. The wind rattled the walls. It occurred to him that maybe there was no intruder, that the chandelier had just shook itself loose from its moorings. And that the second crash had simply been some stray piece of crystal shattering a few moments later.

He let out a sigh of relief, followed by a flash of exasperation. He had paid a good chunk of Gavin's movie money for this place; it shouldn't be falling apart on him. *Talk about shoddy workmanship,* he thought indignantly. *I could have been killed!*

Somebody was getting an angry call tomorrow, if he even waited that long. And that was just for starters; he ought to sue somebody, too.

He paused at the top of the stairs, uncertain what to do

next. His inclination was to go back to bed and let the cleaning woman deal with the mess in the morning. That was what he paid her for, after all.

Then he noticed a light was on in the den downstairs. An amber glow seeped out the doorway, which was cracked partway open. Had he turned off the lamp before turning in? He honestly couldn't remember. Searching his memory, he remembered what else was in the den.

Oh crap, he thought. *The safe.*

The wall safe hidden in the den held plenty of valuables, including gold, jewels, and a substantial quantity of cash, not to mention his passport, fake IDs, and anything else he might need to make a quick getaway. He was living the good life now, thanks to little brother's unintended generosity, but Brad hadn't quite shaken the habit of always having an escape route ready, just in case things went south and he needed to clear out in a hurry.

Plus, he didn't trust banks. Bunch of crooks, all of them.

"Crap, crap, crap," he muttered. Greed overcame caution as he hurried down the stairs, barely remembering to turn off the ground-floor motion sensors first. Barefoot, he stepped gingerly through the strewn crystal slivers. Bat in hand, he shoved open the door and advanced cautiously into the den.

"Hello?" A tremor in his voice betrayed his unease. "There had better not be anybody in here."

The glow from a desk lamp illuminated the den, which appeared to be unoccupied. Brad's eyes searched the room, seeing only shelves of classy-looking hardcover books, all of which had come with the furnishings. A pin-up calendar, tacked to a bulletin board, was his own addition to the decor, as was a deluxe glass-lined humidor full of pricey cigars. Worrisome shadows cloaked the far corners of the room, beyond the radiance of the lamp. A broken vase lay in pieces upon the hardwood floor.

"Hello? Anybody there?"

His gaze went to the phony encyclopedia set that usually hid the safe. To his dismay, he saw that the cast-iron door of the safe was wide open, exposing the contents. His heart missed a beat.

"No, no . . . !"

He glanced around one more time, to make sure nobody was lying in ambush, before dashing over to the violated safe. He rifled quickly through the stacks of cash, travelers checks, and other assets. Much to his surprise, everything still seemed to be accounted for. Even his stash of recreational pharmaceuticals had been left alone. On closer inspection, he discovered only one item was missing: the thumb drive that bitch of an agent had given him in Frankfurt. He scratched his balding head in confusion.

"What the hell?"

"Looking for something?" a female voice asked from above and behind.

His heart nearly jumped out of his chest. He spun around in time to see a skinny blonde drop nimbly from the ceiling, where she must have been hiding all this time. Her slender form was squeezed into a matte-black jumpsuit. She was cute enough, if you didn't mind getting scared shitless.

"Jesus, lady!" he blustered. "Who the heck are you?"

"Took you long enough," she said. "I was afraid I was going to have to smash every breakable in the house."

He noticed belatedly that she was holding a ceramic ashtray in her hand. She tossed it to the floor, where it shattered loudly.

"Stop that!" His nerves couldn't take much more of this. He waved the baseball bat in the blonde's direction. "Who are you? What are you doing here?"

He yanked open a desk drawer with his free hand and groped for the Colt .45 he kept hidden there, parole officer or no parole officer. Trembling fingers searched fruitlessly for the pistol.

The blonde brought a hand out from behind her back. Gloved fingers gripped the missing gun.

"Why don't you drop the bat," she suggested.

He did as he was told. The wooden bat clattered to the floor.

"That's better." She removed the stolen thumb drive from her pocket and lobbed it over to him. "Now we can talk."

"I don't understand." He tried to remember if he still owed any loan sharks or bookies anything. He thought he'd paid off all his debts with the early proceeds from Gavin's book, but it was possible he had forgotten somebody. There had been a lot of markers to pay off. "What's this all about?"

"A demonstration," she explained, "of just how easily we can get past your security . . . or anybody else's."

"We?"

He glanced around in confusion.

"Maybe it would be better if I let my partner explain."

As a rule, Parker preferred simple breaking and entering to grifting. With Sophie's help, she'd gotten better at playing a role—why, she hadn't broken character and stabbed a mark in months!—but she was glad that she didn't have to work Brad all by herself. Let somebody else deliver the sales pitch.

"Partner?" he echoed.

"Check your computer."

He belatedly noticed the laptop sitting open on his desk. It hummed in hibernation mode. He poked a key experimentally.

"Ah, Mr. Lee," Hardison Skyped. "Good of you to join us, mate."

Brad collapsed into a chair in front of the computer. He glowered at the screen. "And you are?"

"Jones," Hardison introduced himself. "Cyrano Jones." Parker thought she recognized the name from one of the old sci-fi shows Hardison had made her watch. He affected a Cockney accent for the occasion. He was proud of the accent and used it every chance he got. "Pleased to make your acquaintance, as it were."

"Enough with the damn games!" Brad said, his temper flaring. "What do you want?"

"To make you aware of our services," Hardison said, "and perhaps assist you in resolving your present difficulties."

"What difficulties? What are you talking about?"

"Let's not be coy, Mr. Lee. We know all about the sequel . . . and who currently has it in their possession." He flashed a winning smile. "My partner and I are prepared to remedy that situation—for a substantial fee."

Brad didn't waste time with denials.

"Yeah, right. What do I need you for?"

"Well, we got to *your* valuables easily enough, didn't

we? We can get you the sequel just as readily, if you'll let us."

"Just like that, huh?"

"Just like that," Hardison promised. "And, as a bonus, we can straighten out your problems with Ms. Gallo once and for all."

Despite Brad's belligerent attitude, Parker caught a flicker of interest in his piggy, bloodshot eyes. Brad toyed with the thumb drive, rolling it between his pudgy fingers. She could tell he was hooked.

Nice, she thought.

For once, the mark was going to think the crew was working for him!

SIX

MANHATTAN

"So there was this douche-bag lieutenant that was getting on everybody's last nerve. *Somehow* a dose of CS powder ended up in the heater of his rag-top Jeep, so when he fired it up, he got some serious tear-gas air-conditioning!"

"Oh my God." Denise cracked up at the story. She wiped tears of laughter from her eyes. "Wow. I can't remember the last time I laughed like that. Or cried for any reason except . . . you know."

She and Eliot were trading stories over dinner at Gavin's favorite Italian restaurant in the Village. Candlelight cast a warm glow over the table. Chamber music played softly in the background. An open bottle of wine rested on the table between them. The dinner was something of a private memorial for Gavin, since Eliot had been unable to attend the actual service. Henri's seemed like the perfect location.

"Yeah," he said. "I know."

A somber mood fell over the table, threatening to dispel the good spirits and humor of the moment before. A melancholy distance entered Denise's eyes as she toyed with the compass around her neck. He had never seen her without the keepsake.

Eliot raised a glass of red wine. "To Gavin."

"To Gavin." She clinked her glass against Eliot's. "And good friends."

Less than a day had passed since Parker's nocturnal invasion of Brad's mansion. The crew had set up shop in a suite at a midtown hotel, but Eliot had taken the night off to spend this time with Denise. His earbud rested, inactive, in his pocket. It was off duty, too.

"So how is the operation going?" she asked.

"It's going," he said, not volunteering any details. He knew she had to be curious, but in general, it wasn't a good idea to let clients get too close to the con while it was under way. They were too emotionally involved, and not accustomed to working outside the law. It was better, and less messy, to keep them at a distance until the job was done.

Most of the time, at least.

Eliot suspected that Nate didn't approve of his socializing with Denise like this. And he probably had a point; Eliot recalled his own thoughts on the importance of keeping one's personal life personal and divorced from the job. He was breaking his own rule here.

"And?" she prompted.

"Everything's going according to plan." He nodded at her plate, hoping to change the subject. "How's your rigatoni?"

She frowned at his reticence, but did not press the issue. He guessed she didn't want to spoil their dinner.

"Delicious," she raved. "The pasta came out perfectly al dente, and the broccoli and cauliflower are cooked just right. Crisp, but tender." She waved her fork at his plate. "How's yours?"

"Not bad." He'd gone with the pork cutlets with pine nuts and prosciutto. "I would have gone a little easier on the capers, and maybe sliced the prosciutto even thinner before wrapping it around the cutlets, but I can't complain. It's still damn good cooking. I can see why you like this place. They know what they're doing."

"Whoa," she said. "Who knew you were such a foodie? I'm impressed."

"Hey, I make a pretty mean rigatoni myself. And you should taste my *tagliolini con asparagi*." He prided himself on his culinary skills, which were considerable. "There's more to me than just hitting people."

"Yes, I'm getting that impression."

She gazed warmly at him across the table, and he experienced the same mixed feelings he had tangled with back in that hotel room in Boston. The candlelight flattered her emerald eyes and red hair. Her fair complexion seemed to glow with its own special radiance. He found himself wishing that they had met under different circumstances. She was a woman worth knowing better.

"Well, I'm no Gavin," he said.

She gave him a cryptic look. "You don't have to be."

Eliot wasn't sure how to respond to that.

The waiter cleared their plates away, then returned with

the check. Eliot snatched it the minute it hit the table. "Don't even think about it," he warned her before she could reach for her purse. "This is on me."

Denise didn't argue the point. "Far be it from me to wrestle a professional butt kicker for the check. Thanks."

Putting on their coats, they stepped out into the cold night air. Cars and pedestrians filled the bustling streets and sidewalks. Horns honked at every intersection. Neon signs cast colored shadows onto the pavement. It was a crisp, clear night. A crescent moon could be glimpsed through the looming skyscrapers. An autumn breeze rustled Denise's hair.

"Brrr." She hugged herself to keep warm. "Feels like winter's coming."

He resisted the temptation to put his arm around her. "Yeah, it's a bit nippy."

Her apartment was only a few blocks away, he knew. He had never been there, but after all that had happened, the address was burned into his brain. Once again, he wished that he had found time to visit while Gavin was still around.

"Walk me home?" she asked.

"Try and stop me."

They headed downtown, walking side by side. Eliot counted down the blocks, feeling a certain tension grow the nearer they got to her place. He wondered what might happen when they reached the home she had once shared with Gavin. He wondered what he *wanted* to happen. None of this was part of the plan.

"You sure you can't tell me more about what you and your friends are up to?" she pried. "Just so I'm not completely in the dark?"

"Trust me. The less you know the better."

She let out a rueful chuckle. "Now you *do* sound like Gavin."

"Sorry."

"Don't apologize." She took his arm. "I know you're just looking out for me, like he did."

He didn't want to think about Gavin right now, and he felt bad for feeling that way. He owed Gavin his life. *But what do I owe Denise—and the job?*

They crossed Greenwich Avenue. Coffee shops, art galleries, and vintage clothing shops were shutting down for the evening. They jaywalked against the light like true New Yorkers. Eliot thought he knew the way, so he was surprised when, as they came to a corner, she abruptly tugged him to the right.

"No," she said forcefully. "Not that way."

He mentally kicked himself. They were nearing the intersection where Gavin had been run down. No wonder she wanted to take a detour.

"All right," he said.

A somewhat roundabout route brought them to a converted brownstone on a quiet side street. A concrete stoop led up to the front entrance. The lights on the third floor were dark. An old woman walking a dog strolled past the corner, but otherwise they had the sidewalk to themselves. Eliot wasn't sure if this was a good thing or not.

"Well, here we are," she said.

"Looks like it."

Despite the October chill, they lingered at the foot of the stoop. An unspoken possibility lingered as well. His gaze darted to the darkened apartment above, then back to Denise. Were they ready to go there?

Should they?

She let go of his arm and turned to face him. Her warm breath frosted before her lips. A wool scarf was wrapped around her neck.

"Tonight was nice," she said. "I needed that."

"Yeah. I had a good time, too."

He wasn't usually tongue-tied around women, but this was different. Denise was a client . . . and Gavin's all but widow. It had only been six months since Gavin's death. His memory hung in the shrinking space between them.

"Do you . . ." She hesitated, but only for a moment. "Do you want to come inside?"

You know I do, he thought, but held back. Denise was still grieving and vulnerable. He didn't want to take advantage of that, even if she wanted him to. "Not sure that's such a good idea."

Her face fell. "I see."

"It's not that—" He searched for the right words. The last thing he wanted to do was hurt her feelings. "It's just that . . . you know."

"It doesn't have to be about the job." She stepped closer, well within reach. The night suddenly didn't feel so cold. Her hair gleamed beneath the streetlights. Her eyes were soft and inviting. "Or him."

He wavered, on the verge of giving in. "Denise . . ."

A horn honked at the corner. Brakes squealed loudly. "Hey, watch where you're going!" a bellicose voice cried out. "You trying to get someone killed?"

Denise flinched. All the blood drained from her face. She looked sick to her stomach.

He reached for her. "Denise?"

"No." She backed away from him. "Maybe you're right. Maybe we . . . should call it a night."

It's too soon, he realized. Maybe it always would be. "You going to be okay?"

"I'm fine," she insisted. She forced a smile to patch over her reaction to the near collision at the corner. "It was a wonderful evening, Eliot." She leaned forward and kissed him on the cheek. "Thank you."

He knew when it was time to go.

"Okay, then."

He walked away quickly, before he could change his mind. Second thoughts strafed him like sniper fire as his feet stomped down the pavement. Every moment of the encounter, every word and look, played on a continuous loop inside his head as he debated whether or not he had made the right call. Was it too late to turn around and go back? If he hurried, maybe he could still catch her before she turned in for the evening. The night didn't have to end this way . . . did it?

What did he want to do? What would Gavin want him to do?

"Damn it."

He was less than a block away when grunts, curses, and the distinctive smack of meat and bone slamming into flesh yanked him out of his own head. Adrenaline jolted his system into overdrive. He knew a fight when he heard one, and where the commotion was coming from.

Denise!

He raced back the way he'd come. Rounding the corner,

he saw Denise tussling with three tough-looking goons who were trying to hustle her into the back of a waiting black limousine. Artfully applied mud obscured the limo's license plate.

Denise was putting up a pretty good fight, much more than her would-be abductors seemed to have expected. As Eliot ran toward the fracas, she drove an elbow into the gut of the goon behind her and, with practiced skill, flipped him over her shoulder into the thug charging her. The men collided loudly and crashed onto the sidewalk, landing in a tangle of limbs and profanities. A third man already had a split lip and bloody nose—Denise's handiwork, presumably. A fallen gun rested on the pavement, where it must have landed after being knocked from one of the assailant's grasp. Bloody Nose scrambled for the weapon.

No way, pal, Eliot thought. He didn't like guns.

Dashing forward, he kicked the gun into the street, under the limo. Bloody Nose swore and took a swing at him. Eliot saw the blow coming from a mile away and yanked his head out of the way while simultaneously checking out his opponent. The guy was a beefy Nordic bruiser who looked like he was descended from a long line of Viking marauders. Cropped blond hair and blue eyes did little to soften his thuggish features. He was built like a tank, with a blocky head, bull neck, and bodybuilder's physique that practically screamed steroid abuse. He had probably four inches and thirty pounds on Eliot. Most people would find him pretty intimidating.

Eliot wasn't most people.

His fist slammed into Bloody Nose's jaw, knocking the other man's head to one side. The thug staggered backward, a stunned expression on his ugly face. Eliot guessed he was more used to hitting than being hit.

Turnabout's a bitch, Eliot thought.

Getting in close, he delivered a couple of rabbit punches to the guy's gut. There wasn't a lot of flab there, just solid muscle. The guy grunted, but didn't go down. Eliot tried to finish him off with an uppercut to the chin, but the thug blocked the blow with his forearm and shoved Eliot away with a meaty hand. He glowered angrily at Eliot, raising his fists.

"Bad idea, Romeo," the thug snarled. A deep, gravelly voice made Arnold Schwarzenegger sound like a castrato. He wiped his bleeding snout with the back of his hand. "Should've stayed out of this."

"Not a chance," Eliot said.

They circled each other on the sidewalk. Eliot threw a couple of feints at the guy's head, but Bloody Nose didn't bite. This gorilla was more than just local muscle, Eliot realized; he'd had some training. But he wasn't Eliot's match.

Few people were.

Bloody Nose blocked a jab, then took another swing at Eliot, who was ready for it. Ducking beneath the blow, he slipped behind the thug and pounded him in the back. Bloody Nose stumbled forward, smashing loudly into the rear of the limo. A string of oaths, all of them unprintable, escaped his lips.

Eliot tackled him from behind, hoping to pound his face against the side of the car, but Bloody Nose threw his head back, butting Eliot in the face with what felt like a hairy cinder block. Eliot reeled backward, momentarily stunned. Blood dripped from his own nose now.

"Take that, pretty boy," Bloody Nose said. Sophie might surmise that the man had issues with his looks. "Looks like you should've minded your own business!"

Pushing off from the limo, he spun around and took the fight back to Eliot. His apelike arms grabbed onto Eliot's head, bending him forward to take a knee to the gut. A stomach full of wine and fine Italian cuisine absorbed the impact as Eliot gritted his teeth and kept on fighting. Doubled over, he took advantage of his hunched position to administer an openhanded blow to the thug's exposed solar plexus, hitting him right where it would deliver the most oomph.

"Awwwk!" Bloody Nose gasped and doubled over as well. Eliot returned the favor by taking hold of the man's thick skull and yanking it down. His knee rose up to meet the thug's already damaged face. Eliot heard a wet, satisfying crunch. The thug yelped in pain.

Bloody Nose became Broken Nose.

Serves you right, Eliot thought, *for going after Denise.*

He swung the thug away from him into a nearby trash can. The man knocked the can over as he reeled across the sidewalk, spilling trash on the sidewalk. Eliot followed up with a roundhouse kick to the jaw that left the guy sprawled upon the pavement. He clutched his nose, moaning.

"This *is* my business," Eliot said.

The fight took longer than Eliot liked. He checked anxiously on Denise, who was holding her own but outnumbered two to one. She had assumed a defensive stance, her weight on her forward leg, open hands held up in front of her. She moved to keep both bad guys in her line of sight, staying aware of her surroundings. Alert green eyes were on guard for attacks. Concentration, not panic, could be seen on her face. Her tactics indicated krav maga training, and maybe a few other disciplines.

How about that, Eliot thought.

The thugs closed in on her from north and south, blocking both ends of the sidewalk. One of them had a cheap crew cut; the other was bald and bearded. Crew Cut nodded at Baldy, who charged at Denise, seizing her attention. She adroitly sidestepped the lunge so that the thug grabbed only empty air. A back fist strike nailed Baldy, who toppled backward. He landed flat on his back.

A flicker of a smile appeared on Denise's face.

The move, as effective as it was, distracted her from her other adversary, who rushed forward to pistol-whip her from behind. Cold steel cracked against her skull and she crumpled to the pavement. Crew Cut kicked her in the ribs.

"Denise!"

Eliot saw red. An empty beer bottle had spilled from the overturned trash can. He snatched it up and hurled it at Crew Cut's gun hand. The missile slammed into the gunman's wrist, knocking the weapon from his grip. Eliot threw himself at the unarmed thug even as Baldy scrambled to his feet to join the melee. It was two against one, again.

Works for me, Eliot thought.

The trick to taking on multiple opponents was to hit hard and fast and never give them a chance to gang up on you. While Crew Cut was still clutching his hurt wrist, and looking around for his lost gun, Eliot took the initiative and punched him in the throat, then shoved him into the path of Baldy, who grabbed on to his buddy instinctively. With Crew Cut coughing and choking and hanging on to his body, Baldy could not get to Eliot. Charging ahead, Eliot rammed into Crew Cut, driving him backward into Baldy. His fist flew over the first man's shoulder directly into the chin of the other, landing a solid blow that left Baldy reeling. He teetered uneasily on his feet, even as Crew Cut sucked down air.

"Crap!" Crew Cut wheezed. "Who do you think you are?"

"More than you bargained for." Eliot figured that the goons had been waiting to get Denise alone, only to find that their simple smash-and-grab had gotten a lot more complicated. *Tough,* he thought.

"Screw this!" Broken Nose hollered, lurching to his feet. "Fall back! Fall back!" He had clearly decided to cut their losses. Clutching his gushing schnoz, he shouted at his buddies. The men piled into the limo, dragging Crew Cut with them. "We'll get the bitch another time!"

Not so fast, Eliot thought. Abruptly finding himself with no one to hit, he started after them, intent on keeping them from getting away, only to be distracted by an anguished groan from the sidewalk. *Denise!* He turned to see her lying facedown on the pavement. A crimson halo spread outward from her head.

"Damn it."

He turned back toward Denise. The limo peeled away, running over the lost pistol in its haste. Eliot hastily took note of the car's make and model. It looked to be a 2010 six-passenger Lincoln Town Car; he'd know it if he saw it again. He scowled as the bad guys made their escape, but seeing to Denise took priority. He prayed that she was only stunned.

First, Gavin. Now Denise, too . . .

He dashed to her side.

"Denise! Talk to me!"

He knelt beside her, cursing himself for leaving her alone on the sidewalk. An excruciating moment stretched on forever until she stirred and lifted her bleeding head from the pavement. He gasped in relief.

"Denise?"

"It's all right, Eliot." She sat up unsteadily, holding a hand to her head. Dark red blood seeped through her fingers from a nasty cut on her forehead. "It's just a head wound. It looks worse than it is."

Possibly, he thought. Cuts to the head could be deceptive that way, and the blood seemed to be venous, not arterial. Just the same, he wasn't inclined to take chances. Peeling off her scarf, he used it to apply pressure to the wound. He checked her eyes for any signs of a concussion. Thankfully, the pupils were not noticeably dilated. His fingers gingerly explored a swollen bump at the back of her skull.

"Ouch," she protested.

"Sorry." He handed her the scarf so she could keep pressing it to her head. Her injuries looked minor, thank God, but he wanted a professional opinion, pronto. "We need to get you to an ER."

She shook her head, which made her wince.

"I'm just shaken up," she insisted. "I'm fine."

"No arguments." He wasn't taking no for answer. "If nothing else, you might need stitches. And trust me, you don't want me handling that." He managed a grin. "I cook much better than I sew."

"Okay," she relented. "I'll take your word for that."

He helped her to her feet. She sagged against him, using him for support. He fished his phone from his pocket and hit the speed dial.

"Damn it, Hardison. Pick up."

He knew the hacker often worked late, doing mission prep. He always complained that Eliot and the others didn't appreciate the long hours he spent at the keyboard, getting their cover stories and aliases online, as well as digging up dirt on their targets. He was probably right, not that Eliot would ever admit it.

"Eliot?" Hardison answered on the second ring. *"What's up? I thought you were taking the night off."*

"Turns out not so much." Eliot glanced down the street, where the limo was nowhere to be been. He guessed it was halfway to Brooklyn or Queens by now. "Looks like Brad's getting desperate. Some goons just jumped Denise, tried to abduct her."

"Seriously?" Hardison sounded appropriately shocked. *"That's messed up, man. What happened? She okay?"*

"I'll give you the full story later. Right now I need you to get me an ambulance or a cab or a horse and buggy . . . you got me?"

He could've called 911, but he figured Hardison was faster and more efficient than some overworked switchboard operator. Hell, Hardison had once managed to take over an air-traffic control tower on a few minutes' notice—and even land a plane or two.

"Is Denise hurt?" Hardison asked. *"How bad is it?"*

"Damn it, just get me that ambulance!"

The geek got the message. *"Okay, I'm locked on to the*

GPS signal from your phone. Stay right where you are. Help is on the way."

That was more like it. "Thanks, man."

"No problem. Anytime, you know. We also serve who only sit and click." Hardison tapped away in the background while he talked at Eliot. *"They really tried to snatch Denise, huh? Just wait until Nate and the gang hear about this. Guess we really rattled Brad's cage."*

"Seems like it." Eliot kicked himself for not seeing this coming, especially after what had happened to Gavin. Just how greedy was Brad? He heard an ambulance siren heading toward them. "Hang on," he told Denise. "I think our ride's almost here."

"Really?" she cracked wise. "What took them so long?" She nestled against him, holding the bloody scarf to her brow. He was glad to see that the bleeding already seemed to be slowing. She gazed into his eyes. "Thanks for coming to my rescue, by the way."

"Looked like you were doing pretty good on your own," he said, holding her up. He eyed her suspiciously. "Where'd an office temp pick up moves like that?"

"YMCA," she supplied. "How do you think I keep my girlish figure?"

"I don't know. You tell me."

"One of these days." A pained smile lifted her lips. She hugged him tighter. "Maybe next time you'll stick around a little longer?"

"Try and stop me."

SEVEN

LONG ISLAND

"Just one more chapter," Parker pleaded. Her eyes were fixed on the screen of Hardison's ebook reader. "Hang on. Yvette has the rebel leader in her sights, but she doesn't know that Dmitri was detained at customs . . ."

Hardison sat at the wheel of a flashy red sports car they had acquired for this occasion. The spiked iron gates of Brad Lee's estate lay at the end of a long private drive. Security cameras tracked their progress. He turned toward Parker, who was tucked into the passenger seat beside him. Exasperation tinged his voice.

"Woman, will you forget about the damn book for a minute?"

Parker scrolled through another page. "But I thought the book was what this job was all about?"

"Well, yes, but—"

"I've only got about thirty pages more," she announced. "I can't wait to read the sequel."

He shot her a look. "Er, you do know there is no sequel, right? Not for real?"

"Then why are we here?" she asked.

Hardison opened his mouth to explain, but decided it probably wasn't worth the effort. Sometimes Parker just took their scams a little too literally. Like the time they had faked Sophie's death and even held a mock funeral for her: it had been weeks before Parker had stopped poking Sophie to make sure she wasn't a ghost.

And, of course, she still wanted to know what happened to that time machine.

"Never mind," he said. "Just stick to the script."

He pulled up to the barred front gate and honked the horn. A mounted security camera swiveled toward them. A moment later, an electronic buzz signaled that they were clear to proceed. The gates swung open automatically.

Parker frowned as they drove onto the estate. "I don't like this. It feels like cheating."

"You can break into the next mansion," he assured her.

"Promise?"

The driveway led to Chez Brad, which was the size of stately Wayne Manor but twice as tacky. There were enough chimneys, dormers, pilasters, columns, ornamental stonework, and other flashy architectural bling to keep a dozen Real Housewives happy. The conspicuous grandeur of the estate was even more ridiculous when you considered that only one greedy ex-con was currently residing there. Living large was one thing; Hardison could appreciate a little pizzazz. But why did one person need ten bathrooms?

"Back again," Parker said. In theory, she had left her hacksaw behind.

They parked the car and headed for the house. Hardison was dressed to impress in a hip urban ensemble, while Parker sported a belted black blazer, tunic, and leggings.

Brad met them at the front door in a blue velour tracksuit that made room for his girth. Imposing marble columns dominated the two-story-high portico. Stone lions guarded the wide front steps.

"Ah, Mr. Lee!" Hardison put on his Cockney accent, which he thought sounded bloody brilliant . . . or maybe smashing. One of those. "So good of you to meet with us like this." He introduced Parker. "I believe you've already met my lovely assistant, Miss Lincoln?"

"Oh, yeah," Brad said sourly. "I remember."

"All of that was just to make your acquaintance," Hardison assured him. "Trust me, you won't regret it."

"Yeah, yeah," Brad said, not wasting breath on pleasantries. "Let's hear what you have to say." He stepped aside to let them enter the foyer, where a naked chain hung from the ceiling. "You owe me a new chandelier, incidentally."

Parker shrugged, unrepentant.

"Forget the chandelier," Hardison said. "With what you stand to make from the sequel, you'll be able to outshine Versailles."

"Ver-what?"

Okay, we're going to need to dumb things down, Hardison realized. He made a show of glancing around cautiously. "So, you're all alone here, as we discussed. No snoopy servants or bodyguards?"

He already knew, from hacking into the security cameras, that Brad had gotten rid of any inconvenient staff or visitors, but there was no point in letting him know that they had the house under surveillance. Better to play the part of an appropriately paranoid felon.

"Yeah, it's just us today," Brad confirmed. "Still don't see why we had to do this here, instead of over the phone or something." He glowered at Parker. "Bad enough she already barged in uninvited."

"I don't barge," she said indignantly. "Barging is for amateurs."

Hardison tried to head off a debate on the finer points of home invasion. "In matters of this nature, I find face-to-face meetings are preferable to conducting delicate business over the phone, online, or in public. You never know who might be listening in." He gestured grandly at the imposing edifice surrounding them. "A more secure environment is always best."

More importantly, they needed to set a precedent for their *next* meeting, which, according to plan, had to take place on these premises. There was also the fact that marks were often more easily manipulated on their home turf, where they were likely to feel more confident and be less on guard. Or so Sophie maintained, and she would know.

"If you say so," Brad said grudgingly.

"I do," Hardison said, taking control.

Brad led them into the same den where Parker had

spooked him before. The wall safe was again hidden behind the shelf of phony encyclopedias. Hardison's nose twitched in distaste; the room reeked of tobacco. Parker glanced nostalgically at the ceiling before perching on the edge of the desk and getting back to her book. Brad looked askance.

"Don't mind her," Hardison said. "She's just along for my protection." He leaned toward Brad and whispered. "Seriously, mate, just leave her be."

Brad gulped. He sat down behind the desk. He lit himself a cigar and puffed on it aggressively, as though daring his visitors to object. "So what's your racket anyway?"

"Think of us as highly skilled facilitators." Hardison planted himself in a wingback chair facing Brad. The smoke from the cigar was obnoxious, but he ignored it for the sake of the con. Exuding confidence, he launched into his spiel. "The saps and suckers, they think they can hold on to what they've got. But smart operators like us, we know better. Nice guys finish last, and sometimes you need some first-rate bad guys on your side to solve problems nobody else can."

"And that's where you come in?" Brad said.

Hardison leaned back in his chair. He chuckled slyly, channeling Nate.

"We provide . . . solutions."

"Uh-huh," Brad said skeptically. "For how much."

"Fifty thousand dollars, and a tiny sliver of the proceeds."

"Fifty thou?" Brad nearly swallowed his cigar. "For what?"

"Not only will we acquire a complete copy of the sequel,

as well as any documents establishing its provenance, but we can also make your problems with Denise Gallo go away for good."

"Oh, yeah. And how you gonna do that?"

"Let me demonstrate." Hardison took out his phone and dialed a number. A second later, a ring tone sounded from Brad's pocket. Confused, he took out his phone and stared at the screen. "Check your messages," Hardison suggested. "You're not going to believe who's calling you."

A video clip played on the phone. Gavin Lee gazed up from the screen with a serious expression on his face. His voice spoke from beyond the grave:

"Hi. This is Gavin James Lee, recording this video will for posterity. Being of sound mind and body, I wish to leave all my worldly estate to my brother and oldest living relative, Bradley Orson Lee." He paused to let this sink in before speaking directly to the camera. "We've had our differences, big brother, but family is family, and I hope this proves that, ultimately, blood is a bond that can't be broken. Take care, bro, and be well. I love you, buddy. Recorded September fourth, 2012."

Brad's eyes bugged out. "Holy crap! Is this for real?"

"Are you kidding me, mate?" Hardison said. "Of course not."

"Then how?"

Hardison put his phone away. He wiggled his fingers.

"A little CGI, a few YouTube videos of your brother giving interviews and doing readings, a new backdrop, some creative splicing and editing of the audio clips, and . . . voilà." He didn't have to fake his pride in the manufactured footage. "I must say, your brother was quite articulate, with an impressive vocabulary. Made my job a good deal easier."

Brad watched the video again. "Okay, that's pretty slick."

"Actually, the rendering still needs a little work," Hardison admitted. He had wanted to tinker with it a bit more, but that business with Denise had cut into his work schedule. "But I can get you a cleaner version later, once we have a deal."

"Yeah, about that." Brad went into haggle mode. "That's a cute trick, sure, but what do I need a phony will for? The courts have already awarded me Brad's estate."

"True, but as long as Denise is out there making noise, you're still going to have to keep convincing nervous business partners that there's no potential complications with the rights—and deal with any bad PR regarding the poor, mistreated girlfriend. This way the whole world will know that Gavin wanted to do right by you." Hardison waved the cigar smoke away from his face. "Plus, of course, there's the matter of the sequel. Don't you want to be able to prove, conclusively and beyond a doubt, that the new book belongs to you and you alone?"

"I suppose," Brad conceded.

"Trust me, this is in your best interests," Hardison said. "And, if I may say so, a much more elegant solution than any crude snatch-and-grab."

"Yeah," Parker interrupted. "What were you thinking there?" She shook her head disdainfully. "Amateurs."

"Huh?" Brad scowled. "What the hell are you talking about?"

"Please," Hardison scolded him. "Like you didn't have anything to do with that attack on Denise Gallo the other night."

"Attack? What attack?"

"Did you really think we wouldn't hear about that?" Hardison wagged a finger at Brad. "Thought you could just have your hooligans snatch a woman off the street and that would be the end of it? You're going to have to do better than that, Mr. Lee."

"Are you crazy?" Brad's face flushed crimson. He lurched to his feet. "I swear to God, I don't know anything about any attack! What happened to Denise?"

"She's fine, no thanks to those discount goons you hired, which just goes to show that you get what you pay for." Hardison took Brad's outburst in stride, calmly lecturing him like a professional adviser dealing with a clueless client. "You're in the big leagues now, Mr. Lee. Maybe that kind of strong-arm tactic worked back when you were boosting autos and knocking over 7-Elevens, but it's no way to secure your claim on a valuable piece of intellectual property. Frankly, Brad, I'm a bit disappointed in you."

"I keep telling you, I didn't have anything to do with it!"

Hardison wondered if Brad was telling the truth. He hoped not, because that would mean that somebody else was after Denise, like maybe the mysterious Tarantula? Hardison made an effort to shove the mystery out of his mind for the present. There would be time enough to ponder the question later. Right now he needed to stay in character, and Brad's guilt or innocence had no bearing on how this con needed to play out.

"If that's your story, fine," he said as Parker snorted in

disbelief. "The point is, if you want this problem taken care of the right way, you need to hire professionals."

"For fifty K?"

"And a modest percentage," Hardison reminded him.

"I don't know," Brad hedged. "That's a lot of money."

"Wouldn't be worth our time if it wasn't." Hardison plucked Brad's cigar from his fingers and ground it out in an ashtray. He fixed a steely gaze on the recalcitrant mark. "But what you need to ask yourself, Mr. Lee, is how much is that sequel worth to you?"

YESTERDAY:

"You were holding out on me, pal," Nate accused Brad, posing as Max Dunfee of Antipodes Press. "You told me in Frankfurt there was no sequel."

He was on the phone to Brad, pacing back and forth in the deluxe hotel suite that was serving as the crew's temporary base of operations in New York. An array of screens had been set up in the central living room. Sophie was stretched out on the couch behind Nate, while Hardison and Parker were sharing a bowl of microwave popcorn over by the bar. Eliot was off guarding Denise; he had barely left her side since the attempted abduction. Nate hoped he wasn't getting too involved with their client. That seldom worked out well.

"Er, I was just playing my cards close to my chest," Brad lied. "While I figured out the best way to peddle the book, you know."

Brad was lounging in a hot tub, unaware that his

sweaty, beet-red form was currently filling up a large portion of the screens in front of Nate and the others. Hardison had detected the presence of the hidden camera aimed at the hot tub when he'd tapped into the mansion's electronic security system, and Parker had verified its existence while prowling the mansion a few nights ago. Nate didn't need to rack his imagination to figure out what sort of X-rated activity the camera was intended to catch, but that was irrelevant; what mattered was that the camera was working for him now.

"Well, the news is out," Nate said. "That's for sure."

He wasn't exaggerating. Thanks to some well-placed rumors on industry Web sites and message boards, the whole world knew about the alleged sequel, supposedly titled Assassins Remember. *Sophie brandished the latest copy of* Variety. *A front-page headline read* STUDIOS SNIFF AFTER ASSASSINS SEQUEL. *One of the screens charted Internet searches regarding the sequel.* Assassins Remember *was currently a trending topic on Yahoo. Fans were already speculating feverishly about the plot.*

"Tell me about it," Brad said. "My phone's been ringing off the hook."

"I can imagine," Nate said, *although he didn't need to. They had been tracking Brad's incoming calls and e-mails since the news broke, and, yes, Brad was getting positively buried in offers and inquiries from genuine publishers, agents, big-name directors, movie stars, and studios. And the best part was, Nate and the crew hadn't even needed to fake all this interest.* Assassins Remember *really was a hot property now.*

Too bad it didn't exist.

"So this is the real deal?" Nate asked. "An actual sequel written by your brother before he died, not some ghostwritten knockoff like you were talking about before?"

"It's for real," Brad said. "The last thing my brother ever wrote."

"Then you're sitting on a gold mine, my friend." Nate wanted to keep reinforcing that idea every chance he got. Brad was not somebody who required a subtle touch. "So when do I get a chance to read this future bestseller?"

"Um, soon," Brad hedged. "Just getting all my ducks in a row, you know." He got out of the tub and walked over to a nearby fridge in his birthday suit. Sophie averted her eyes from the fleshy spectacle. Parker made a face. "And, naturally, I'm getting lots of other offers."

"I'm sure! But hey, when you're looking at the international market, don't forget your friends in New Zealand—and those beers we had in Frankfurt." Nate let Max sound a little desperate to land the book for Antipodes. "I can't talk figures right now, not before I have a chance to review the manuscript, but I can tell you that if *Remember* is half the book that *Forget* was, this could be a very big book for us—and we would pay accordingly."

"So I keep hearing," Brad said. "Gotta run. More calls coming in."

"I'll bet." Nate stayed on the line as long as he could. "Don't forget. We want to see that manuscript. And the sooner the better."

"I hear you," Brad said, a tad impatiently. "Loud and clear."

He hung up on Nate.
His phone kept ringing.

"All right," Brad said. "We have a deal . . . if you can get me that sequel."

Hardison beamed at him. Parker put down her ebook.

"You can count on us," Hardison said.

EIGHT

LONG ISLAND

For credibility's sake, they let Brad stew for a couple days. They couldn't make stealing the sequel seem too easy; he might get suspicious, or just start wondering why he was paying so much. In the meantime, he continued to be barraged with legitimate offers regarding *Assassins Remember*, without the Leverage crew needing to lift another finger. Hardison actually felt sorry for raising the hopes of Gavin's fans—it was like teasing people with the possibility of new *Deep Space Nine* episodes—but not enough to call off the con.

"You got it?" Brad asked eagerly. "The new book?"

"Was there ever any doubt?" Hardison strode up to the front door of the mansion, carrying a leather briefcase. He grinned at Brad. "We always deliver."

Parker trotted up the steps beside him. She stumbled on

the top step and fell toward Brad. "Oops!" She grabbed on to him briefly to steady herself, then shoved him away. She gave the steps a dirty look. "You should get that fixed."

"Get what fixed?"

She didn't explain. "You're lucky nobody's broken their neck yet!"

"Never mind that." Brad clearly couldn't care less about the steps—or Parker's neck. He eyed the briefcase hungrily. "Is that it? What have you got there?"

"Look at you." Hardison chuckled. "As greedy as a kid on Christmas. Well, naughty or nice, Santa has definitely come through for you this time." He raised the case and patted it. "We hit the mother lode: computer files, a printout of the manuscript, plus Gavin's own handwritten notes and outlines, just to prove he really wrote it."

"Wow," Brad said, impressed. He reached for the case. "Let me see."

"Not so fast." Hardison kept a tight grip on the handle of the case. "There's still the little matter of our payment. In cash, as agreed."

"Oh, yeah. That." Brad's enthusiasm dimmed several watts. "Don't worry. I've got the money, although it wasn't easy coming up with that much dough on short notice, I'll tell you that."

"You'll make it all back with the sequel," Hardison promised. "And much, much more."

"That's the idea," Brad said. It was unclear if he was agreeing with Hardison or trying hard to convince himself. He gestured toward the door. "Come on, then. Let's go inside. As soon as I make sure those are really the goods, and that you're not trying to pull a fast one on me, you can have your dough."

"Now we're talking," Hardison said. "I look forward to completing our transaction."

In truth, he had no intention of letting Brad look at the "sequel" too closely. A couple of sample chapters were one thing, but even with Eliot's help, they could hardly expect Denise to churn out an entire novel in a matter of days, so they had just cobbled something together by cutting and pasting scenes and chapters from a dozen different spy thrillers they had pirated online. Hardison had personally searched and replaced to make sure all the names and proper nouns were consistent throughout, but it would be a literary miracle if the plot made any sense at all. As an exercise in creative plagiarism, the Frankenstein-like patchwork job looked like a real book at first glance, just in case Brad insisted on skimming it right away, but no way would it bear a close reading.

Fortunately, it didn't have to.

Hardison checked his watch. *Anytime now* . . .

Right on cue, a blue sedan, with a spinning red bubble light atop its roof, zoomed up to the front of the mansion. A police siren wailed as the unmarked vehicle squealed to a stop only a few yards away from the portico.

"What the heck?" Brad exclaimed.

"Hell, no!" Hardison feigned distress. He turned on Parker. "Were we followed? You were supposed to make sure we weren't followed!"

"Don't blame me!" she snapped. "Why is it always my fault?" She glanced around frantically, as though considering making a run for it, but the mansion's open front lawn offered little in the way of cover. She lunged at Hardison, brushing against Brad. Her finger jabbed Hardison's chest. "Damn it, I told you this location was too risky! We should've used that old fallout shelter instead. The one in Death Valley!"

"Wait!" Brad looked alarmed. "What's happening?"

"Don't say anything!" Hardison said urgently. He hastily lobbed the briefcase into some nearby bushes. "Let me handle this, okay?"

The car's door slammed open and Eliot emerged, dressed in a police uniform. His long hair was hidden beneath his cap. A surly expression made it clear he was not to be messed with. His right hand rested on the gun holstered at his hip.

"Nobody move!" he ordered. "Stay right where you are."

Brad instinctively threw up his hands, then lowered them sheepishly. This wasn't the first time he'd been confronted by the law. "Um, what's this all about, Officer?"

Before Eliot could explain, the car's back door was flung open and Sophie joined the scene. She stormed up the steps and pointed angrily at Hardison and Parker.

"You see, I told you those thieves would be here . . . with him!" Her dark eyes shot daggers at Brad. She was utterly convincing, more so than she ever was onstage. "I knew you were lowlife scum, Brad, but I never thought that even you would stoop so low!" She looked like she was about to slap him. "Your brother would be ashamed!"

"That's enough, Ms. Drury." Eliot got between Sophie and Brad. "Let me handle this."

"Handle what?" Brad asked. "What's this all about . . . and how did you get past the front gates?"

That would be me, Hardison thought smugly. It had been easy enough to reprogram the security system so that Eliot and Sophie could buzz themselves in. Not that Brad was likely to figure this out anytime soon. He was about to have bigger things to worry out.

"You gonna give me a hard time, buster?" Eliot challenged Brad. He waved a forged document in Brad's face. "This warrant says I go where I please, you got that?"

"Yeah, yeah," Brad said, backing off. A guy had to be pretty ballsy—or stupid—to stand up to Eliot when he was being his intimidating self. Brad was no Starfleet science officer, but he wasn't *that* dumb. "Whatever you say, Officer. I'm just trying to cooperate . . . fully."

"Is that so?" Eliot snorted. "Then maybe you can explain how it is that you're in the process of receiving stolen goods from these two?"

Brad tried to look innocent, but it didn't come naturally. "Stolen?"

"We have evidence," Eliot said. "*Ironclad* evidence of this young lady breaking into Ms. Drury's private residence and escaping with certain items that did not belong to her." He spun Parker around and slapped some cuffs on her. "As well as proof that this other gentleman acted as her accomplice and getaway driver."

Hardison distanced himself from Parker, who pretended that the cuffs were actually a problem for her. He hid his own hands behind his back, out of sight and mind. "*Moi?* Why, I barely know this—"

"Stop. Don't even start with that." Eliot glared at Hardison in a manner that, frankly, was all too familiar. "Where's the briefcase?"

"Briefcase?" Hardison played dumb. He looked at Brad. "You know anything about a briefcase?"

"Over here, Officer!" Sophie rummaged through the bushes and emerged with the briefcase. She ran back onto the porch. "I saw him try to get rid of it as we pulled up!"

"Gimme that," Eliot ordered. He tried the combination lock, which refused to yield. He thrust the case at Hardison. "Open it!"

Hardison stared at the case like he had never seen it before. They had to make this look good; he couldn't cave too readily.

"I'm sure I don't know . . ."

"Open it," Eliot snarled.

Brad exchanged a worried look with Hardison. He looked like he was about to throw up.

Hardison dragged it out. "But—"

"Open it."

Sighing in defeat, Hardison unlocked the case. The bottom half dropped open, spilling a thick manuscript and several spiral notebooks onto the porch. A flash drive landed at Eliot's feet. Loose pages began to blow away.

"You thieving pirates!" Sophie exclaimed. She rushed to gather up the loose pages before they could get too far. A breeze threatened to carry off Chapter Two. "How could you do this? Steal the fruits of a dead man's genius?"

"This your property, ma'am?" Eliot asked. He retrieved the fallen flash drive and carefully placed it into a plastic evidence bag.

"You bet your badge it is!" Sophie declared. She skimmed the first few pages just to make sure, taking just long enough to make it believable. She looked up from the pages with a vindictive expression. "We've caught them red-handed!"

"Wait a sec!" Brad protested, backing away from Hardison and Parker as though they were radioactive. He was already perspiring heavily. "I don't know anything about this!"

"He made me do it!" Parker blurted, nodding at Brad. "It was all his idea!" She rattled her cuffs. Hardison knew it had to be killing her to act like she couldn't get out of them. "I . . . I'm the victim here!"

"Oh, yeah?" Eliot said sarcastically. "And how is that?"

Parker's brow furrowed. She frowned sullenly. "Give me a minute. I'm working on it."

"I swear to you, Officer, I had nothing to do with this." Brad tried and failed to look innocent. Agitated, he wrung his hands. "I didn't know anything about a break-in!"

"And these people just happened to show up on your doorstep?" Eliot said skeptically. "With a stolen manuscript by your brother in hand?"

"Um, well . . ." Brad wiped sweat from his brow as he struggled visibly to come up with a plausible explanation. "They said they had some unpublished material by my late brother. How was I supposed to know they'd stolen it?"

"You lying pig!" Sophie accused him. "You knew exactly who really had Gavin's book. I told you all about it in Frankfurt!"

"Back off, ma'am," Eliot warned. He held up his palm like a traffic cop. "Let me handle this. I'm not going to tell you again."

"But you don't believe him, do you?" Sophie sneered at Brad. "The man is a convicted criminal. Check his record!"

Brad swallowed hard. "That's all ancient history, Officer. I'm clean now, I swear to God." He gestured frantically at Hardison and Parker. "These are the only thieves here, Officer. Not me!"

Hardison gave him a wounded look. "Really, mate? You're throwing us under the bus now? That's what you're doing?" He shook his head sadly. "I expected better of you, Brad. I really did."

"I was hypnotized!" Parker came out with. She hopped up and down to get everyone's attention. "That's right! I was hypnotized . . . or brainwashed! He washed my poor, innocent brain!"

You know, Hardison thought, *that would explain a lot.*

"Listen to her, Officer! She's crazy!" Brad was getting more desperate by the moment. His voice went up several octaves. "They're making this all up. It's their word against mine!"

"Says the sleazy ex-con who ought to be in jail," Sophie said, wrinkling her nose in disgust. She regarded him as she would a slug—or a slush pile. "You think your word means anything?"

"Shut up, you bitch!" Brad snapped. "You're not helping!"

"Watch it, mister!" Eliot grabbed on to Brad's tracksuit and shoved him up against one of the looming Corinthian columns. His fists bunched up the velour fabric. "Just 'cause you live in some big, fancy-pants mansion doesn't mean you can act like a punk. You hearing me?"

"Yes, Officer," Brad whimpered. "It won't happen again."

"It had better not." Eliot backed off and let go of Brad's suit. "I'm watching you, mister."

The chastened ex-con gasped, struggling to catch his breath. He sagged against the ostentatious marble column.

"Look, Officer—" Hardison squinted at Eliot's badge. "Officer Kolchak, I understand that you're a busy man. Is it too early to start cutting a deal? I'm prepared to give evidence against Mr. Lee here in exchange for a good word with the D.A. I'll spill my guts like a sliced halibut—"

"Wait!" Brad cried out. "Be quiet!"

"Sorry, chum." Hardison shrugged apologetically. "It's every thief for his self now." He glanced at Parker. "Hell, I'll even throw in my female associate as a bonus."

"Hypnotized!" she repeated. "Did I mention I was hypnotized?"

"Just check out his den," Hardison suggested. "I'm willing to bet that you'll find a suitcase with fifty thousand dollars in unmarked bills. All part of our deal."

It was a safe bet. He had personally watched Brad assemble the cash via a hijacked webcam. The payoff money was right there, just waiting for Eliot's bogus search warrant. And Brad knew it.

"Um, I can explain that." Brad tugged on his collar. "That's . . . a charitable donation I was getting ready to make, anonymously, to, um, the Boy Scouts."

"The Boy Scouts? Seriously?" Hardison rolled his eyes. "Okay, now you're just embarrassing yourself, mate." He turned back toward Eliot. "There's more, Officer. Subpoena his phone records and e-mails. I think you'll discover that

Mr. Lee here has already been negotiating to sell the very book we just . . . acquired . . . from Ms. Drury's residence."

"And why not?" Brad blustered. "The book belongs to me anyway!" He appealed to Eliot. "Even if what they're saying is true, and I'm not saying it is, I was just trying to recover my own property, which was being illegally withheld from me. Maybe, hypothetically, I didn't go about it the right way, but you can't arrest a guy for stealing his own property." He looked hopefully at Eliot. "Can you?"

Eliot confiscated the briefcase and its contents from Sophie, who surrendered them with a show of reluctance. He regarded Brad dubiously. "You saying this book belongs to you?"

"Yes! And I can prove it." Brad pulled out his phone and called up a certain video clip. "My brother, who wrote the book, willed his entire estate to me." He held the phone up to Eliot. "Listen!"

Gavin's voice issued from the phone:

"Hi. This is Gavin James Lee, recording this video will on September fourth, 2012. Being of sound mind and body, I wish to bequeath my entire estate, including all rights to my complete literary output, to my girlfriend, collaborator, and soul mate, Denise Maria Gallo." He sighed audibly. "Denise, sweetheart, I'm hoping you'll never see this video, but I want to make sure you won't lose everything we've worked for, just in case something happens to me. You're my best friend and partner, and the only person I trust to look after our work. I love you."

"Wha—?" Brad stared at the phone in shock. "Wait a second. That's not right. That's not what it said before . . ."

A FEW MINUTES AGO:

Parker trotted up the steps beside Hardison. She "stumbled" on the top step and fell toward Brad. "Oops!" She grabbed onto him briefly, supposedly to steady herself, while deftly lifting his phone from his pocket. Backing away, she gave the steps a dirty look. "You should get that fixed."

While Hardison chatted with Brad, keeping him occupied, she turned her back on them and quietly deleted the first version of the will from Gavin's phone. She then discreetly dialed Nate, who transmitted the new version to the phone.

"You got it?" he asked in her ear.

She checked to make sure Video Will 2.0 had arrived safely.

"Yep," she whispered beneath her breath.

In theory, a built-in worm would cause any backup copies of the original phony will to delete themselves from wherever they were being stored. Now all she had to do was wait for the right opportunity to put the phone back where it belonged.

She didn't have to wait long . . .

Eliot's car came roaring up the drive, right on schedule. She winced at the blaring sirens.

"Oh, no." Hardison acted alarmed. He turned on her in a way she would never tolerate if it had been for real. "Were we followed? You were supposed to make sure we weren't followed!"

"Don't blame me!" she snapped. "Why is it always my

fault?" She brushed against Brad, replacing the phone, while play-arguing with Hardison. She jabbed his chest with her finger to sell the scene, just like Sophie had suggested. "Damn it, I told you this exchange was too risky!"

"Wait!" Brad looked alarmed. "What's happening?"

You're being played, *she thought. That's what.*

"I don't understand," Brad said, bewildered. "That's all wrong."

"I don't know. It sounded very clear-cut to me." Sophie stepped forward and plucked the traitorous phone from Brad's fingers. He was too numb to put up a fuss. She handed the phone over to Eliot for safekeeping. "So how long have you been sitting on Gavin's last will and testament, Brad? Concealing your own brother's final requests? That's low even for you."

"No!" Brad sputtered. "That's a fake!" He pointed at Hardison. "This is some sort of trick. He faked that will, but now he's changed it somehow!"

"Whoa there!" Eliot said. His eyes narrowed ominously. "Did I hear you right? Did you just confess to taking part in a conspiracy to commit a fraud?"

"What? No!" Brad's face fell as he realized he was digging himself even deeper into a hole. He feebly attempted to backpedal. "That is, I mean . . ."

"So what is it?" Eliot demanded, getting all up in Brad's face. "That will genuine or not?"

"Well, um . . . you see . . ."

"You weren't trying to deceive a police officer, were you?"

"No, never! It's just that . . ."

Brad looked like he didn't know whether he was coming or going, which was precisely what they were after. "I . . . um . . ." Tongue-tied, and terrified of saying the wrong thing, he stammered incoherently. "The thing is . . . you see . . . it's just . . ."

"Answer me!" Eliot growled. He unhooked a second pair of handcuffs from his belt. "Or I'm taking you all down to the station right this minute!"

"No, please!" Brad squealed. A two-time loser, and then some, he was looking at serious jail time if he got convicted again, not to mention the almost certain revocation of his parole. No doubt visions of concrete walls and prison cells were closing in on his imagination. Brad wasn't the kind of tough guy who could fend for himself in a hard-core penal environment. He sounded scared out of his wits. "There must be a way we can work something out."

"Well, actually . . ."

Sophie moved in for the kill. She let an avaricious gleam light up her eyes. Her voice took on a calculating tone.

"Officer Kolchak, this matter has already taken up too much of your valuable time. I don't wish to burden you or the judicial system any more than necessary." She gently took Eliot's arm and batted her lashes at him in a way that would probably turn Nate fifty shades of green if it hadn't been part of a con. "And, as much as I'm loath to admit it, Brad *is* my client's boyfriend's brother. I'm sure she wouldn't want to see him behind bars . . . again."

A flicker of hope appeared on Brad's face. It was a thing of beauty.

"What are you suggesting, ma'am?" Eliot asked.

Sophie regarded Brad coolly. "I'm prepared to drop all charges—if Mr. Lee returns my property and agrees not to contest Gavin's will." She smirked at Brad. "I'll want that in writing, of course."

Eliot took his time thinking it over, letting Brad sweat.

"Well, Mr. Lee," he said finally. "What do you say?"

Brad hesitated, no doubt torn between his plans to cash in on his brother's legacy and the daunting prospect of going back to jail for a long term. For a second, Hardison worried that they might have hyped the imaginary sequel too much. What if Brad couldn't bring himself to part with those profits, no matter what?

"Don't give in, mate," he called out, attempting a little reverse psychology. "All you need to do is stick it out for another ten to twenty, maybe a trifle more, and hope that those royalties are still waiting for you. Prison's not so bad. You've done time before." His face lighted up. "Hey, maybe we can be cell buddies?"

"Hypnotized," Parker repeated. "I'm just saying, hypnotized."

"Shut up, you two." Eliot leaned on Brad, literally playing the bad cop. "Make up your mind, buster. I've got better things to do than sort out who owns some stupid spy novel. I've got real killers and rapists to catch, damn it."

Brad looked plaintively at Sophie. "Fifty-fifty?"

"No deal," Sophie said, enjoying the upper hand. "You had your chance to play nice. It's all or nothing now."

Brad was up against a wall and he knew it. A pitiful whimper escaped his blubbery lips.

"Okay, okay," he caved. "The book's yours."

"Both books," Sophie clarified. "Gavin's entire literary estate."

"Yes." He dragged the word out like he was coughing up a hardcover. He stared glumly at his feet. "Both books. You win." He glanced back over his shoulder at the looming mansion. "Should've known it was too good to be true."

You don't know the half of it, Hardison thought.

"Fine," Eliot said impatiently. He handed the briefcase over to Sophie. "Are we done here?"

"So it appears." Sophie strolled back toward the waiting police car. "Can I prevail upon you for a ride to the train station?"

"Why not?" He shook his head in disgust. "All of this over a dumb book. Intellectual property, my ass. Don't call me again unless there's a dead body or a broken window." He rolled his eyes. "A spy novel, for Pete's sake!"

"You should read it." Parker handed Eliot back his cuffs, which she had deftly slipped out of. "I couldn't put it down."

He glared at her in a very believable fashion.

"C'mon, girl." Hardison took her arm and guided her toward their borrowed sports car. "I don't know about you, Miss Lincoln, but I think we've overstayed our welcome." He waved a cheery good-bye at Brad. "So long, mate. Sorry things didn't work out."

"I'll fax you the necessary paperwork," Sophie called out from the drive. "Do be a dear and sign it right away. I wouldn't want to have to ask Officer Kolchak to make a return trip."

"Nah, that wouldn't be a good idea," Eliot said. He gave

Brad a look that had made stronger men soil their undergarments. "Trust me on that."

Brad nodded. They left him standing on the porch of his mansion, which he probably wouldn't be keeping much longer. He looked well and truly defeated.

"Good job, everyone," Nate congratulated them over the comms. *"That was almost too easy."*

Hardison looked around for some wood to knock on. He rapped his knuckles against a convenient shrub.

Don't jinx it, he thought.

NINE

MANHATTAN

"Oh my God, you did it! This is fantastic!"

Denise was overcome with emotion as she met with the Leverage crew in their hotel suite to hear the good news. Tears of happiness filled her eyes as she hugged Eliot, who had personally escorted her to the meeting. The rest of the team were also on hand to enjoy the moment, seated around a polished walnut coffee table in front of a toasty fireplace. Sunshine filtered through filmy curtains. Less than four hours had passed since the con at Brad's mansion, and they already had what they wanted. *Assassins Never Forget* belonged to Denise now.

"Thank you so much!" she gushed. "All of you!"

A frown crossed Eliot's face as he hugged her back. He wished he felt better about this victory, but Gavin was still dead—and important issues were unresolved.

Don't think about that now, he thought. *Let her have this moment.*

"It was our pleasure," Nate insisted. He waited for Denise and Eliot to disengage before presenting her with a manila envelope. "Enclosed is a faxed release from Brad, granting you all rights with regard to Gavin's estate." A former insurance investigator who knew the ins and outs of fine print, Nate had personally drawn up the paperwork. "Just show that to your lawyer tomorrow morning, and I'm sure he'll be able to straighten everything out."

Denise clutched the envelope to her chest. "I don't believe it. It doesn't seem real."

"Believe it," Sophie told her. "Gavin's work—everything you accomplished together—is all yours. Just as he would have wanted."

"Too bad the sequel's not as good as the original," Parker said. She was perched at the bar, poring over the patchwork manuscript they had brought back with them. She frowned at the pages. "Seriously, this book doesn't make any sense at all."

Denise looked understandably baffled. "But—"

"Just go with it," Eliot advised her. "It's easier that way."

Denise took his word for it. Getting back to the matter at hand, she opened the envelope and skimmed the enclosed document. A flicker of worry furrowed her brow.

"What if Brad changes his mind?" she asked. "Is there any chance he could fight this?"

"It's always possible," Nate conceded, "but between the 'will' and this signed release, he would be on extremely shaky ground, unless he wants to admit hiring Hardison to fake Brad's will in the first place."

"You mean, hiring 'Cyrano Jones,'" Hardison corrected Nate. "Respect the alias, man."

"Sure," Nate said. "No tribble."

Hardison eyed Nate with new respect. Eliot resisted a temptation to punch them both.

"Don't worry about it," he told Denise. "Brad raises a fuss, Officer Kolchak will pay him another call."

And that's if he's lucky, Eliot thought.

His fists clenched at his sides.

Their words seemed to reassure Denise. A grateful smile replaced her look of anxiety.

"Thank you," she said again. "I'll talk to my lawyer in the morning, have him get in touch with the various publishers and studios." Her eyes brimmed over. "This is like a dream come true, or, on second thought, more like waking up from a nightmare. I promise to make sure the profits go to support human rights, just like Gavin and I always intended."

"I'm glad we could remedy this situation for you," Nate said. "That's what we're here for."

Knowing Nate, Eliot suspected that their leader was already thinking ahead to their next play. More than any of them, probably, Nate was driven to fight back against a system that often screwed over people who deserved better. Sophie did her best to keep him balanced, and to get him to stop and smell the flowers now and then, but Nate was a man with a mission, and he wasn't one to sit on his laurels for too long.

Eliot knew the feeling. He had unfinished business, too.

"Well, I won't keep you any longer," Denise said. "I'm sure there are plenty of other people who need your help."

Eliot walked her to the door, where she lingered on the threshold. She questioned him with her eyes, uncertain if he would be accompanying her back to her apartment. "Should I wait for you?" she asked softly. "Are you going my way?"

He had been sticking close to her, in more ways than one, since the attack outside her apartment. Truth to tell, he had been spending every night at her place, and not just playing bodyguard. It still felt awkward, especially when he thought of Gavin, but it felt right, too. Life was short and it wasn't just about Gavin anymore. It was about Denise and what she needed and wanted now. And, yeah, it was about his feelings for her, too. Denise was a beautiful, vital woman with whom he'd forged a real connection. It wasn't fair to deny that out of respect for a ghost—or so he kept telling himself.

Too bad he couldn't tell her everything.

"Maybe later," he told her. "I've still got some stuff to take care of here."

That flicker of anxiety returned, almost as though she knew he wasn't being entirely honest with her. "Anything serious?"

"Nope," he lied. "Just some shoptalk—about another job."

She eyed him carefully, not entirely convinced he was on the level. "Okay, I'll leave you to it." She moved in closer and lowered her voice. "Don't be long, okay? I feel like celebrating."

"Count on it," he said.

That was all she needed to hear, apparently. Despite the audience elsewhere in the room, she pulled him in and planted a passionate kiss on his lips. For a second, he forgot all about any other pressing matters as he held her and kissed her back. Intoxicating moments passed before they finally broke apart.

"I'll be waiting," she promised.

She closed the door behind her as she left. Eliot turned to face his friends, who regarded him with varying degrees of amusement and/or embarrassment. Sophie looked pleased as punch, Hardison snickered and gave him a thumbs-up, Nate sighed and looked at the ceiling. Parker was oblivious.

"What?" he challenged them. He swept his gaze over the others, daring them to say anything.

"None of my business," Nate said, shrugging. He nursed his afternoon scotch. "I just hope you know what you're doing."

Me, too, Eliot thought.

Sophie smirked, enjoying the situation a little too much. Her eyes twinkled. "I'm not saying anything."

"About what?" Parker asked. She looked up from the manuscript.

"Eliot and Denise," Hardison explained. He winked at her conspiratorially. "They're sharing . . . pretzels."

It was something of a private joke between them.

"Oh, that." Parker shrugged. "I thought we already knew that."

"We did," Nate said. "So let's move on." He put down his drink and got serious. "So, I take it we're not telling Denise the rest of the story? What Hardison just turned up regarding Gavin's accident?"

"Not yet," Eliot said. Nate had privately alerted him earlier, when Eliot was with Denise, that Hardison had tracked down some disturbing new evidence about the night Gavin died. Eliot had chosen to keep Denise in the dark until he found out more. "She's happy now. Why spoil it?"

"All right," Nate agreed. "That's your call—for now."

The celebratory mood evaporated as Eliot sat down on the couch in front of the blank, transparent screens. The rest of the team settled in for the briefing as well. Eliot assumed that the others had heard some of this before, but he wanted to get the full story from the beginning.

"Show me," he said.

Hardison claimed his remote and fired up the screens. He drew the drapes to cut down on the glare. Looking directly at Eliot, he launched into the briefing:

"As you know, Nate asked me to look into that supposed hit-and-run 'accident,' which turned out to be easier said than done. Despite my best efforts, which y'all know are nothing to sneeze at, I couldn't find any video coverage of the actual collision. No CCTV footage, no amateur YouTube videos, no ATM security cameras . . . nada. Which, honestly, raised some red flags right there. It was like the hit-and-runner deliberately chose an intersection that was conveniently out of view of any inconvenient cameras. All I could find was this."

A crime photo of the intersection appeared on the central screen. A portion of an ambulance intruded in the lower right corner. Hardison had mercifully cropped the image to avoid any shots of Gavin's lifeless body.

Eliot appreciated the effort.

"Check out those heavy black skid marks just in front of the crosswalk," Hardison said. "Looks to me like somebody peeled out in a hurry, going from zero to sixty just as Gavin was crossing the street in front of them."

The skid marks looked fresh as hell. "That was no accident," Eliot realized. "Gavin was murdered."

"So it appears," Nate agreed.

"And in cold blood," Sophie added, appalled. Although a career criminal, she disapproved of violence . . . and homicide, in particular. She had once told Nate that she could never be involved with a killer. "How despicable."

That was putting it lightly. Eliot seethed with tightly controlled fury. For a second, he was back in a humid Sumatran rain forest:

"Eliot! Behind you!"

A flashbulb went off in the jungle, distracting the sentry. Startled, he swung his gun toward the flash, away from Eliot.

"You're welcome," Gavin said.

"Tell me you know who did this," Eliot said darkly.

"To be honest with you, man, I wasn't getting anywhere until those guys in the limo tried to grab Denise. Then I started looking for a suspicious black limousine matching your description."

"A 2010 six-passenger, black Lincoln Town Car," Eliot spit out. His jaw clenched as he remembered how close the limo had come to carrying off Denise. If he had been a few minutes slower, or if she had put up less of a fight . . .

"Right," Hardison said. "Which matches the tread marks at the crosswalk, by the way." He had clearly done his homework. "Now take a look at this."

He clicked his remote and a familiar black limousine appeared on the screen. The limo was parked at a curb somewhere in Manhattan, on what looked like a commercial side street well after sundown. A time stamp in the corner caught Eliot's attention. He recognized the date and time.

"That's traffic-cam footage taken the night Gavin died, around the time his book signing was breaking up," Hardison confirmed. "That limo is parked just up the road from the bookstore."

"Like they were waiting for him," Eliot realized.

"Is it the same limo?" Sophie asked. "The one you saw outside Denise's apartment?"

"Maybe." Eliot stared at the footage, searching his memory. He had been too busy dealing with Denise and those thugs to take a really good look at the vehicle, but, yeah, that might be it. He looked at Hardison. "What else you got?"

"More," the hacker said. "A lot more."

Manipulating the remote like a virtuoso, he called up a quick shot of the same limo cruising down a nocturnal city street. Eliot thought he recognized the neighborhood. It wasn't far from Denise's place.

"That's about five minutes before the 'accident,'" Hardison explained. "Running parallel to Brad's own route home."

Sophie shook her head in dismay. "It's like it's stalking him."

"Probably had a spotter keeping an eye on him," Nate speculated. "Keeping the limo informed of his movements."

"Yeah," Eliot said. "That's what I'd do."

In fact, he had taken part in similar setups, back in

the bad, old days. That didn't make him feel any better about what was about to happen to Gavin. The net had been tightening around his friend and he probably hadn't even known it.

Or had he suspected, in his final moments, that he was in danger?

Assassins Never Forget . . .

"It was a perfect opportunity," Nate observed. "They knew when and where Gavin would be heading home that evening. Wouldn't be too hard to figure out the most likely routes—and plan accordingly."

"This is why I never use the same route twice," Parker said. "Ever."

Eliot believed it. For years, she had maintained at least six fake addresses in Boston while actually calling an empty storage unit home. Even after she joined Nate's crew, it had been months before any of them actually found out where she lived. He still remembered the first time he laid eyes on her place, which had been more sparsely furnished than the average bomb shelter.

"Skipping ahead," Hardison continued. "Here we are three minutes *after* the collision, two blocks further west."

On the screens, the black limo was speeding away from the scene of the crime. Nate leaned forward, squinting at the display. He put on his reading glasses.

"Can you give us a better look?" he asked.

"Way ahead of you." Hardison froze an image of the limo heading toward the camera. A blurry smudge could now be seen at the front of the vehicle. "Let me enhance that for y'all."

The blur resolved itself into a close-up of the limo's

damaged front end. A substantial dent, that Eliot was pretty sure hadn't been there before, marred the limo's elegant lines. The crumpled metal gleamed wetly.

"Is that blood?" Sophie asked, making a face.

"Looks like it," Eliot said. Freshly spilled blood had a distinctive sheen to it, even on a crappy video feed. He glared furiously at the limo on the screen. He knew whose blood he was seeing.

Gavin's blood.

Nate stayed on point. "What about the driver?"

"On it."

Shifting the image away from the dented hood, Hardison zoomed in on a glimpse of the windshield. Magic pixels brought a pair of faces into resolution. Eliot spotted no trace of remorse on either man's face.

"Eliot?" Nate asked.

"I don't recognize the driver," Eliot said, "but I know the guy in the passenger seat." It was Broken Nose, back when his proboscis was still intact. He recognized the gorilla's homely mug. "He's one of the guys who jumped Denise."

Silence fell over the suite as the obvious implication sank in.

"Okay," Nate said finally. "No way is that a coincidence. We're talking conspiracy here."

"But who is behind it?" Sophie asked. "Brad?"

"That's who my money's on," Hardison said. "He's the one who made a killing, no pun intended, off Gavin's death. And who needed to get the sequel from Denise. I'm guessing he planned to hold her hostage until her agent"—he looked pointedly at Sophie—"came through with the goods."

"Shouldn't have bothered," Parker said, disdainfully flipping another page. "This book sucks."

"Hey," Hardison said indignantly. "You see what you can come up with on short notice? I did the best I damn could."

Parker cocked her head. "What's this got to do with you?"

"I like Brad for this," Eliot said. "Who else could it be?"

"What about Gavin's anonymous whistle-blower?" Sophie asked. "Tarantula?"

"Tarantula is just a shadow at this point," Nate said. "No name, no motive, and no obvious reason to go after Denise." He put aside that red herring. "Brad is still our prime suspect. When in doubt, look for who benefits."

"So?" Parker asked. "We already beat Brad, right?"

"We got the book back, that's all." Eliot stood up and paced restlessly, too angry to sit still. "It's not enough, not if he actually had Gavin killed."

This was why he couldn't fully enjoy their victory earlier. Just stealing back the book would have been fine if this had only been about Brad screwing Denise out of Gavin's legacy, but the stakes had just been raised, big-time. Somebody needed to pay for Gavin's murder—and tricking Brad out of some book royalties was not nearly punishment enough.

He knew Denise would feel the same way, but would he be doing her a favor by telling her the truth at this point? He hated the idea of lying to her, especially now that they had gotten so close, and yet . . .

This was her life, her story. In more ways than one.

"So what's the verdict, Nate?" Sophie asked. "Are we still on this job? Maybe looking at a longer game?"

"I'm not sure," he admitted. He looked expectantly at Hardison. "Is there anything we can use to pin Gavin's death on Brad?"

"I can keep looking," the hacker said glumly. "But don't get your hopes up. Brad has an airtight alibi for the night Gavin died, and he was home sleeping when those goons went after Denise. And there's been no sign of a certain black limo at his mansion, at least not since we started keeping tabs on him."

"What about the limo?" Eliot asked. "Where did it go after hitting Gavin?"

Just give me an address, he thought vengefully. *And aim me like a weapon.*

"I followed it as far as the Brooklyn–Battery Tunnel," Hardison said, "but the coverage got spotty after that. Too many residential neighborhoods and side roads in Brooklyn, you know; it's not like Big Brother is watching every block in Flatbush and Crown Heights. I'm guessing they stayed away from the main drags to avoid . . . well, people like me."

Parker looked for the bright side. "But we know they're in Brooklyn?"

"Not necessarily," Eliot said. "There are plenty of ways out of the borough. They could have just been taking a roundabout route to the Bronx, New Jersey, or God knows where."

"What if we search his financials?" Sophie suggested. "Look for evidence of any payoffs around the time Gavin died, or limousine rentals, or body-shop repairs, or something? Where there's significant money involved, there's usually a paper trail."

"Not this time," Hardison said. "I already tried all that, with the help of several bottles of orange soda and a heaping helping of gummy frogs. Brad's spent a lot of money on a lot of dubious stuff—we're talking escorts, gambling, and some gamy Ukrainian Web sites that made me want to give my poor hard drive a Silkwood shower—but there's no smoking gun linking him to Gavin's death . . . or the attack on Denise. Sorry."

"That's a problem," Nate said. "We need a way in here."

"I can go through it all again," Hardison said, sighing wearily. He worked the remote, replacing the traffic-cam footage with a blizzard of credit-card bills, canceled checks, bank statements, credit reports, deeds, titles, and other financial records, including a handwritten IOU scribbled on a cocktail napkin. "Maybe I missed a hidden account, but frankly, Brad didn't seem all that sneaky. For all we know, he met those guys at a bar or strip club and just paid them cash under the table." He huffed indignantly. "Did I ever mention how much I hate low-tech lowlifes? Backward cavemen don't give me anything to work with."

Ordinarily, Eliot would have snickered at the hacker's frustration. He preferred things old-school himself. But not when it meant that Gavin's killers might get off scot-free. Right now he'd sign up for Facebook if it meant catching the bad guys responsible for his friend's death.

"Just find me proof," he said. "I'll handle the rest."

Various scenarios, more brutal than elaborate, were already playing in his mind. Even if they couldn't track down the murder limo's nameless driver, he already knew where

Brad was, and how to get to him. Sometimes the direct approach was the most effective—and final.

"I know what you're thinking, Eliot," Nate said. "And I don't blame you for wanting to take matters into your own hands, but that's not how we work. You know that."

Eliot didn't want to hear it. "Don't get in my way, Nate." He was in no mood for a lecture. This wasn't Nate's call, not this time. "I've killed men before, and for worse reasons."

"Yes, but we don't know for sure that Brad's responsible for Gavin's murder. Slow down and let us do this right."

"What if I don't want to wait? I'm not you, Nate. Maybe you've got the patience to work out some complicated, long-term, ironic way to get back at the people who've wronged you, but that's you." He recalled that it had taken Nate *years* to exact poetic justice on the insurance firm responsible for his son's death. "Me, I'm more hands-on."

"Don't sell yourself short," Nate said. "You're more than just a hitter. Let's be smart about this." Nate called upon Hardison again. "You still hacked into Brad's computers and home security?"

"Does a Timelord regenerate?" Hardison asked rhetorically. "When I hack something, they stay hacked."

"Good," Nate said. He went into action like a general mobilizing his forces. "Keep watching him and record every minute, twenty-four/seven. Parker, you help him. The more eyes the better. If Brad *was* involved with the attacks, he's bound to slip up eventually, especially now that he's losing everything. Desperate people make dumb mistakes. If we're lucky, maybe he'll lead us to that smoking gun . . . or limo."

A troubling thought snuck up and ambushed Eliot. "You think he might go after Denise again?"

"Why?" Parker asked. "What would he gain from that?"

"Gavin's estate, perhaps, if something happened to Denise," Sophie speculated. "Or so he might hope."

Eliot didn't like the sound of this, not with Denise currently heading home alone. He remembered how close she had come to being abducted before. That murder limo was still out there.

"What's Brad doing now?" he asked urgently. "Show me."

Nate nodded at Hardison, who obliged by clearing the screens and calling up a live feed from Brad's mansion. It was a little after four in the afternoon; with any luck, Brad would still be cooling his heels at home.

"Please, God, not the hot tub again," Sophie prayed. "I'm still trying to expunge those visuals from my mind."

"You and me both," Hardison agreed.

It took him only a moment or two to locate Brad, who was pacing back and forth in the mansion's oversize, luxury kitchen. Stainless-steel appliances that looked as though they had never been used crowded the granite counters. A built-in refrigerator and freezer matched the kitchen cabinets. Unwashed dishes were piled high in the sink. Judging from the angle of the shot, Brad's hijacked laptop was sitting open on a nearby counter or table.

Food and drink had taken over the massive kitchen island. A half-eaten pizza, chocolate cream pie, and a demolished six-pack suggested that Brad had attempted to drown his sorrows with booze and comfort food, or maybe he just wanted to empty the pantries before they were repossessed.

Cigar stubs filled up an overflowing ashtray. Tendrils of smoke rose from the fallen warriors. You could practically smell the tobacco over the screens.

"No, I'm not joking," Brad said aloud. He sounded more than a little agitated, no surprise given his recent reversal of fortunes. A Bluetooth earpiece was clipped to his ear, and he was smoking up a storm. He seemed to be desperately trying to milk some money out of the sequel while he still had a chance. "Cash up front, that's what I'm saying. Transfer the money tonight and the book's all yours. You can snatch it right out from beneath the noses of everyone else . . . like a preemptive strike, you know?"

"That shameless toad," Sophie observed. She took out her own phone. "Time to leak the news about Denise getting the rights back."

Not a bad idea, Eliot thought, although Brad already seemed to be having trouble closing the deal.

"What do you mean you need to see the book first? It's *Assassins Remember,* what else do you need to know?" Brad angrily ground a cigar stub into the marble counter. Multitasking, he harangued the guy on the other end of the line while checking his e-mail for any takers. His sweaty, porcine face leaned into the screen, causing Sophie to recoil instinctively. "Fine," he said sourly. "Just think of it as a reading fee. Give me a down payment right now and I'll e-mail you the first three chapters."

Whoever was on the other end of the line didn't seem to be buying it, much to Brad's exasperation.

"Yes, I said a reading fee," he blustered. "You got a problem with that?" He waited for a response. "Hello? Hello? You still there?"

Eliot watched Brad redial. As much as he enjoyed seeing the guy sweat, he was more relieved to see that Gavin's no-good brother didn't seem to be targeting Denise at the moment.

Unless the black limo is already heading back toward her place, he fretted. *Maybe I should head on over there?*

"I don't know," Sophie said. "I'm not seeing any smoking guns. Just a lot of smoking."

"Me either," Nate replied, "but this could take time. We may need to be patient while we come up with a new avenue of attack."

"I could break into his mansion again," Parker volunteered, with a hopeful tone in her voice. She got twitchy when she wasn't scaling a building or wiggling through an air duct. She'd once stolen the Hope Diamond and put it back just because she was bored. "Poke around a little more."

"I'll keep that in mind," Nate promised.

Meanwhile, Brad was still trying to drum up business, without much success. "What? Where did you hear that?" He stomped around the kitchen, barely able to contain his exasperation. He tugged on what was left of his hair. He finished off a beer and angrily hurled the bottle into the sink. He lit another cigar. "Look, I don't know what you've heard about Gavin's old squeeze getting the rights, but—"

Sophie smiled smugly as she put down her phone. "Amazing how fast a well-placed leak can travel these days."

"I'm surprised he's not on the phone to you already," Hardison said to Nate. "To 'Max Dunfee,' I mean."

Nate checked his messages. "New Zealand must be low

on his list, but I suspect I'll hear from him before the night is out."

"That could be our opening," Sophie suggested. "For the Viking Horn Reversal, perhaps, or the Blurry Morning After scam?"

A familiar look of concentration came over Nate's face. "I'm working on it."

Eliot decided to leave the plotting to the experts. He had better places to be. He headed for the door. "I'm going to check on Denise," he announced. "Just to be safe."

"Uh-huh," Parker said. "Enjoy the pretzels."

Eliot chose to ignore that. He was halfway out the door when a sudden commotion, coming from the video wall, stopped him in his tracks. He spun around and stared at the monitors.

Four armed thugs, wearing ski masks, burst into Brad's kitchen, menacing him. A Glock was shoved in his face. A gloved hand yanked off his Bluetooth device and flung it against a wall. Another hand shoved him against the counter.

"You're coming with us!" the gunman announced. He sounded like he had a cold—or maybe a broken nose. Eliot recognized his stance and posture from the fight outside Denise's apartment. "Don't give us any trouble!"

"Hardison?" Nate asked urgently.

"The mansion's security just went down," the hacker reported. He called up a diagnostic on a screen. "Somebody's disabled it at the source." He frowned at the scrolling data as he tried to regain control of the system. "That's just rude."

Sophie watched the shocking home invasion unfold in

real time. "Should we be calling the police?" She must have realized how odd this sounded, coming from her, because she quickly added, "They *do* serve a purpose sometimes."

"Or maybe we should just let Brad get what's coming to him," Eliot said grimly. He headed back into the suite, his gaze glued to the screen, where Brad was backed up against a granite counter. "Looks like Brad's buddies might take care of one problem for us."

I could live with that, he thought.

"Who are you?" a terrified Brad asked the invaders. "What do you want?" He cowered against the counter, turning his ashen face away from the muzzle of the gun. He gaped at his attackers' concealed faces as though trying to penetrate the wool masks with X-ray vision. His cigar slipped from his fingers. "Is this about that poker game in Atlantic City? I paid that off weeks ago . . . I think!"

Hold on, Eliot thought. Brad didn't seem to know who the invaders were. Did that mean he hadn't had anything to do with Gavin's murder after all? Eliot's suspicions reluctantly switched gears. It was starting to look like Brad might actually be innocent, at least where a certain "accident" was concerned.

So who were the actual killers working for?

"Move it!" Broken Nose demanded. He ground out the fallen cigar beneath his heel as his men dragged Brad toward the door. Brad squirmed helplessly in their grasp, unable to break free.

"Please!" he squealed. "Just tell me what you want!"

"Tarantula."

Brad's jaw dropped.

"But . . . I don't know anything about that!" He seemed

to recognize the name, which implied that he had learned a thing or two about his brother's work, not that it was doing him any good right now. He shouted frantically, "I don't even know if Tarantula is real!"

"Yeah," Broken Nose said, unconvinced. "We'll see about that."

He signaled one of his men, who pistol-whipped Brad from behind. Eliot fumed, remembering how Denise had been whacked the same way, possibly by the same guy. He wished he could leap through the screen and shove that pistol right up the thug's—

"Ouch," Sophie said. "These guys play rough."

"Tell me about it," Eliot said.

Brad sagged limply between the two thugs holding him. His chin drooped onto his chest. Eliot didn't envy the men having to support Brad's deadweight. He would have walked the man out at gunpoint before knocking him out. These guys were too vicious for their own good.

And Brad's.

Broken Nose reached for the laptop. He closed the lid and the screen in the team's suite went blank.

"Hardison!" Nate said sharply.

"Working on it," the hacker said. "I need to reboot the mansion's security cameras."

By the time Hardison managed to fire up the outdoor cameras, the men were tossing Brad into the back of a distinctive black limo. Eliot noted darkly that the dent in its hood, left over from the collision that killed Gavin, had long since been repaired. The blood had also been washed away.

Doesn't matter, he thought. *I know it's there.*

The limo raced away from the estate, through the open front gate. Hijacked cameras tracked the vehicle's departure until it quickly zoomed out of range. Hardison's screens showed nothing but a stretch of empty road.

The murder limo had gotten away . . . again.

The crew stared at the useless video, watching the dust from the limo's departure settle. Brad had just been abducted before their very eyes.

"Okay," Sophie said, "I didn't see that coming."

Nate frowned. His grim expression gave Eliot serious competition.

"No," he said. "Neither did I."

TEN

MANHATTAN

"So Gavin's death wasn't an accident?"

"Doesn't look like it," Eliot confessed to Denise.

He had rushed to her apartment right after Brad's kidnapping, just in case she was in danger, too. Along the way, while urging the taxi to go faster, he had decided that it was too risky to keep her in the dark any longer. She needed to know what had happened to Brad—and how badly matters had escalated.

"I'm sorry for not telling you earlier," he said. "We didn't know for sure until tonight."

Slightly more than an hour had passed since Brad's abduction. The sun was just starting to go down. Eliot had drawn the curtains to discourage spies or snipers and had made sure every window was locked. A fire escape outside the bedroom window made him nervous. He peered out through the drapes at the street below.

"I see," she replied.

Her muted reaction surprised him.

"To be honest," he said, "I expected you to be angrier . . . and more shocked."

She smiled ruefully. "You're not telling me anything I didn't already suspect. I think I've known all along that Gavin was murdered. I just didn't want to admit it."

"And you don't mind that I kept this from you?"

She shook her head. "I understand about secrets, and keeping quiet to protect the people you care about." She fingered Gavin's "lucky" compass. "Maybe if Brad and I hadn't been so hell-bent on dragging Tarantula's secrets into the light, Gavin would still be alive. And Brad wouldn't be in danger."

"Hey, you can't blame yourself for any of this." He reached out to comfort her. "It's not your fault."

"Isn't it?" She stepped away from him, denying herself his embrace. "If I had stopped Gavin, talked him out of trying to expose all that nasty black-ops business instead of egging him on and encouraging him, none of this would have happened!"

"Listen to me," he said. "You didn't kill Gavin. You didn't drag Brad into this. None of this is on you, you got that?"

He knew all about guilty consciences and how they could fester over time; it wasn't something he'd wish on anybody, let alone Denise. She had enough to deal with already, maybe even more than she was willing to admit.

"I wish I could be sure of that," she said. She plopped down onto a secondhand love seat and buried her face in her hands.

"Be sure." He sat down beside her and placed his arm around her shoulders. "We're going to get these guys and make them pay for what happened to Gavin, I promise."

"But how?" she asked. "And what about Brad?"

Eliot glanced at his watch. It was a quarter after six. The kidnappers might have made it back to their lair by now. Chances were, Brad was currently on the receiving end of a harsh interrogation. Eliot didn't envy him. If his abductors really did want information on Tarantula, they were bound to be disappointed. Brad didn't know anything about his brother's sources, which meant that the bad guys were going to have to look elsewhere, closer to home.

"Nate figures the kidnappers will be in touch," Eliot said. "He's usually right about these things."

"In touch with who?" Realization dawned in her eyes. "Me?"

Eliot nodded.

"So here's what we have to do . . ."

Nate's prediction was right on target.

The call came shortly after midnight as Eliot and Denise were having a late-night snack. Both of them were too tense to even think about turning in for the night. Denise started at the ring.

"You expecting a call?" he asked her.

She shook her head.

"Let me handle this," he suggested. She handed him her phone and he checked the caller ID, which listed the caller as unknown. Letting the phone keep ringing, he popped his earbud into place.

"Hardison? You reading me?"

"I'm here, man. Just waiting on you," the hacker said. *"The bad guys call Denise already? They're not wasting any time."*

"Nope," Eliot agreed. For once, he had been hoping Nate was wrong.

"You ready on your end?"

"The tap is in place," Hardison promised. He had already linked his own hardware to Denise's phone, in anticipation of this call. *"Let's hope it's your buddies from the limo."*

"They're no friends of mine," Eliot said. He answered Denise's phone. "Hello?"

"Who is this?" an electronically distorted voice asked. *"Not the lovely Ms. Gallo, I take it."*

Eliot went on high alert. Telemarketers didn't need to disguise their voices. The phone was set on speaker and he put it down on the counter so that Denise could listen in.

"If this is about Brad, you can talk to me."

"Interesting," the voice commented. *"I don't suppose I have the privilege of addressing the infamous 'Tarantula' himself."*

For a second, Eliot considered saying yes, but he wasn't sure what the long-term ramifications of that might be. Nate and Sophie were better at improvising scams and false identities on the fly. He had no idea if claiming to be Tarantula would open up the right can of worms. And what if the bad guys already knew more than they were letting on?

"Deny everything," Nate joined in. He must have been sitting up waiting for the ransom call as well. *"Keep them guessing."*

Eliot appreciated the advice.

"Think again," he said. "I'm just a friend." He hoped Hardison was getting all this. "What do you want?"

"What we all want, ultimately. Peace of mind." The unknown caller chuckled wryly; the artificial distortion could not conceal his cultured tone and speech patterns. They weren't dealing with another Brad here. *"Assassins Never Forget* made certain parties uncomfortable. It hinted, albeit in fictionalized form, at matters that would have been better kept out of print. Those same parties, including myself, are naturally concerned about the contents of the sequel—and the identity and whereabouts of Gavin's anonymous informant."

Eliot didn't bother asking the caller who he was. "Who ordered Gavin killed? Was that you?"

"Let's just say we thought the matter was contained after Gavin's unfortunate accident. Imagine our dismay when we found out about the sequel."

Great, Eliot thought. *This is all our fault. We painted a great big target on Denise—and everyone else connected to the make-believe book.*

It was surely too late to admit there was no sequel. The crew had done too good a job of spreading the word.

"Assassins Remember," the voice continued. *"A most worrisome title, I must say. Some things are best forgotten."*

"Yeah, I get it." Eliot struggled to control his temper. "You and your friends have dirty laundry you don't want aired. So what do you want with Denise?"

"We just had a long, if somewhat fruitless, conversation with Brad Lee. He insists that he knows little or nothing about the sequel or Tarantula, and that Denise is the person we should be talking to about Gavin's work. Indeed, it seems that he was never in possession of the sequel at all, unlike Denise."

Eliot mentally kicked Brad in the crotch. He should have known that creep would throw Denise under the limo.

"Don't even think about trying to snatch Denise again," he warned. "Or it will be more than your flunky's nose that gets broken next time."

"Ah, this is the chivalrous gentleman that came to the fair lady's rescue the other night. I suspected as much," the voice said. *"Ideally, it won't be necessary to put Denise in jeopardy once more. We don't want her, only the manuscript and Tarantula. And we're prepared to offer Brad's safety in exchange."*

"And what makes you think I care one bit about what happens to Brad?" Eliot said coldly. It wasn't hard to sound like he didn't give a damn. "He's a lowlife scumbag who tried to screw Denise over."

"But he is Gavin's brother," the voice pointed out. *"I assume that counts for something."*

"I wouldn't bet on it."

"That's unfortunate for Brad, then. It's clear to me now that he knows less than nothing, which means that he has no value except as a bargaining chip. But if you would rather he disappear, I can easily accommodate you . . ."

Eliot and Denise exchanged a worried look. Despite everything, neither of them wanted more blood on their hands. Not even Brad's.

"Wait," Eliot said. "How do we know that you haven't gotten rid of Brad already?" He knew the drill; this wasn't his first hostage negotiation. "I want proof of life."

"Naturally. I expected as much," the voice replied. *"I trust that Denise is listening as well? There's somebody here who wants desperately to speak to her."*

The electronic distortion was switched off. Brad's voice erupted from the phone:

"Denise? Anybody? You gotta help me here! These guys mean business. They want the sequel—and this Tarantula dude—and they're not going to take no for an answer." There was no mistaking the naked fear and desperation in his voice. Sobs and sniffles punctuated his frantic pleas. *"Please, you gotta do what they ask! I know you don't like me, and I don't blame you, but my skin's on the line here! You can't let them kill me. Please, I'm begging you. I wish I'd never gotten mixed up in this!"*

Now you tell us, Eliot thought. *A bit late for that, pal.*

"Please!" Brad squealed. *"Do what they say! Don't let them kill—"*

He was cut off abruptly.

Damn it, Eliot thought. *I really didn't need to hear that.*

And neither did Denise.

The first voice picked up where he'd left off:

"A heartrending plea, don't you think? Are you truly willing to trust Brad to my tender mercies, which I assure you are neither of the above?" The mystery caller spoke as

though he already had Eliot's number. *"I don't think so. You strike me as something of a white knight."*

"Trust me, I'm more gray than white."

"Be that as it may, I want the new book—and Tarantula. Do we have a deal?"

"Not so fast," Eliot said. "What if we don't know who Tarantula is? Or how to contact him?"

"Then Brad will soon be reunited with his brother."

Denise bit down her knuckles, stifling a gasp.

"Hold on. Let's talk about this!"

"This is not a negotiation. You have forty-eight hours. I'll be in touch to arrange the terms of the exchange. And, please, don't bother trying to trace this call. We have taken the necessary precautions. Good-bye."

"Wait!" Eliot blurted. "We're not done here!"

"Yes, we are."

The line went dead.

"Hello, hello?" A dial tone mocked Eliot. He fought an urge to throw Denise's phone across the apartment. He cupped a hand over his ear. "Hardison! Tell me you ID'd the caller."

"Sorry, man," the hacker replied. *"These guys know what they're doing. They covered their tracks by bouncing the signal through a dozen networks, spoofed numbers, digital scramblers . . ."*

"We get it," Eliot said, cutting off the geek speak. "We're dealing with professionals." Which made sense given their interest in Tarantula and the black-ops secrets that had been outed in Gavin's book. This job had moved out of the relatively bloodless world of the book racket into far more dangerous territory.

"That's what I'm saying," Hardison agreed. *"Call the Ghostbusters. We're talking spooks here."*

"Okay. I'll keep you posted."

Eliot popped out his earbud so he could converse with Denise in private. She watched him anxiously, having heard his half of the back-and-forth with Hardison. She leaned against her tiny kitchen counter, hugging herself.

"He couldn't trace the call?" she asked.

Eliot shook his head. "'Fraid not." He offered her a sliver of hope. "But give him a shot. I hate to say it, but Hardison's pretty good at that digital juju. If there's some geeky, googlely way to pick up their trail, he'll find it." He double-checked his earbud to make sure it wasn't transmitting. "But if you quote me on that, I will disavow every word."

She managed a slight smile before the severity of the situation weighed her down again. This afternoon's jubilation had not lasted long.

"Brad's right," she said. "He's a cheat and a scumbag and no friend of mine. But I don't want his death on my conscience."

Eliot guessed that, rightly or wrongly, she was already carrying a bigger load of guilt than she ever bargained for. He knew how it felt not to like what you saw in the mirror. A troubled conscience could be a heavy burden.

"I get that."

She sighed. "So now what do we do?"

He knew the answer to that at least.

"We talk to my friends."

———

"The question has to be asked," Sophie said. "How far do we want to go to save Brad Lee of all people?"

The crew had convened at the hotel suite to hash out their next moves, if any. They were seated around a long conference table. It was early the next morning and a continental breakfast was going largely ignored. Sophie would have liked a few more hours of sleep.

"As far as we have to," Nate said. "Brad may be a slob and a jerk, but those aren't capital offenses. We can't just let him be murdered."

"I understand that," Sophie said. "I truly do. But before we rush into anything, we should take a moment to recognize the very real hazards involved. If we're truly dealing with black-ops assassins, this entire job just became a good deal dicier. We need to take that into consideration."

Sophie often found herself cast in the role of the voice of caution. The other members of the crew were all gifted in their own unique ways, but they each had their issues:

Nate was probably the smartest man she had ever met; she was frequently blown away (and, yes, occasionally turned on) by the way that brilliant mind of his worked. He was like a grand master at chess, always thinking several moves ahead. But alcohol, and the demons in his past, made his judgment suspect at times. His need to win, and enforce his own brand of justice on an unfair world, could lead him to take unnecessary risks, especially after he'd had a few too many stiff drinks.

Eliot tended to be more pragmatic, most of the time. You could usually trust him to keep a level head, no matter the crisis. But Gavin's death had hit him on a personal level, and his obvious involvement with Denise complicated matters further. Sophie couldn't trust him to talk sense to Nate this time around. He was in too deep.

Hardison knew technology like nobody else, and had promise as a grifter, but he sometimes let his enthusiasms get the better of him. Real life was more complicated than a comic book or computer game, and you didn't get another life if your cockiness got you killed. Hardison was so smart he could outsmart himself, which was the last thing they needed when going up against professional killers.

And Parker . . . well, Parker was crazy.

Which leaves it up to me, Sophie thought, *to make certain that we all know exactly what we're getting into.*

"Look, I don't want any of you to put yourself in danger on my account," Denise said. She sat at the end of the table, next to Eliot. "You've already done so much for me already. Brad is my problem. You can walk away from this."

Denise had insisted on taking part in the meeting. It was against protocol, but Nate had gone along with it, which made Sophie suspect that he was already formulating some sort of scheme that required Denise's involvement. Sophie wondered what he had in mind—and how dangerous it might be for all of them.

"The hell with that," Eliot said. He rested his hand on her arm, not caring who was looking. "We're not going anywhere." Flinty eyes challenged the rest of them to disagree. "Right?"

Nate spoke for the crew, as he was prone to do.

"This is our responsibility, too," he reminded everyone. "We invented the imaginary sequel that brought the kidnappers out of the woodwork and nearly got Denise nabbed as well. The way I see it, this job's not done until we get to

Gavin's killers—and see to it that they don't hurt anyone else."

"We're with you, man," Hardison chimed in. "The con continues. Bring on part two."

"Sequels suck," Parker said. "But sure, I'm in."

Sophie was very good at sizing up the feel of a room. She could usually tell just by stepping into a boardroom or sales conference whether a company was turning a profit or not. She saw the writing on the wall.

"Very well, then," she said, going along with the consensus. In truth, she hadn't felt comfortable abandoning Denise, or even Brad. She had simply wanted to inject a healthy dose of caution into the proceedings. "It seems we're doing this. But what precisely are we doing?"

Nate stepped up to the plate.

"As of this moment, we have two new objectives: ransom Brad and turn the tables on Gavin's killers." He tapped his watch. "We have exactly forty-one hours and eight minutes. Hardison, set the clock."

"I'm on it, man."

Denise dabbed at her eyes. "Thanks so much . . . again. And, please, don't keep me in the dark this time. I want to help, however I can."

"I may take you up on that," Nate said. "Sooner than you think."

Sophie could practically see his brain working the problem, taking it apart and analyzing it from every angle. She couldn't wait to see what he came up with.

"You're already putting together a plan, aren't you?"

"Possibly," he admitted. A carafe of hot coffee rested on the table. He refilled his mug. "But first we need to know who our target is." Cup in hand, he circled the table to come up behind Hardison, who was tapping away at his laptop. "Hardison?"

Hardison grinned up at him, like a cyber-wizard about to pull a digital rabbit out of the Internet. The indefatigable hacker had clearly been busy.

"I may have something for you there."

"Y'all remember this footage," Hardison said, waving his clicker like a pointer. He had to admit it, he enjoyed these moments in the spotlight. "Taken by a traffic cam a few blocks away from the 'accident,' and ingeniously enhanced by yours truly."

The crew, plus Denise, was seated before the screens while Hardison got his emcee on. The monitors offered a glimpse of the murder limo's driver, as seen through the town car's front windshield.

Denise, who hadn't seen the face of the driver before, stared stonily at the screen. Her jaw clenched. Her whole body was tense. Her face flushed. You didn't have to be able to read people as expertly as Sophie could to see that she was barely keeping a lid on some serious anger. Throw in some gamma rays and she'd be Hulking out on them for sure.

Not that Hardison blamed her. The bad guys had run down the love of her life.

If somebody had Parker killed . . .

"Yeah, I remember," Eliot said tersely. He also looked like he wanted the homicidal driver in his sights as soon as possible. "What about it?"

"Well, I've had my own, custom-made facial-recognition software running overtime for the last fifteen-plus hours." That was time enough to compare the driver's face print to literally millions of photographs. "It took a while, for reasons I'll get around to, but I finally got a hit."

He clicked the remote and the screens divided themselves between the enhanced traffic photo and a series of color shots of what appeared to be the same man, albeit a few years younger. The stills were obviously undercover surveillance photos taken by a telephoto lens from long distance. The photos showed a lean, elegantly dressed man getting into a waiting black limo. A lucky gust of wind blew off his trilby hat, exposing a gaunt, aristocratic-looking face that bore a distinct resemblance to the driver of the murder car. He had a long, angular face with thin lips, a sharp nose, and calculating gray eyes. Wispy brown hair, going gray at the temples, led up in a widow's peak atop his high forehead. He lingered outside the limo, scowling impatiently, while a flunky retrieved his hat.

"A tad younger," Sophie observed, "but he could be the same man."

"No need to guess," Hardison bragged. "Let science settle this."

He split the screen between the driver and the man in the spy photos. Green dots mapped their respective faces. Lines connected the dots. In less than a minute, the program coughed up its ruling.

CONFIRMATION: 88.6%, a dialogue box reported.

Eliot grunted in approval. "Close enough for government work."

"Funny you should say that," Hardison said. "'Cause our friend here does a lot of work for a lot of governments. Almost all of it off-the-record."

Nate signaled Hardison to speed it up. "Cut to the chase."

Really? Hardison thought. *That's how it is? We're backseat-driving my pacing now?*

He didn't like being rushed, and was tempted to drag out the suspense a few moments longer, but the look on Denise's face—and Eliot's—convinced him that now was not the time. This was too important to both of them.

"Meet Anton Beria," he said. "Or, if you want to be more precise about it, the *late* Anton Beria. That's why it took my programs so long to ID him. He's not listed in any current databases because he's supposed to be dead."

Eliot glared at the photo of the limo driver. "Looks alive enough to me."

He sounded like he wanted to remedy that situation.

"Tell us about him," Nate prompted.

"Not much to tell—officially, that is. His paper trail is shorter than my pull list at the comic-book shop, and Bigfoot has had more photos taken of him than this guy. Most of what I dug up—and it wasn't easy—is more whispers than hard biographical data. Born in Hungary, educated in the UK, became a naturalized American citizen back during the Reagan years. Officially, he was a lobbyist for an obscure diplomatic think tank that's rumored to have been a front for a private black-ops outfit that specialized in putting down revolutionaries, reformers, and troublesome opposition leaders. Noted for his 'flexible' political loyalties;

at one point, he's said to have taken contracts from Pakistan and India simultaneously."

"Okay, that's ballsy," Eliot said. "And pretty shady."

"Beria has deep connections to the U.S. intelligence community as well," Hardison continued. "CIA, NSA, Homeland Security . . . you name it. Built up a track record that's impressive or scary, depending which end of the sniper scope you're at. You want an inconvenient agitator eliminated, or an uprising nipped in the bud, he's your man—at least until he conveniently died of a stroke three years ago, right before a congressional investigation into his activities. Did I mention that he died on his yacht, outside international waters, and that his body was buried at sea?"

"How very neat and tidy," Sophie said.

"Tell me about it," Hardison said. "I'm going to have to remember that one."

It wasn't hard to fake a death, especially in certain parts of the third world, where a death certificate could be bought for the price of a large pepperoni pizza. Hardison had phony death certificates for every member of the team, just in case they ever had to drop off the map permanently. Unknown to Eliot, the cause of his death was listed as auto-erotic asphyxiation.

Hardison intended to be far away when that bomb dropped.

"Take it from a former insurance investigator," Nate said, "faking one's death is surprisingly common. I cut my teeth on phony life insurance scams, usually perpetrated by the grieving 'widow.' Dying is the easy part. What trips people up is staying dead. Wait long enough and they almost always resurface to deal with unfinished business . . . like maybe a novelist whose book cut too close to the truth?"

"Sounds like one of the characters in the book," Sophie observed. "The nameless spymaster who ran things from behind the scenes, his true identity known only to his closest lieutenants. Not even Yvette ever found out who he really was."

"I remember that part," Parker said. She laughed out loud. "That was hilarious."

Everyone stared at her. Denise looked baffled.

"What?" Parker asked, noticing the funny looks she was getting. "It was a comedy, right?"

"Moving on," Nate said. "Eliot, you ever had any dealings with this guy?"

It was a reasonable question. Even more than the rest of them, Eliot had dealt with some pretty questionable characters in his day, people who didn't mind hurting people— and worse. Eliot didn't like to talk about it, but they all knew he had cracked more than safes and software. And knew people for whom life was all too cheap.

"Not that I remember," he said. "This Beria guy may have been too far back in the shadows. Just to be clear, I was always more of a hitter, not a spook or assassin."

Denise regarded him warmly, a sad smile on her lips. "I never doubted it."

"I don't suppose there's any point in reporting Brad's kidnapping to the police?" Parker asked. "A crazy idea, I know, but maybe Bonanno can do something?"

Detective Patrick Bonanno was an honest Boston cop who had worked with the Leverage crew before. He had been known to look the other way when it came to bringing down serious bad guys.

"Not his jurisdiction," Nate said. "But even if we could convince the authorities that Beria is still alive, and that's a seriously big if, he's probably untouchable."

"More than probably," Sophie said. "A man like that, with friends and connections in high places, can get away with murder . . . and kidnapping."

"Which means it's up to us," Nate said. "As usual."

"Truth," Hardison said. "Too many bad guys are getting away with too darn much. We should probably think about franchising."

Nate tabled that suggestion for now. He walked over to Denise.

"What about you?" he asked her. "You ever catch a glimpse of Beria? He look familiar to you?"

She stared at Gavin's killer. "No. Absolutely not."

"You sure about that?" Eliot asked gently. "You never saw him around? With Gavin . . . or anywhere else?"

"No," she repeated. "Not once."

Hardison watched Nate and Eliot question Denise, curious to see what happened next. There was a definite undercurrent to the discussion, almost as though they were interrogating her. Sophie observed the exchange with interest, too.

"Okay," Nate said, letting up. "I figured it couldn't hurt to ask." He turned back toward the video wall, and the shots of Anton Beria, past and present. "Take a good look at him, people. We have a new target."

"Just point me at him," Eliot growled. "Any idea where this slimeball is hiding?"

"Not really," Hardison said. "His last known location was the bottom of the ocean, remember? In a body bag."

That wasn't what Eliot wanted to hear. "Great. So we still don't know where Beria and his goons are holding Brad." Frustration practically radiated from him. "So what are we supposed to do now?"

As always, Nate had an answer.

"Now we write a book."

ELEVEN

MANHATTAN

"But we can't write an entire book in less than forty-two hours," Sophie protested. "It's impossible."

"No, just an exercise in teamwork," Nate said with a smirk. He had it all figured out. "A decent-size thriller is—what?—one hundred thousand words?" He swept his gaze over his crew. "There's four of you. That's approximately twenty-five thousand words apiece. And we already have the first three chapters, so that gives you a head start."

The cut-and-paste job they used to fool Brad wasn't going to pass muster in this case. That patchwork manuscript was never meant to bear close inspection; it had just been a glorified prop in their plan to entrap Brad. But Beria and his crew were different. Unlike Brad, who had been more interested in selling the sequel than in reading it, Beria actually cared about the contents of the manuscript.

They had to assume that he would examine the text more closely—which meant they needed a real book.

"But we're not writers, Nate," Hardison pointed out. "We can't just churn out a spy thriller overnight."

"Are you sure about that?" Nate asked. "I've seen all of you, even Parker, invent entire characters and backstories on the fly." He walked around the table, singling them out one by one. "Sophie, you're a master at that. You can spin new identities and narratives out of thin air, often at a moment's notice."

"It's a gift," she admitted.

"And, Hardison," Nate continued, "you have an extremely active imagination when it comes to crafting cons. Remember all the effort you put into developing your persona as a master jewel thief, 'the Iceman'? Or that whole Snake River Massacre treasure hunt you devised to fleece those gold swindlers?"

"But you didn't like either of those," Hardison reminded Nate.

"No," Nate insisted. "I just thought they needed a little fine-tuning. You have a tendency to go overboard sometimes, but that doesn't mean you don't have a highly creative mind."

Hardison beamed at the compliment. He looked around to make sure the others were listening. "See, that's what I keep telling y'all."

Eliot snorted and rolled his eyes.

"But I don't know anything about *stories*," Parker objected. "I'm a thief, not an author. I barely know what makes real people tick, let alone made-up ones."

"You're underestimating yourself," Nate said. He knew

Parker was going to be a hard sell, but he figured he could convince her if he reminded her of all the progress she had made over the last few years when it came to relating to people. "Remember when you had to pose as that methhead heiress? Or as Alice, the friendly juror? You were *creating* there, improvising on the spot. Now you just have to do it at a keyboard."

And quickly, he added silently.

Finally, he turned to Eliot, who maintained a poker face. His stony impression made it clear that he wasn't about to be conned himself.

"You got a pep talk for me, too?" Eliot asked.

Nate shook his head. "Don't need one. You and I both know how quick you are at thinking on your feet. And you already helped Denise produce those first three chapters." He winked at Denise. "Nice work, by the way. Very convincing."

"If you say so," she muttered. "We did our best."

"And you will again," Nate said confidently. "And for even bigger stakes: a man's life."

"I'm sure we all appreciate your faith in us," Sophie said. "But what on earth are we supposed to write about?"

He had the perfect response, straight from the writing handbooks.

"Write what you know."

He spelled it out for them.

"Sophie, you'll handle the characterization. You write all the emotional, character-driven scenes. As a grifter, and a great one, you have a flawless grasp of what motivates people—and how to push their buttons. Just apply that same understanding of human nature to our characters."

"Fine," she agreed. "But nobody dare cut my love scenes."

I wouldn't dream of it, Nate thought.

"Hardison, you'll handle all the high-tech business. This is a spy thriller. I'm sure we can work in plenty of wiretapping, electronic surveillance, hacking, and so on. Feel free to show off your expertise and the latest, cutting-edge, state-of-the-art spy tech. Give the book a real air of authenticity."

"Real tech done right?" The hacker's eyes lit up at the prospect. "You've got the right man there. Did I ever tell you about the time I impersonated the technical consultant on *Aliens vs. Terminators*?" He sighed. "They really should have listened to me."

"I'm sure," Nate said, hoping to head off a lengthy postmortem on the movie. "This time the technobabble is all yours. Go to town."

"Oh, I will," Hardison enthused. He scratched his chin. "Did you know the Pentagon is already developing robot hummingbirds for covert surveillance? And using bees to detect plastic explosives? That could make for some seriously cool spy-fi scenes, especially if we upgrade things a generation or six . . ."

Nate let him brainstorm away. He hadn't been worried about Hardison; he'd known the enthusiastic young hacker would get into the spirit of the thing. The only challenge was going to be preventing Hardison from getting too farout. *I'll have to keep an eye out for time machines,* Nate thought. *And wormholes.*

"Eliot, you'll do the fight scenes, of course. You know better than most what actual hand-to-hand combat feels like. Put the reader in the middle of the fight, describe what it's like to take a punch or take down an opponent. Do it blow by blow and the fight scenes will ring true."

And fill up plenty of pages, Nate thought.

"Fine," Eliot said. "But I'm not giving away my best moves."

Nate moved on to Parker. She eyed him warily.

"Parker, you're the pro when it comes to heart-pumping stunts and action scenes. Let Eliot handle the fisticuffs. I'm counting on you for exciting scenes of people diving off buildings, scaling walls, and breaking into maximum-security facilities. Maybe even a high-speed motorcycle chase or skydiving sequence."

Parker nodded, looking a little less apprehensive.

"What about Tasers? Can I write about Tasering people?"

"Knock yourself out," Nate said. "You're our adrenaline specialist. Give the reader plenty of jolts."

"We're not still talking about Tasers, are we?"

"Stick to words this time," Nate advised. "They can be pretty shocking, too, if you use them right."

With any luck, he thought, *Anton Beria has a big shock coming . . .*

"What about you?" Sophie asked him. "You've laid out the division of labor very neatly, but what exactly are you contributing to this proposed opus?"

"That's easy," he said. "I'm the editor."

"Of course you are," Sophie said drily.

"I'll provide you with a basic outline," he elaborated, "so that we're all on the same page, as it were." He already knew one crucial plot point that needed to be included in the book. "Then we'll divide up the book according to your respective specialties and pass the chapters back and forth as each of you fleshes out the parts assigned to you. I'll be reviewing the work in progress throughout, to make sure that the story stays on track."

And that nobody gets too "inspired," he thought.

"Just remember, this is a collaborative effort. We don't have time for creative differences or outbreaks of artistic integrity." He made a point not to look directly at Sophie, or Hardison, or anyone in particular. "So check your egos at the door. We have a sequel to write . . . and a killer deadline."

"What about me?" Denise asked. "Where do I fit in?"

"You're the last stop on the assembly line," Nate said. "You'll do a final pass on the finished manuscript, smoothing out any stylistic inconsistencies and making it read like it was truly written by the author of *Assassins Never Forget*."

Denise nodded. "By Gavin, you mean."

"No," Nate said. "By the real author."

He gazed pointedly at Denise.

"What?" She sat straight, feigning confusion. "I don't understand. What are you implying?"

Eliot turned toward her.

"It's time, Denise," he said softly. "We can't afford to play games anymore. You need to come clean."

"Games? What are you talking about? I don't—" She slumped back into her seat, unable to deny it any longer. She looked at Eliot. "How long have you known?"

"I started getting suspicious when we were writing those early chapters together," he confessed. "Like I said, you have a very distinctive style. Then, when I saw you hold your own against that goon squad, I guessed that you weren't just an ordinary temp."

She smiled weakly. "Didn't buy that YMCA story, huh?"

"Not for a second," Eliot said. "I didn't say anything, because I figured you had your reasons, but things are becoming too complicated. It's probably better if we get everything out into the open."

She glanced around the table. "What about the rest of you? When did you figure it out?"

"Eventually," Nate said. "The pieces were all there. You just had to assemble the puzzle."

"It all made sense," Sophie said. "Once you knew what to look for."

"Hold on." Parker was still confused. "If Gavin didn't write the first book, who wrote the sequel? And why do we need to write another one?"

"Because it's all part of the con," Nate told her.

"Okay," Parker said. "That works."

Denise look embarrassed at being exposed.

"I'm sorry," she said, mostly to Eliot. "I didn't want to lie to you, but . . ."

"Gavin was your front," Nate supplied. "He posed as the author, making public appearances as such, so that you could fly under the radar."

"That's right," she confirmed. "He was a photographer, not a writer. I did all the writing and let him take the credit." Her voice cracked and she wrung her hands. The guilt came pouring out of her. "It's my fault he was doing that stupid book signing. It should have been me."

Parker cocked her head. "So why wasn't it?"

"Because Denise Gallo doesn't exist," Nate said, unable to resist showing off how much he had already figured out. He had a reputation as a mastermind to maintain. "Isn't that right, Hardison?"

"You called it," the hacker said. "Don't get me wrong. You did a pretty good job fabricating a new identity." He tipped an imaginary hat to her. "But once Nate pointed me in the right direction, it wasn't hard to figure out that 'Denise Gallo' came out of nowhere a few years ago."

"In 2007, to be exact," Denise said. "I guess I should've seen this coming. Eliot said you were good."

"He did?" Hardison grinned at Eliot. "Hey, thanks for the props, man."

"I have no idea what she's talking about," Eliot said.

"See, that's your problem, man. You need to own your feelings. Get more comfortable expressing yourself."

"How about I express you out the nearest window?"

Nate cleared his throat. "Focus."

"Anyway," Hardison said, getting back on point, "the only thing I couldn't uncover was who you were before."

"Someone else," Denise said. "Tarantula."

FIVE YEARS AGO:

"I don't like it, Okata. Why so hush-hush?"

"Because you're an assassin?" her handler quipped. Daniel Okata was a stocky, silver-haired operative in his late fifties. A patch covered his left eye. Old burns scarred his left cheek. A lightweight black jacket fit him snugly. "A certain degree of cloak-and-dagger comes with the territory."

Vicki Rhodes, a thirty-year-old brunette with striking green eyes, was staked out on the roof of a Paris office building. She wore black as well. It was a clear summer night and the City of Light shone all around them, but this particular rooftop was comfortably dark and inconspicuous. It also overlooked the offices of Le Monde, *a leading French newspaper. Although it was almost midnight, lights were still visible on the upper floors of the newspaper building, where workaholic editors and reporters were burning the midnight oil and racing to make their deadlines. Vicki had taken a few journalism classes in college; she knew how consuming it could be.*

This doesn't feel right, *she thought. A Parisian newspaper office hardly seemed like a breeding ground for terrorists, so what were she and Okata doing here?*

"I understand about keeping secrets," she said. "I don't understand why secrets are being kept from me—by my own people." *Months of frustration spilled out of her.* "It doesn't make sense. Why haven't I been briefed on the target yet? I don't like being kept in the dark."

Okata shrugged philosophically. He was not one for drama. She wasn't sure she had ever heard him raise his voice.

"This is an unusually sensitive matter," *he explained, without really doing so.* "Our superior felt that this time around, things were best handled on a need-to-know basis."

"I'm about to kill someone," she said. "Don't you think that constitutes need to know?"

"Soon," *he promised. His eyes narrowed as he scrutinized his balky protégée.* "What's really bothering you? Don't tell me you're having doubts about the work?"

That's putting it mildly, *she thought.*

Okata had recruited her right out of college. In the aftermath of 9/11, and the anthrax mailings and the London bombings, it had been clear that America—and the world—needed protecting from some seriously dangerous people. Okata had appealed to her patriotism and sense of duty, as well as, to be honest, a certain restless yearning for excitement. A championship marksman, with a talent for languages and creative thinking, Vicki had struck the older man as having the potential to become a world-class sniper—and one without any military record or paper trail. Perfect for covert operations conducted off the books.

Okata had personally supervised her training. He had been a master sniper himself, until a booby trap in the Philippines cost him an eye and his depth perception. For the last five years, he had aimed Vicki at a series of terrorists, conspirators, warlords, rebels, pirates, and insurrectionists, all of whom, she had been assured, posed significant threats to American lives and security. She'd never had any direct contact with Okata's shadowy superior, but she knew she was employed by a private black-ops group that did contract work for the U.S. government and its allies. Plausible deniability was their stock-in-trade.

At first, the work had been exciting and fulfilling, if occasionally messy. She had really felt she was making a difference. But doubts had recently undermined her resolve and troubled her conscience. Some of her targets—victims?— had not struck her as clearly identifiable threats. Her assignments seemed to be drifting into some uncomfortably gray areas. Unsettling questions kept her up at night.

Just because a foreign opposition leader had an anti-

American bias, did that make him a supporter of terrorism and a legitimate target? Where exactly was the line between a dangerous "ecoterrorist" and a radical environmentalist? Was she really defending America, or just taking out anyone who challenged the entrenched power structures?

Okata assured her that all of their targets had been thoroughly vetted, but as her personal body count piled up, she found herself less and less inclined to trust that decision to higher-ups she had never even met. She needed to know *why* she was pulling the trigger.

Like tonight.

"Doubts? You bet." A long leather bag rested at her feet. She unzipped it to reveal her weapon of choice: an M24 sniper rifle. She hefted the weapon and double-checked to make sure its sight was properly calibrated. "So, you ready to tell me who our target is?"

Okata checked his watch, as though timing the revelation down to the minute. He handed her a pair of high-powered binoculars.

"Fifth floor down, third window to the right."

She located the window in question. The binoculars zoomed in on a Gallic-looking middle-aged reporter seated in front of his computer. His sleeves were rolled up and his tie was undone. He consulted a small spiral notebook as he tapped away at his keyboard. A coffee mug sat within arm's reach, along with an ashtray. A family photo, depicting the wife and kids, occupied a position of honor on his desk. The man glanced up at a clock on the wall, then went back to typing. Vicki gasped as she recognized his profile.

"Wait a second," she said. "That's René Leroux, the investigative journalist. I read his exposé on those escaped Balkan war criminals." Lowering the binoculars, she turned to confront Okata. "He's a reporter, not a terrorist!"

"He might as well be," Okata said mildly, seemingly unconcerned by the distinction. "He's been poking his nose into our business, which is making our friends in D.C. and elsewhere more than a little nervous. And that could interfere with our work."

That didn't explain what they were doing lurking outside his office with a sniper rifle at the ready. "But he's just doing his job."

"His job will give aid and comfort to the enemies of freedom. At this very moment he's waiting for a call from an anonymous whistle-blower who has information on that safe-house bombing in Budapest six months ago." He gave her a knowing look. "You remember that one, don't you?"

I wish I didn't, she thought. She had merely provided backup on that mission, maintaining a defensive position on a rooftop while the demolition team went about its work, but the resulting explosion, which was conveniently blamed on a radical left-wing labor organization, had produced far too much collateral damage for her piece of mind. She still had nightmares about it.

"Yes, I remember."

"Then you know what's at stake. Leroux follows that lead, it could point him toward you and me and the people we work for. And that means more terrorists would be able to act with impunity."

Vicki remembered the photo on the journalist's desk.

"But he has a family! We can't just kill him, not for reporting the truth."

"You're missing the big picture," Okata insisted. "You need to settle down, focus on the mission, and follow orders. Just like you always have before."

The rifle in her hands was feeling heavier every second. She racked her mind, searching for a way out. "But if he's assassinated, won't that just raise some pretty big red flags, and maybe bring down even more heat on us?"

Okata smiled serenely. "We have that covered."

He had brought a leather satchel to the mission. He laid it down on top of the humming ventilation fan and undid the clasp.

Vicki tensed. "What's that?"

"Evidence pointing to one Henri Paquet," he said. "A local crackpot and conspiracy theorist. Seems he's been sending vaguely threatening e-mails to the paper for some weeks now—or at least someone has been sending them under his name and from his address. Poor Henri! We couldn't have asked for a better patsy."

Okata opened the bag and began strewing the phony "evidence" about the rooftop.

"Paranoid flyers and newsletters with his fingerprints on them," he enumerated them, "a soda can with his prints and DNA, a sandwich crust rescued from his trash." Okata shook his head in mock disapproval. "Sloppy, sloppy."

Horrified, Vicki picked up one of the fallen newsletters. DON'T BELIEVE LIES!!! *a garish headline screamed in French.* THE TRUTH BEHIND THE MEDIA'S SECRET EXTRATERRESTRIAL AGENDA!!!

"We're framing him?" She couldn't believe her ears. Paquet might well be a nut, but that didn't mean that he deserved to take the fall for a murder. "But won't he deny everything?"

"Trust me," Okata said coolly. He finished planting the evidence. "That's not going to be an issue."

He didn't need to spell it out. Paquet was already dead or soon would be. Another piece of collateral damage, sacrificed for the greater good. Or so she had often been told.

"But you don't need to worry about that. Your job is to take out Leroux." Okata looked out over a safety railing. "A tricky shot, but nothing you haven't pulled off before. Just do your job."

"No! Not this time," she blurted, her course suddenly clear to her. "This is the last straw. I'm through."

Okata sighed. "Are you sure about that?"

"Are you kidding? Killing a journalist? Framing an innocent . . ." Her voice trailed off as a ghastly suspicion hit her like a kill shot. "Hang on! Why are you telling me all this? What happened to need to know?"

She started to swing the rifle around, but Okata was way ahead of her. His trusty Beretta was already pointed at her head.

"Please keep your rifle pointed at the right target," he instructed. "My aim might not be what it once was, but close-range is no problem."

She understood now. "This was a . . ."

"A test," he confirmed. "There were concerns that you were going soft on us, especially after your reaction to the Budapest incident." He shook his head sadly. "A shame, really, after all the time and trouble we put in to training *you, and after such a sterling track record. I guess you can take the girl out of the humanities but you can't take the humanity out of the girl."*

You came close, *she thought.* Too close.

She held on to the rifle. "So now what?"

"You're going to take the shot, and then we're going to go somewhere for a nice, long chat about your future with the organization."

She guessed that future would be short. "Why not just use me as a patsy—and leave Paquet be?"

"Too risky," he said. "You have too many links to our group. We can't have people looking into your past and recent activities." He sounded as though he had already considered that option. "Better that we just finish the mission and catch our flight."

A single-engine Cessna was waiting for them at a small private airfield just outside the city. The plan was to skip the country as soon as the hit was complete, crossing the Channel to the UK, where Okata would be debriefed on their mission. A bed-and-breakfast in Dover was already booked under an assumed name. Vicki had been looking forward to decompressing after the hit, but it seemed that had been wishful thinking.

She suddenly remembered one of her favorite movies, Hitchcock's North by Northwest, *and how the suave villain played by James Mason had famously observed that some problems were best disposed of from a great height and over water. She suspected that she wasn't meant to make it all the way across the Channel.*

And I probably can't count on Cary Grant to rescue me.

"Leroux should be receiving his call any minute now,"

Okata said, a trace of impatience creeping into his usual placid tone. "We shouldn't delay any longer. Get on with it."

She figured that the only reason he hadn't disarmed her was that he still needed her to take the shot. Like he said, his aim wasn't what it used to be.

"And if I don't?"

His face hardened. He kept his pistol aimed at her. "Then Leroux will outlive you, at least for the time being."

"You'd really shoot me? My own handler?"

Part of her still couldn't believe it. He'd had her back for the last five years. She had trusted him with her life.

"We're snipers," he reminded her. "That's what we do."

She stalled for time. "We can't talk about this?"

"Shoot first, talk later." He came up behind her, his gun aimed at her back of her skull. "Without further delay, please."

He came a little too close.

There's that depth-perception problem again, *she thought.* She rammed the butt of the rifle into his chest, knocking him backward. His handgun went off, the bullet whizzing past her head.

One shot was all she gave him.

She flipped the rifle in her hands, like a majorette twirling a baton. The muzzle flared. A silencer muffled the sharp report.

He crumpled against the churning ventilation fan. Blood soaked through the front of his jacket. It was a kill shot, but not a clean one. She had done better in the past, but these were special circumstances.

"*Guns have two ends,*" she said. "*You should've remem-*
bered that."

"*You can't just turn your back on us,*" he gurgled, his
voice wet and halting. "*We'll find you wherever you run.*"

"*We'll see about that.*"

"*They won't forget this.*" He coughed up blood. "*Assas-*
sins never forget . . ."

His eyes glazed over. He slumped lifelessly onto the
rooftop.

She vowed that he would be her last victim.

Vicki hurled the rifle away from her. Her career as an
assassin was over, but she needed to move fast if she wanted
to make a clean break. A desperate exit strategy popped
into her mind. It was a drastic ploy, which would change
her life forever, but possibly the only one available to her.

She quickly gathered up the dummy evidence framing
Paquet and stuffed it back into the satchel. She had bought
Leroux time, but she didn't want Paquet to go down for
Okata's murder instead. Let the authorities find a mystery
along with a body.

Good-bye, Daniel, *she thought.* Looks like you trained
me too well.

She raced down a service stairway, taking the steps two
at time, until she reached the ground floor and exited into
an alley behind the building, where she ditched the incrim-
inating satchel in a Dumpster. Their getaway car was
parked a few blocks away. Thankfully, there was no driver;
due to the "sensitivity" of the mission, the hit team had
been kept to a minimum.

A short, tense ride brought her to the airfield, where the

GREG COX

Cessna 172 Skyhawk was fully fueled and waiting. The pilot, a grizzled vet named Malone, greeted her on the tarmac. He blinked at her in confusion. "What happened? Where's Okata?"

"He's not coming," she said, racing toward the plane. "And neither are you."

Seeing only a friendly, he wasn't expecting the karate chop that dropped him like deadweight. A kick to the head guaranteed that he wouldn't be springing right back up again. She wondered just how guilty he was.

As guilty as her?

"Sorry."

She left him unconscious on the tarmac, grateful that she hadn't needed to murder him as well. There was too much blood on her hands already. She was done with killing . . . almost. There was still one more person left on her hit list:

Vicki Rhodes.

Her training had included flight lessons, just in case something happened to a pilot. Climbing into the cockpit, she fired up the Cessna and set its propeller spinning. Within minutes, she was in the air and heading for the Channel as planned.

Chances were, Okata's body would not be discovered until morning at the earliest, but by now her unknown superiors were surely wondering why Leroux was still alive. She prayed that her former employers wouldn't send another team after the nosy reporter, but she couldn't worry about that. She maintained strict radio silence all the way to Calais. Her bosses would just have to worry and wait.

Let them stew, *she thought bitterly.*

The Channel came into view, with the white cliffs of

*Dover visible across the way. Vicki switched on the auto-
pilot and shrugged into her parachute. The plane was already rigged to self-destruct in the event of capture. She set
the timer for ten minutes, time enough for the plane to get
safely out over the water.*

Time to play D. B. Cooper, *she thought.*

*She threw open the plane's hatch. Violent wind currents
invaded the cabin. Committing herself to her rash course
of action, she tossed herself out of the Cessna while it was
still over land. She plunged toward the French coastline
below. All sense of falling evaporated as she reached terminal velocity, roughly a hundred and twenty miles an
hour. A sudden jolt yanked her upward as the chute de-
ployed.*

*She was still drifting toward the ground, scanning for a
relatively safe landing spot, when the plane exploded over
the Channel. A blazing fireball erupted in the night. Flam-
ing debris plunged toward the choppy water below.*

No body would ever be found.

Rest in peace, *she thought as she parachuted toward an
unknown afterlife. She silently bid farewell to the woman
she had been, and a life she could no longer live with. She
had no idea what happened next, only that Vicki Rhodes
was dead and had to stay that way.*

I'm going to need a new name, *she realized.*

"So you faked your own death in order to put that life behind you," Nate said, summing it up. The whole crew had
been hanging on Denise's words. "Lot of that going
around."

"It wasn't as easy as it sounds," she said. "We're talking plastic surgery, forged documents, a whole new identity." She ran a hand through her flaming-red locks. "Generous quantities of henna."

"Next time go with wigs," Sophie advised her. "Better for quick changes."

"I just wanted to start over," Denise said. "Get away from all the death and deceit and double-dealing. And then I met Gavin and, for a while there, it really did seem like I had a chance at a normal life with a great guy."

"Okay, I get that," Hardison said. "But how come, after going to all that trouble to bury your past, you would want to dig it all up again in your book?"

Nate thought he knew the answer. "Your conscience was troubling you."

"That's right," Denise said. "*Assassins Never Forget* wasn't just a catchy title. It was the story of my life. I couldn't forget what I had done, what was still going on out of the public eye, by renegade black-ops groups like the one I'd worked for. I had to come clean somehow, if only to confess and get it off my chest. I couldn't sleep at night unless I tried to make things right . . ."

"And so 'Tarantula' was born," Nate said. "Gavin's 'anonymous' informant."

She pulled back her hair to reveal a cobweb tattoo on the back of her neck. "I got this one night in Santa Fe after too much tequila." She let her hair fall back into place, concealing the telltale ink. "It was a private joke between Gavin and me. He was the only person who knew about the tattoo."

Nate couldn't help wondering if Eliot had ever glimpsed

the tattoo during his sleepovers at Denise's place. There was no tactful way to ask.

"And Gavin knew about your past?" Sophie asked. "About Vicki."

"Not at first, but yes, eventually. I couldn't hide it from him. We shared everything else. He deserved to know the truth about me." Her voice was strained, but she held it together. "It was Gavin's idea to put himself forward as the author so I could stay safely in the background."

It all makes sense, Nate thought. "That's why you never got married, why there was no will, why only Gavin's name appeared on the book contracts . . ."

"Why I never showed my face at his public appearances," Denise said, finishing Nate's sentence. "It was all about maintaining a low profile so as to avoid raising any red flags where my new identity was concerned, and to keep anyone from connecting me to the book. Between Gavin acting as the front, and us disguising the book as fiction, we figured we could avoid attracting the wrong kind of attention." She choked up. "But instead I got Gavin killed."

"You didn't kill him," Eliot said forcefully. "Beria did." He gestured at the surveillance photos of Anton Beria. "He the guy you worked for, before?"

"Maybe," Denise said. "I never met the man at the top. I mostly dealt with my handler." She winced at the memory. "Everything was strictly compartmentalized, on a need-to-know basis."

"Like with terrorist cells," Eliot said. "So that if you're captured or interrogated you can't rat out the entire operation."

"Exactly," Denise said. "I swear to you, I wasn't lying before, not about that. I don't know Beria. As far as I know, I've never met him."

"And he's never met you," Nate observed. "Interesting."

He wondered just how much plastic surgery Denise had undergone to bury her former identity. Enough that Beria had failed to recognize her as the late Vicki Rhodes? Possibly. But did Beria still think Vicki was dead—or had he figured out that Tarantula was Vicki? Nate wished he knew for sure just how much Beria knew or suspected. Opposition research was key to a good plan, but Beria was far too murky a target, and there were too many outstanding question marks for Nate's liking.

Good thing I've got a plan for every scenario, he thought. *I hope.*

"Maybe I should just exchange myself for Brad," Denise suggested. "He wants Tarantula? All right; at least nobody else will get hurt because of me."

"Forget it," Eliot snarled. "That's not happening."

"But this is my mess," she insisted. "I'm the one he wants."

"Oh, we're going to give him Tarantula," Nate said. "Don't worry about that." He winked at Sophie, who caught on immediately, as he knew she would. "But first we still have a book to write . . ."

Hours later, the suite had been converted into a prose factory. Everyone, including Denise, was sequestered in a corner, tapping away at one of six networked laptops. Hardison had set up a wireless link between the computers so that scenes and chapters could be passed along the assembly line as each author completed a section. As planned, all roads led to Denise, who was hard at work imposing her singular voice and style on the collaborative effort. A "Do Not Disturb" sign hung on the door outside. The drapes were drawn to cut off the outside world. Room-service trays and pizza delivery boxes were scattered like debris all over the suite. Yellow legal pads were covered with notes and character sketches. Oceans of black coffee had been consumed. A fresh pot was brewing in the kitchen.

They were going to need it.

Nate sat at the bar, sipping a whiskey as he monitored the book's progress. He was starting to understand why so many authors and editors became alcoholics. Pulling a book out of the ether was enough to drive anyone to drink.

They had been at it nonstop for at least ten hours and the strain was starting to show. Beria's deadline was bearing down on them like an unstoppable avalanche. A large digital display on the video wall counted down the hours, minutes, and seconds. Nate frowned at the countdown. They had already fallen behind on their word counts . . .

"Pick up the pace, people," he called out. "You're not writing the Great American Novel here."

"Is that a thing?" Parker asked. "Is there a prize?"

"Just keep writing, Parker. And faster, if you don't mind."

"Slave driver," she muttered under her breath. "I bet there's a prize."

Nate lifted his eyes from his laptop to check out the crew. Everyone seemed to be searching for their muse in their own way.

Parker was choreographing her complicated action

scenes with the aid of toy vehicles and action figures she had foraged from a local dollar store. As Nate watched, a G.I. Joe fell to his doom after being knocked off the arm of the couch by a hang-gliding My Little Pony. Parker chuckled evilly as the action figure hit the floor. She typed feverishly. "Take that, Double Agent Triple-X!"

Nate peeked at her current output. Sure enough, a rogue assassin had just plummeted to his death in the Swiss Alps.

Whatever works, he thought.

He shrugged and hit save.

Meanwhile, Hardison seemed to be holding up so far. No surprise there; the hacker was accustomed to marathon sessions in front of a computer screen. Empty bottles of orange soda littered the floor around his feet. He finished off one bottle, tossed it aside, and reached for another. Nate made a mental note to schedule another bathroom break soon.

A bowl of brightly colored gummy frogs rested at Hardison's elbow. He stuffed a handful of candies into his mouth, then washed it down with a swig of soda. Nate practically got a sugar rush just watching him, but didn't suggest that Hardison ease up on the sweets. They all had their vices and Nate was no one to talk.

He poured himself another whiskey.

Hardison's latest pages scrolled past Nate's watchful gaze.

Uh-oh.

"Hold on, Hardison," he called across the room. "What's all this about an artificial intelligence . . . from a parallel universe?"

"All based on sound scientific theories," Hardison proclaimed, a tad defensively. "Hold on, let me send you some links backing me up here."

Nate's e-mail chimed. He ignored the message.

"Just dial it down, Asimov."

Hardison backspaced through the offending passages. "Everybody's a critic," he grumbled, loud enough for Nate to hear. "This stuff was gold, I'm telling you, twenty-four karats of Nebula-quality scientific extrapolation. We're talking bestseller, boys and girls."

Save it for the next book, Nate thought. *I doubt if Beria's a sci-fi fan.*

Sophie jumped to her feet and started acting out a scene, complete with multiple voices and accents.

French: "For the love of God, Dmitri. Why do you have to be so cold and emotionally unavailable, even to the people who truly care about you. Stop pushing me away!"

Russian: "The mission is all that matters, Yvette. You should know that by now. I am who I am. I lost my heart a long time ago, when Sasha was murdered by those terrorists. All that's left is the work."

French: "I don't believe that. Maybe that hollow-man act fools other people. Maybe you've even fooled yourself. But I know you, Dmitri. Better than you know yourself. You're not really dead inside. You're alive, Dmitri, alive!"

German: "But not for much longer, *mein freund*!"

French: "Gustav! No! Put down that machine gun!"

Sophie threw herself in the path of an invisible assassin. A look of mortal terror contorted her face, followed by a grimace of pain. She clutched her chest as though shot.

Russian: "Yvette!"

French: "Don't forget me, Dmitri! Never forget . . ."

Nate winced. This was a little on the nose, in more ways than one.

"Damn it, Sophie!" Eliot barked. He pounded away at his keyboard like it was an enemy to be subdued—or maybe just a manual typewriter. "Do you have to keep doing that out loud? Some of us are trying to concentrate here!"

"I'm sorry," she said. "But it helps me bring my characters to life. I can't just type the dialogue. I need to hear it, speak it, feel it . . ."

"Well, hear it, speak it, and feel it somewhere else," Eliot said. "How am I supposed to write a fifteen-page fight sequence involving multiple combatants, a sniper, and a grizzly bear with you making all that racket."

"Racket?" Sophie said indignantly. "I'll have you know that scene is the heart and soul of the book. How is the reader supposed to understand Yvette's complicated love/hate relationship with Dmitri unless every line comes straight from my heart?" She threw up her hands in frustration. "I've opened a bloody vein here, people. I'm bleeding onto the page!"

"You are?" Parker said, putting down the action figures. She peered at Sophie's screen with interest. A puzzled look came over her face as she looked in vain for any literal gore. Disappointed, she turned back toward her own work. "And people think I'm the crazy one . . ."

The way things are going, Nate thought, *she's going to have plenty of company.*

"Calm down, everyone." He strolled to the center of the suite and raised his voice to be heard over the bickering.

"Look, I understand. You're all tired and irritable and running on fumes. But we've got to hold it together." He glanced at the countdown. "We still have fifty-two thousand words to go—and only thirty hours left."

A chorus of groans greeted his update. It wasn't exactly the response he'd hoped for. Even Denise was slumped over her keyboard, looking utterly fried. Sophie collapsed into a comfy chair. She looked up at Nate, her face a portrait of surrender. Red-rimmed eyes implored him.

"I just can't do it, Nate," she moaned. "I can't write anymore. I don't have anything left."

"I don't believe it." He knelt by the chair, talking to her one-on-one. "You're Sophie Devereaux. You once worked a PBS telethon for seventy hours straight while posing as a blind tap dancer."

"Don't remind me," she said. "I still cringe whenever I hear 'Puttin' on the Ritz' after dark."

"The point is, you're a trouper. Fatigue has never slowed you down before. You keep going until you get the job done."

"But that's different," she protested. "Yes, when I'm grifting I can stay in character for days if I have to, but that's what I do. I'm an actress, not a writer."

"So play a writer."

"What?"

"You heard me. Pretend you're playing the part of a writer with a tight deadline."

She sat up straight, struck by the notion. She opened her mouth to raise an objection, but paused and thought it over instead. A speculative look came over her face, along with an unmistakable gleam of interest in her eyes. Nate recognized that gleam; she got it whenever she was developing a new character.

"Am I a good writer or bad writer?"

"A *fast* writer," he stressed.

"And what's my motivation?"

Nate smirked.

"Your coldhearted, hard-as-nails, son-of-a-bitch editor."

She smiled slyly as they shared a moment.

"Yes, I can see that."

|||||| **TWELVE** ||||||

MANHATTAN

END, Denise typed. She hit save.

"That's it," she announced, taking her hands away from the keyboard. She sounded like she couldn't believe it. "I think we're finished."

"Oh, thank God," Sophie exclaimed, slumping in her seat. She couldn't remember the last time she'd felt so tired, so drained. Her eyes drooped heavily; it was a struggle to keep them open. Her brain felt foggier than her old London stomping grounds. She didn't even want to think about what she must look like in a mirror. "I think I died a couple hours ago."

Parker leaned over and checked her pulse. "Nope," she reported. "Not this time."

"Tell me about it," Hardison said. Like the rest of them, he was showing the telltale effects of hours of nonstop wordsmithing. His eyelids drooped, as though he was having trouble keeping them up. He needed a shower and a shave. Reaching wearily for his umpteenth bottle of orange soda, he paused and reconsidered. An incredulous look came over his face. "Whoa. I'm all soda-ed out. I honestly can't face another drop."

"That's scary," Parker said. She stared at him as though he had just been replaced by an alien impostor. She backed away. "Hardison isn't Hardison anymore."

"I'm not sure there's much left of any of us." Eliot cracked his knuckles. He stretched his stiff neck. "I'm through with this writing crap. Give me a bare-knuckle cage match in Bangkok any day."

Even Nate had switched from booze to black coffee. His eyes burned.

"Look, I know it was hard on all of you," he said, "but we did it. We have a book . . . and none too soon."

The electronic countdown had only four minutes and thirty-two seconds to go. The forty-eight hours were almost up.

"I can't believe we actually pulled it off." Denise marveled aloud. She yawned and rubbed her eyes. "That was quite the marathon."

Eliot walked over and massaged her shoulders. "How you bearing up?"

"To be honest, I'd kill for a hot shower and a long nap, maybe at the same time." She ran a hand through her hair. "I feel like an absolute zombie—and probably smell like one, too."

Hardison chuckled, as though at a private joke. "Funny you should mention zombies . . ."

Before he could elaborate, a ring tone brought the suite to a hush. All eyes turned toward Denise's cell phone, which was resting on the conference room table, next to her laptop. The countdown on the video screens hit 00:00:00.

"Right on schedule," Nate said.

Denise reached for her phone.

"No," Nate said. "Let Sophie take it."

He nodded at her and she took a deep breath to clear the cobwebs from her brain. A rush of adrenaline combated her fatigue. She stretched and took the phone. It was already set on speakerphone so that the others could listen in.

Showtime, she thought. "Hello?"

An electronically distorted voice delivered a chilling pronouncement: *"Your time is up."*

Sophie declined to be intimidated by such theatrics.

"Mr. Beria, I presume?"

They were taking a calculated risk, revealing that they had already ID'd Beria, but Nate had decided it was worth the gamble. With any luck, using his name would throw Beria off his game and perhaps even serve to bring him out into the open. He might be less likely to remain in the shadows if there was no longer any point in concealing his identity.

At least that was the idea.

"Guilty as charged," he admitted after a brief pause. There was a click on the line as he dispensed with the electronic distortion. A cool, icy voice with a cultured Mid-Atlantic accent emerged from the phone. *"It seems you have the advantage on me. May I ask whom I have the pleasure of addressing?"*

That was her cue.

"You can call me . . . Tarantula."

She couldn't resist milking the moment for all it was worth. How often did she get to play an international woman of mystery?

Other than every day, that is.

"Ah, the late Mr. Lee's highly indiscreet informant," he replied. *"I don't suppose you'd care to volunteer your real name, simply to put us on an equal footing?"*

"What's the rush?" she said, stalling. They still didn't know whether Beria suspected that Tarantula was actually the supposedly deceased Vicki Rhodes. "There will be plenty of time to get to know each other once we've concluded the business at hand."

"Indeed," he agreed. *"I look forward to having a long and illuminating discussion with you in the very near future. In the meantime, are you prepared to exchange yourself—and the sequel—for poor, petrified Brad?"*

"Yes." Her voice caught in her throat as she channeled Denise's guilt and acute sense of responsibility. "Too many people have ended up in harm's way because of my secrets . . . and my past. I can't let anyone else pay the price for my sins."

Her dialogue actually came from Chapter Sixteen of *Assassins Remember,* which she had written herself, but Beria didn't need to know that.

"A commendable attitude," Beria said. *"I'm glad that you're being so reasonable about this. This matter is between you and me. There's no reason for any hapless civilians, such as Brad, to get caught in the cross fire."*

She glanced over at Hardison, who was diligently

attempting to trace the call to its origin. Probably a wasted effort, considering Beria's black-ops background and expertise, but it was worth a try. Maybe Beria had gotten rusty.

"And you have the manuscript in hand?" he asked. *"The complete text of* Assassins Remember*?"*

"Yes, of course." She shuddered, recalling all those long hours at the keyboard. It was a miracle that she hadn't developed carpal tunnel syndrome. *You have no idea what I went through to be able to say that. What we all went through.*

Parker had actually dozed off on the couch. Sophie felt a pang of envy.

"Let's make this exchange," she said. "When and where?"

"Trinity Churchyard in lower Manhattan, three A.M. *You are familiar with the location?"*

"Naturally."

The historic graveyard, which held the bones of such luminaries as Alexander Hamilton and Robert Fulton, was located in lower Manhattan near Wall Street. Sophie had occasionally taken lunch there while running stock-market scams.

"Excellent," Beria said. *"Come alone, and don't forget the manuscript."*

"Alone? You can't be serious." Sophie knew that Tarantula would never agree to such terms, and neither would she. "I need some sort of backup to ensure that you carry out your side of the bargain, and to escort Brad to safety if and when you release him."

"You are hardly in a position to dictate terms," Beria reminded her. *"We have Brad. His continued existence depends on your cooperation."*

"True, but I'm not going to sacrifice myself without taking a few reasonable precautions—for Brad's sake." She let a note of exasperation creep into her voice. "Don't insult my intelligence. We're both professionals. We know how these things are done."

"Far be it from me to behave unprofessionally," he conceded. *"Let us each bring one bodyguard for our own protection. Is this acceptable?"*

Sophie glanced at Eliot, who nodded. So far, things were playing out according to plan. She felt better knowing that Eliot would be watching her back, and be on hand if things got physical.

"Yes. That will do," she said. "But we're not finished here. It's been forty-eight hours since we've had proof of life. I'm not going anywhere, let alone a deserted cemetery after dark, unless I know Brad's still alive and in one piece."

Beria chuckled. *"You* have *done this sort of thing before, haven't you? Very well. Stay on the line."*

He put Brad on.

"Please," the terrified hostage sobbed. *"I don't know who you are, but you have to do what they want."* He clearly didn't recognize Sophie's voice without her New York agent intonations. *"It's not fair! I never asked for this. I don't know anything about tarantulas or assassins or whatever Gavin was mixed up in. I just want to—"*

He was cut off in midsentence.

"Was that sufficient?" Beria inquired.

"Quite."

"Then we're nearly done here," he said. *"One last thing: we will have the location under surveillance between now and then. So do not think that you will be able to case the site in advance and arrange some manner of surprise. We will expect you at three, and not before."*

He hung up.

Sophie put down the phone. "Hardison?"

He shook his head. "No dice. It was just like before. He routed that call through Timbuktu and back again. It was like trying to find Carmen Santiago, blindfolded and without a map."

"Spellcheck," Parker muttered in her sleep, her fingers twitched as though she was still typing in her dreams. "Gotta check the spelling . . ."

Nate let her sleep. They could her fill her in later.

"All right. It's on," he said. "Everybody get some food or coffee if they need it. This isn't over yet and we all need to be at the top of our game, despite the fact that we just spent the last two days writing a book." He looked Sophie over, examining her for signs of fatigue. "You up for this?"

She liked that he was concerned about her. It gave her hope for Dmitri.

"Don't worry about me," she assured, acting less exhausted than she was. She hoped her performance was convincing. "I'm Sophie Devereaux, remember?"

He treated her to a rare smile. "How could I forget?"

Denise reclaimed her phone.

"I'm still not happy about Sophie taking my place," she

said. "Why can't I meet with Beria instead? I'm not just a ghostwriter, you know. I'm Tarantula. This used to be my world."

"Not anymore," Eliot growled. "You worked too hard to get out of it."

"Right," she said bitterly. "And look how that's turned out."

Nate adopted a conciliatory tone. "Nobody doubts your abilities, or your determination, but if you want us to fix this, you need to let us do it our way. And that means using Sophie. You have to believe me when I tell you that she's the right person for the job."

Sophie appreciated the show of support, but knew that there was more to it. Between Denise's guilt over her past and Gavin's death, the remorseful author was too emotionally involved. They couldn't trust her to stick to the script—and not try to sacrifice herself for all the wrong reasons at the wrong time. Sophie knew better than to tell Denise that, however, so she tried another angle.

"It's simple," she explained. "Nate is a control freak and he's never worked with you before. He's not going to be happy unless he's calling the shots, and using his own crew." She shot a preemptive look at Nate. "Well, am I wrong?"

Nate scowled, feigning offense.

Never fails, Sophie thought. *When you can't tell the truth, tell a truth.*

"But you have to let me do something," Denise persisted.

"You've already done enough," Eliot assured her. "We could have never written that book without you."

"But . . ."

"But nothing," Eliot said firmly. "Look at me. Do you trust me?"

She sighed. "Yes."

"Then trust that we know what we're doing. We're going to get Brad back, and see that Beria pays for Gavin's murder. You have my word on that."

His promise, and the gruff sincerity with which it was delivered, seemed to appease Denise. "All right," she said, giving in. "We'll do it your way." She gave Sophie a thumbs-up. "Good luck being me."

"Thanks," Sophie said. *Here's hoping we don't let you down.*

Nate checked his watch. "Okay, it's twelve-thirty. We have two and a half hours before the meet. And you know what that means."

Time to squeeze in a nap? Sophie hoped. Her adrenaline rush was wearing off at an alarming pace. An adjacent bedroom called out to her.

"We still have time to give the book one last polish."

Sophie contemplated murder.

Nobody would ever miss an editor . . .

Two-plus hours later, she and Eliot approached Trinity Church on foot. The towering Gothic Revival edifice, which had once been the tallest structure in Manhattan, was located at the corner of Broadway and Wall Street. Sleeping skyscrapers and office buildings lined the quiet streets of the financial district. It was nearly three A.M. in a part of lower Manhattan not exactly known for its nightlife and all the bars and restaurants were closed. The Wall Street crowd would be showing up in a few hours, but for now the sidewalks were deserted. A damp October fog reminded Sophie of home, shrouding the neighborhood in mist and reducing visibility to an ominous degree. She had to admire nature's stagecraft; it was the perfect setting for the scene they were about to enact.

Almost curtain time, she thought.

Despite a bad case of sleep deprivation, she felt primed and ready. This was a part she was born to play: a glamorous ex-spy with a shady past and guilty conscience. What more could any self-respecting actress ask for?

She was dressed for the part in a belted Burberry trench coat and black leather boots. A gloved hand held the handle of the same black leather briefcase she had confiscated from Brad mere days ago. A miniature button cam was discreetly pinned to the lapel of her coat, allowing Hardison and the others to see and hear everything she did in real time. She cupped a hand over her ear.

"We're almost there," she said, checking in. "Are you still reading this?"

"Everything's copacetic at this end," Hardison reported from "Lucille," his mobile base of operations. *"We're good to go."*

"Easy for you to say," Eliot grumbled. He had put less thought into his wardrobe. A wool cap, leather jacket, flannel shirt, and jeans insulated him from the cold and damp while still serving to reinforce his intimidating persona. A second button cam, pinned to his cap, provided Hardison with an alternative view. Eliot strode beside Sophie, alert to his surroundings. His sharp eyes scanned the misty city streets. "I don't see you walking into an obvious trap."

Nobody trusted Beria and his goons to carry out their side of the bargain. The elusive spymaster clearly didn't like loose ends, as demonstrated by Gavin's murder and Beria's ruthless pursuit of the sequel. Some sort of double cross had to be in the offing; Sophie would have been willing to bet the Crown Jewels on it, assuming Parker hadn't lifted them first.

Good thing we've got our own plans, she thought.

"Look at it this way," Hardison told Eliot. *"At least you'll probably get to hit somebody. That always makes your day."*

"Don't tempt me." Eliot started to say more, but then he whirled around and lunged into the fog behind him. A startled yelp escaped the mist as Eliot grabbed on to a lurking figure and threw him up against the sooty stone wall of an office building. "You really think you can sneak up on us, mister?" Eliot drew back his fist. "Think again."

It was the peeper. The one from Frankfurt and before.

With all the drama surrounding Brad's kidnapping, Sophie had almost forgotten about the nameless stranger who had been spying on her in Boston and Frankfurt, but she recognized the scrawny, bespectacled lurker at once. He had on his usual green hoodie. He clutched a leather-bound album of some sort to his chest. A backpack hung from his shoulders, padding his back as Eliot pinned him to the wall. His hood fell back, exposing a mop of greasy, black hair. He grimaced in discomfort.

Sophie found herself thrown for a loop. She stared at the lurker.

What was he doing here now, of all possible times?

This was not part of the plan.

"Please! Don't hit me!" the man begged. "I don't mean any harm! I never did! This is all just a big misunderstanding!"

Eliot kept him pressed to the wall, practically lifting him off his feet. He got in the lurker's face. Sophie watched from a safe distance, giving the crew a good view from her button cam.

"Talk fast," Eliot growled. "Who are you? How come you were following us . . . again?"

"My name's Larry . . . Larry Meeker." The words spilled from him in a torrent as he desperately tried to spit them out before Eliot lost patience. "I just wanted to meet Ms. Devereaux." He peered past Eliot at Sophie, his bulging eyes wide behind his Coke-bottle glasses. "That's all, I swear!"

Sophie flinched at her real name. Well, the name she currently went by, that is. How much did Meeker know about her, if that was indeed *his* actual name?

"Why?" she asked. "Why me?"

"I . . . I . . . I'm your biggest fan!"

Eliot blinked in surprise. He lowered his fist. "Huh?"

"Wait a sec," Hardison chimed in via the coms. *"Sophie has a fan?"*

"I can hear you," she reminded them both. "You needn't sound so surprised."

Truth be told, she didn't know whether to be suspicious or flattered. She approached Larry cautiously, intrigued despite herself. "You know my work?"

"Ohmigod, yes," Larry said. "I'm a huge fan, have been

ever since I caught you in that off-off-off-off-Broadway production of *Death of a Salesman* a few years back." He practically glowed at the memory, enthusiasm overcoming his fear of Eliot. "You were the sexiest Willy Loman ever!"

Sophie was pleased he remembered. She had put a lot of thought into that characterization. "Well, I thought it was important to explore Willy's innate sensuality . . ."

"And I saw every single performance of your *Sound of Music*," he raved. "Both of them!"

Sophie sighed, wishing that particular production had run longer. "I'm not sure the critics truly understood my interpretation of Maria. It was very clear to me that she was secretly tone-deaf . . ."

"The heck?" Hardison said.

Sophie ignored him.

"And I had the front row all to myself for your recent one-woman show in Boston," Larry said. "It was incredibly moving. I wept when Madame Curie started glowing in the dark . . ."

"That was you?" Sophie asked. She remembered a solitary figure sobbing uncontrollably in the front row, obscured by the glare of the footlights, but she had been too deeply in character to take note of his appearance.

He nodded. "I went through an entire box of Kleenex. And I was your standing ovation!"

"That's it," Hardison commented. *"It's official. There are fanboys for everything."*

"Enough," Nate said, shushing him. *"Sophie. What's your take on him?"*

She looked at Eliot while replying to Nate.

"Believe it or not, I think he's for real."

She gestured at Eliot, who backed off a bit. His baleful gaze and expression made it clear that Larry was still on probation as far as he was concerned.

"Don't try anything," he warned. "I'm watching you."

"It's all true, I swear," Larry insisted. "Here! Let me show you my scrapbook." He cast an apprehensive look at Eliot, who grudgingly allowed him to offer the album to Sophie. "It's a true labor of love, you'll see."

Sophie took the scrapbook. Flipping through it, she was surprised (and more than a little tickled) to find an impressive collection of playbills, head shots, theater listings, candid spy photos, and other Sophie Devereaux memorabilia. There only seemed to be one thing missing.

"No reviews?" she asked.

"I'm waiting for some good ones." He blanched at his faux pas. "Ohmigod, please don't take that the wrong way. It's just that . . . the world doesn't appreciate your acting like it should!"

"I know!" Sophie agreed. "It's baffling!"

Eliot coughed, like something was stuck in his throat. *Must be the fog,* Sophie thought.

"But I don't understand," she said. "Why have you been following me all over the world? Why didn't you just approach me before?"

"I've wanted to," he confessed. "But I kept chickening out. I meant to in Frankfurt, but then you spotted me and I lost my nerve. I didn't want you to think I was some sort of creepy stalker."

"God forbid," Eliot muttered.

Larry looked nervously at Eliot. "Then your bodyguard

took off after me and I just panicked. And then there was that scary blonde in the dog costume . . ."

"Scary?" Parker reacted, her indignation coming through Sophie's earbud loud and clear. *"I was adorable."*

"My personal assistant," Sophie explained. "She's a furry."

"I'm still confused about one thing," Larry said. "What exactly were you doing at the book fair anyway?"

"Researching a role. Nothing I can talk about yet, of course."

"Oh," Larry said, sounding disappointed. "Not even a hint?"

"I'm afraid not." She steered the conversation back to more immediate matters. "But you still haven't explained what you're doing here now, at three in the morning?"

He blushed.

"Hoping for your autograph?"

"At three A.M.?"

"I finally worked up my nerve. I was just about to speak up—really!—when your bodyguard grabbed me." He winced, likely a bit bruised from his run-in with the wall. "Like I said, it was all a big misunderstanding!"

Eliot snorted. "Yeah, right."

"His story checks out," Hardison reported. *"I just ran his name through my search engines. He's a retired computer programmer from Seattle. Cashed out during the tech boom several years back. He's single, lives alone, and apparently has way too much time and money on his hands, no offense to Sophie. His interests include theater, travel, and, apparently, a certain tragically undiscovered British*

201

actress. You should see the fan page he's working on . . . or not."

"A fan page?" Sophie wanted to hear more. "I have to ask you, Larry, which of my various roles is your favorite? Feel free to elaborate."

"Well, it's hard to choose. You've done so much great work." He pondered the matter, giving it all due consideration. "But if I have to pick just one—"

"Never mind that," Nate said, staying on point. *"We don't have time for this. Get rid of him—quickly."*

He was right, of course. As gratifying as it was to hear from a devoted fan, she had a job to do and Brad's life was on the line.

"On second thought," she said, "I'm afraid now is not a good time. I'm running late for an appointment."

"Now?" Larry asked. "At almost three in the morning?"

"Look who's talking," Eliot said.

"What can I say?" Sophie said. "An actress is always on call, no matter the hour. I'm on my way to . . . a movie shoot."

"Wow!" Larry said. "Is it a big part?"

"I'm not at liberty to discuss it. Confidentiality agreements, you know." Eliot tugged impatiently on her arm. "Well, it was wonderful meeting you, but I must be going . . ."

She started to return his scrapbook.

"Your autograph?" he reminded her.

"Right." She rooted through her pockets. "I'm not sure I have a pen on me."

"Use mine." He produced a premium brass fountain pen from his vest pocket and flipped the scrapbook open to the front page, where a gilt-edged sheet of high-quality vellum awaited her signature. "'To Larry, my biggest fan,'" he suggested. "'With love.'"

Sophie fumbled with the scrapbook, looking about for a surface to write on. Time was ticking away and they needed to wrap this up.

"Eliot, if you don't mind . . ."

"I don't believe this," he groused, turning his back to her. "Just hurry up, damn it."

Bracing the book against Eliot's back, she hastily signed it.

"'With love,'" Larry prompted.

Eliot snarled. "Don't push your luck."

"There!" Sophie finished off her signature with a flourish, then handed the autographed scrapbook back to Larry, who accepted it as though he was receiving the keys to the city. She let Eliot drag her away. "Got to dash. Ta!"

They left Larry on the sidewalk, admiring his prized new possession. Sophie glanced back over her shoulder, but swiftly lost sight of him in the fog.

"Is he following us?" she asked.

"Not if he knows what's good for him."

Sophie consulted her watch. It was nearly three already. They had to sprint down the sidewalk, running late for their rendezvous. She shoved their encounter with Larry to the back of her mind in order to concentrate on the challenges ahead. Beria was waiting for Tarantula. They didn't want to disappoint him.

Trinity Churchyard appeared before them. The cemetery was located north and south of the church itself, an imposing Gothic pile whose soaring stone steeple and spires contrasted sharply with the looming temples of Mammon dominating Wall Street. Weathered gravestones and monuments rose from the mist-covered cemetery. Time had eaten away at many of the inscriptions, rendering them all but illegible. Rectangular stone sarcophagi, the size of benches, were scattered among the standing headstones. Skeletal sycamore trees had already shed their leaves, adding to the eerily autumnal atmosphere. Paved pathways wound through the historic grave sites, most of which were centuries old. Sophie had read up on the churchyard before setting forth tonight, so she knew that the oldest gravestone dated all the way back to 1681, making it the oldest in New York City. There were no new graves; the churchyard had run out of vacancies more than a hundred and fifty years ago.

A spiked metal fence surrounded the historic cemetery, but it struck Sophie as more symbolic than functional. Parker would snicker at the very idea of the low, cast-iron fence actually keeping anybody out. A sign posted the churchyard's hours: WEEKDAYS, 8:30 TO 6; WEEKENDS, 8:30 TO 4. At the moment the dead were closed for business.

Arriving at the western entrance on Trinity Place, they tried the gate and found that it had already been conveniently unlocked for them. It swung open at their touch. Oiled hinges didn't even squeak.

"We're going in," Sophie reported.

"*So I see,*" Nate said. "*Break a leg.*"

Eliot led the way as they cautiously entered the churchyard. The thick fog swirled among the weathered granite tombstones. Bony tree branches stretched overhead. Sophie was reminded of that low-budget horror movie the crew had hijacked in Eastern Europe a few years ago, only this time the fog was real. She hoped tonight's performance proved just as memorable.

Minus the Serbian gunrunners, of course.

They found Beria sitting on a metal bench in the north yard, not far from the chapel entrance. A polished ebony cane rested across his lap. As agreed, he was accompanied by only a single bodyguard: a beefy, blond steroid case with a bandage across his nose. He glowered at Eliot, confirming Sophie's suspicions that this was one of the thugs who had attempted to abduct Denise.

"How's the nose?" Eliot taunted him.

The thug bristled. "Just you wait, pretty boy. I'm gonna pound your face into—"

"Shush, Carl," Beria said, silencing the goon. "Don't let him bait you."

The scowling muscleman had custody of Brad, who looked distinctly worse for wear. A black eye and split lip testified to his brutal treatment. He was wearing the same blue tracksuit he'd had on when he was kidnapped; dried blood speckled the velour fabric, which clearly hadn't been washed or ironed in days. Stubble carpeted Brad's jowls. His thinning hair was a mess. His hands were bound behind his back. Sheer terror shone in his teary eyes, which bugged out when he recognized Sophie and Eliot. Confusion momentarily dispelled the petrified look on his face.

"Miss Drury? Officer Kolchak?"

"Shut up!" Carl cuffed Brad in the head. "You know the rules. No talking!"

Brad whimpered and fell silent.

Interesting, Sophie thought. *Is there a reason they want Brad to keep quiet? Is there something they don't want him to tell us?*

She and Eliot exchanged a look. She could tell he was thinking the same thing.

"You're late." Beria rose from the bench. He rested the tip of his cane against a three-hundred-year-old grave marker. He was a lean, almost cadaverous figure, wearing a heavy wool peacoat, leather gloves, and trilby. "I was starting to think that you had abandoned Brad to his fate."

Sophie shrugged nonchalantly. "Sorry. There's never a cab when you need one." She glanced around the cemetery. "Interesting choice of venue."

"It seemed an appropriate place to bury the past, once and for all," Beria said, "and unlikely to be occupied at this hour, at least by the living." Raising his cane, which appeared to be more of an affectation than a necessity, he pointed out the security cameras mounted to the gates and a nearby tree. "Do not concern yourself with the cameras, by the way. Budget cuts." He lowered his cane. "Pity."

"But convenient," Sophie said. "After all, it wouldn't do for there to be photographic evidence that the late, unlamented Anton Beria is still alive and kicking."

"Indeed," he said. "Nor another imprudent bestseller."

Sophie slipped deeper into the skin of Tarantula, playing the part to the hilt. "I suppose I should be flattered that you made a personal appearance. What brings you out of the shadows, so to speak?"

"Alas, delegating such tasks has proved ineffective of late." He cast a reproachful look at Carl, who looked suitably chastened. "Sometimes one simply has to take matters into one's own hands."

"Like when you ran Gavin down?" Eliot snarled.

Beria didn't deny it. "Ah, the white knight." He addressed Eliot. "I trust the lovely Ms. Gallo is well? How chivalrous of you to comfort her in her grief."

Eliot's expression darkened. "Leave her out of this."

Sophie admired his restraint, now that they were finally face-to-face with Gavin's killers. It had to be taking everything he had not to tear into them right here and now. She knew he wanted to.

"And how is it that you came to trust Gavin with your secrets?" Beria asked Sophie. "What precisely was the nature of your relationship?"

Sophie overlooked his insinuations. "Shall we get on with this?"

"As you wish," Beria agreed. "I'm certain Brad would appreciate any speed on our part." A sardonic smile betrayed a cruel sense of humor. "I suspect he's tired of our hospitality."

Brad nodded energetically, keeping his mouth shut.

Carl smacked him anyway.

"Show of hands, people," Eliot said. He raised his own empty hands to demonstrate that he was unarmed. "Just to keep everyone honest."

Beria rested his cane against the bench and did the same. Carl and Sophie followed their example. It was always possible, of course, that someone was carrying a concealed weapon, but at least they would have to draw first before getting the drop on anyone. That was probably the best both sides could hope for outside of setting up metal detectors at the gates of the churchyard, which might have been a tad conspicuous.

"Good enough," Eliot declared, watching Carl carefully. "But everybody keep their hands in sight."

"Let us begin with the book," Beria suggested. He nodded at the briefcase Sophie was carrying and gestured toward a sarcophagus located between the two delegations, equidistant from both. Its table-size lid had been worn smooth by the passage of time. "Whenever you're ready."

Sophie stepped forward and laid the briefcase down atop the sarcophagus. She unlocked the case.

"There's a hard copy inside," she explained, "as well as an electronic version installed on a tablet. GPS-disabled, of course."

She retreated from the tomb, leaving the case and its contents behind. Carl watched Beria's back as the cold-blooded spymaster came forward to inspect the ransom. It was too dark to read the printed manuscript without a flashlight, so he claimed the tablet, with its illuminated screen, instead.

"Pardon me while I look this over," he said.

Sophie held her breath as he scrolled through the freshly manufactured sequel, hoping that it would pass muster, at least for the time being. A look of concentration came over Beria's gaunt features as he perused the text. Eliot tapped his foot impatiently. Brad couldn't help whimpering a little. The suspense was obviously killing him, even if Beria and his goons hadn't yet. Sophie tried to speed things along.

"I certainly hope you don't intend to read the entire novel before we go any further," she commented, taking pains not to let a trace of anxiety show. She didn't want to make Beria suspicious by seeming *too* impatient. "It's rather a long book."

"So I see," Beria said. Declining to be rushed, he continued to inspect the sequel. "Have no fear. I am merely conducting a random spot check of various pages, to ensure that it is the same book all the way through."

Thank heavens we wrote the whole thing, Sophie thought. But which pages exactly was Beria examining? There were a few parts they didn't want him reading just yet . . .

"Very good," he said finally. He placed the tablet back in the case and closed the lid. "That should suffice."

"Satisfied?" Sophie asked.

"For now." He took possession of the briefcase and withdrew from the sarcophagus, returning to his original position by the bench. "I fully intend to pore over the text at my leisure later, but a cursory examination suggests that the sequel is clearly of a piece with the first book—and unmistakably the work of the unfortunate Gavin Lee."

Thank you, Denise, Sophie thought. In theory, the actual author was presently sharing the van with Hardison, who was under orders to keep her under close watch until tonight's operation was concluded, one way or another. The last thing they needed was for the former spy and assassin to try to take matters into her own hands.

That could only complicate matters, and possibly get somebody killed.

"So far, it appears, you have fulfilled your end of the bargain." Beria placed the briefcase on the bench, within easy reach. "Now there is the little matter of exchanging prisoners."

It was not necessary to haggle over the procedure; there were plenty of precedents for such trades. Sophie walked slowly toward Beria, leaving Eliot behind, while Brad, unable to control himself, practically scampered toward "Officer Kolchak" and safety. He didn't even bother thanking Sophie as they passed each other briefly. Never mind that she was apparently sacrificing herself for his sake.

Wanker, she thought.

Maintaining an icy cool bordering on hauteur, Sophie turned herself over Beria and his hulking accomplice. Carl quickly frisked her, shamelessly copping a feel in the process.

"Watch the hands," she objected. "This is a prisoner exchange, not a date."

"You must forgive Carl," Beria said. "Useful, yes, but a gentleman he is not."

"You'll have to let me know when one arrives," Sophie said archly.

"Now, now," Beria said, his thin smile fading. "You should know better than to insult your host. I might take it amiss."

Eliot took custody of Brad. "Is that all? We done here?"

"I'm afraid not."

He rapped his cane against the grave marker at his feet. Abruptly, the chapel doors slammed open and two more goons burst into the churchyard, brandishing guns. The men drew their weapons on Eliot and Brad. Carl came forward to search Eliot, and was surprised to find him unarmed.

"Hey, chief," Carl called out to Beria. "This dude's not carrying."

"Don't like guns," Eliot explained. "Don't need them."

Carl snickered. "Says the guy who just got caught with his pants down." He guarded Eliot while the other two men took charge of Brad and Sophie. "Too bad you left the red-head at home. I would've liked to get my hands on her."

"She'd kick your ass," Eliot said. "Again."

Meanwhile, Brad couldn't believe his bad luck as he got dragged back across the churchyard toward Beria.

"Oh God," he moaned. "I thought it was over . . ."

"What's this all about?" Eliot demanded. "You got what you wanted."

"Not entirely." Beria looked over his prisoners. "I'm afraid that you and Brad will be accompanying us as well."

"But why?" Sophie asked. "We had a deal."

"Don't be naive," he scolded her. "There are still too many loose ends and open questions to be dealt with before I can consider this matter concluded." He squinted at Sophie, examining her features. "I'm not even certain who you are yet, or where exactly the white knight fits into the picture." He peered at Eliot, who glared back murderously. "For all I know, you're actually Tarantula."

"Step a little closer," Eliot said, "and let's see how hard I bite."

"I think not." He leaned on his walking stick. "In any event, I have yet to enjoy *Assassins Remember* in its entirety, so I am not about to sacrifice any bargaining chips— or potential sources of information—until I have a clearer picture of what secrets may be hidden in these very troubling books and how exactly they came to be written." More ice crept into his eyes and voice. "You'll find that I have a very low tolerance for unanswered questions."

Now you're sounding like Nate, Sophie thought. *That can't be a good thing.*

"What do you want to know?" she said. "Just ask me."

"Oh, I will," he promised, "and at length. But now is not the time or the place for such an in-depth interview . . . or interrogation." He snapped his fingers at a guard, who paged their ride. Beria retrieved the briefcase from the bench. "Let us be on our way."

He took the lead as his men escorted the three hostages toward the Broadway exit. A hefty brute with a bad crew cut escorted Sophie, gripping her arm hard enough to leave bruises. Through the fog, she saw the murder limo pull up to the curb, waiting for them. A rear door slid open.

"Get going," Carl ordered. He prodded Eliot with the muzzle of his gun. "We haven't got all night."

Before they reached the gate, however, the quiet of the downtown streets was disturbed by a cacophony of unusual noises emanating from somewhere just beyond the cast-iron fence. Anguished moans and groans, along with animalistic grunts and growls, heralded the approach of dozens of shambling figures, who came lurching out of the mist from all directions, converging on the churchyard. They poured out of nearby doorways and subway entrances in a seemingly endless stream. All at once Broadway went from being deserted to overpopulated.

"Chief?" Carl glanced about apprehensively. He appeared understandably confused and maybe even a little spooked. "What's this?"

Beria scowled. "I don't know."

Emerging from the fog, the figures came into view. Brad gasped at their ghastly appearance. Pallid faces, gray as death, bore crazed, contorted expressions. Rotting flesh, sometimes hanging in ragged shreds, added to the horror. Feral yellow eyes, bulging from sunken sockets, contrasted with the blank white orbs of other pedestrians. Lurid red stains smeared gnashing teeth and gaping jaws. Bloody wounds and injuries made the newcomers look like refugees from a casualty ward—or maybe a morgue. Their ragged attire, which ranged from disintegrating tuxedos and bridal gowns to casual wear and sports uniforms, was splattered with grime and gore. A bloody hatchet was half buried in the skull of a shuffling cheerleader whose ashen face was twisted in a grotesque rictus. Loose entrails dangled from the slashed abdomen of a drooling construction worker; his cracked hard hat offered a glimpse of exposed pink brain. He gnawed on a severed arm.

"Holy crap!" Carl exclaimed. "What the hell is this?"

Nothing much, Sophie thought. *Just a zombie flash mob. Right on schedule.*

EARLIER:

"Why zombies?" Eliot asked.

Hardison looked up from his keyboard, where he was busy hyping the upcoming flash mob all over the Internet. He gave Eliot a look of sheer disbelief, amazed that the hitter even had to ask.

" 'Cause it's a graveyard, man. Besides, zombies make everything better."

Privately, Hardison was glad that he would be manning Lucille during the flash mob, instead of visiting the church-

yard himself. He didn't like cemeteries, probably because of that one time he was buried alive.

"Zombies, huh?" Eliot peered dubiously over Hardison's shoulder. "You really think anyone is going to show up for this shindig?"

Hardison grinned. "Trust me on this . . ."

The living dead, or reasonable facsimiles thereof, swarmed through the gates of the churchyard by the dozens. Some lurched awkwardly, as though beset by rigor mortis, their arms stretched stiffly before them like the Frankenstein monster. Blackened nails groped and pawed at the misty night air. Others loped like animals, or dashed to the front of the mob, squeezing their way past their fellow undead revenants. The zombies howled and moaned like souls in torment. Many carried severed heads, limbs, or random body parts.

"Running zombies," Hardison observed. *"That's just wrong, man."*

The zombie hordes kept on coming, blocking the way out of the churchyard. There seemed to be no end of them; within moments, the cemetery was packed with wannabe zombies. Eliot wondered just how far Hardison had spread word of this freaky graveyard get-together—and why so many presumably sane adults were taking part. Not that Eliot was complaining. He had to admit that a zombie invasion made a good distraction.

"Chief?" Carl turned to Beria for guidance, looking away from Eliot for just a moment. "What should we—"

That was all Eliot needed. He spun around and swept

Carl's gun arm to the side. Carl's hand smacked into a stone angel and the gun went flying into the fog and chaos. A blow to the chin sent Carl stumbling backward into a cluster of moaning zombies. "Hey, watch it, dude!" a walking corpse broke character to protest. "I know it's dark and all, but—"

Carl elbowed the zombie, then lumbered back toward Eliot. The hitter made a beckoning motion. He raised his fists.

"Ready for a rematch, big guy?"

"Brains, brains . . ."

Among the horde was a slender blond zombie in a blood-stained nurse's uniform. Cavernous black shadows were painted beneath Parker's eyes. Her greasy complexion was gray-going-on-green. The phony blood on her teeth left a funny taste in her mouth; she kept wanting to lick it off. Only her eyes were their usual shade of hazel. She had passed on the tinted red contact lenses Hardison had tried to press on her. The fog and the dark were tricky enough. She needed to see what she was doing.

"Brains . . ."

Unnoticed amid the other zombies, she shambled up to the nameless thug guarding Brad. Her stun gun slid from her sleeve into her grip. Electricity crackled, the zap drowned out by assorted growls and groans, and the thug hit the ground with a thud. She grabbed Brad by the wrist.

"Come on," she said, momentarily forgetting to drop her hoarse zombie voice. She cleared her throat. "It's time to go."

Utterly bewildered as he was, it took him a moment to recognize her as the agile thief who had broken into his mansion days ago. He blinked in surprise.

"Miss Lincoln?"

The thug guarding Sophie saw his cohort collapse. He hesitated, torn between helping Carl, hanging on to Sophie, and chasing after Brad. Judging from his baffled expression, he had never tried to abduct anyone during a zombie walk before.

"Hey!" he blurted. "What's going on—"

Sophie drove her heel into his instep, eliciting a yelp of pain. His grip loosened and she yanked her arm free.

"Clear!"

Parker jolted him with her Taser. He stiffened before falling over backward onto the ground, only inches away from the goon she had zapped a few moments ago. A carpet of fog obscured their unconscious bodies. She left them resting in peace.

Sophie scrambled away from her captor.

"Come on!" Parker called to her.

"I'm right behind you!" Sophie shouted back. "Just get Brad out of here."

Parker frowned. She didn't like leaving Sophie behind, but figured her friend could keep up. Saving Brad was their primary objective after all, although Parker wasn't entirely sure why. She assumed it had something to do with being the good guys.

"Brains . . ."

Parker dragged Brad through the cemetery, only to find the zombies getting in the way. Hardison had done too good a job promoting this flash mob. Between the fog and the headstones and the hordes of shambling undead, it was impossible to make a clean escape. There were too many zombies crammed into the cemetery already, with more flooding in every moment. Parker shuddered. The mob scene was claustrophobic in a way that, for her at least, air ducts and cramped crawl spaces never were.

"Get me out of here, please!" Brad sobbed. "This is too much!"

Parker had to agree. She glanced back over her shoulder, looking for Sophie, but could barely spot the other woman in the chaos. For a second, she thought she spied Sophie's dark brown hair, but then the milling zombies got between them, blocking the fleeing grifter from view. Sophie was swallowed up by the zombies, although not in the cannibalistic sense.

"Nate!" Parker reported over the comms. "I lost Sophie . . . I think."

"Stick to the plan," Nate advised. *"No matter what."*

Parker wasn't sure about that. Wasn't Sophie more important than Brad?

"But . . ."

"Keep moving, Parker."

"What are you waiting for?" Brad wailed. "I thought you were saving me!"

Parker briefly considered zapping him, but he was way too heavy to carry. *Too bad he's not skinnier,* she thought, *or a dwarf.*

Next time we should rescue a midget . . .

"Working on it," she muttered.

The crush of zombies had them hemmed in on all sides. A zombie nun, cradling a zombie baby doll, ambled into

Parker's path. Bloody saliva dripped grossly from the nun's lips. Cloudy white contact lenses covered her eyes. Groaning hoarsely, while wandering aimlessly through the headstones, she appeared to be in no hurry to get out of Parker's way.

"Excuse me," Parker said, for form's sake. "Excuse me."

The zombie ambulated slowly. She was clearly of the nonrunning variety.

"Excuse . . . oh, never mind."

The stun gun sparked. The nun dropped. Parker stepped over the fallen zombie, dragging Brad behind her. Wielding the Taser like a machete, she cleared a path through the crowd. Stunned bodies fell away to the left and right, all but unnoticed in the general commotion.

"Easy there, girl!" Hardison protested. *"Maybe a little less maximum overkill?"*

"You got a better idea?" she retorted. "Besides, they're just zombies."

She zapped her way toward the far gate.

"Brains!" she chanted. "Yummy brains!"

Eliot was grappling with Carl in the middle of the mob. He fumed in frustration; it was hard to have a decent fight with zombie wannabes crowding him on all sides, forcing him to fight in close quarters where the bodybuilder's size worked in his favor. Eliot was faster, but he had little room to maneuver. Tombstones and milling undead cramped his style.

"Damn it, Hardison," he griped. "There are too many zombies. You overdid it again!"

"Zombies are all about numbers," Hardison replied. *"You got to expect that, man."* He was watching the horrific spectacle via Eliot's button cam. *"Talk about a turnout, though. Not bad for a weeknight! Can I raise the dead or what?"*

"Let me get back to you on that," Eliot growled, "after I take care of this guy."

He chopped at Carl's thick neck with an edge-of-hand strike, but Carl parried the blow with his shoulder, grunting as he did so. He seized Eliot in a bear hug, trying to crush the breath from him. Thrashing and kicking, Eliot worked one arm free and jammed his palm under Carl's cinderblock jaw, driving his head backward until Carl was forced to loosen his grip. Eliot twisted loose and bought some breathing room with an elbow strike to Carl's wounded nose. Fresh blood gushed from the injured snoot, making Carl look like one of the gory zombies infesting the cemetery. The beefy enforcer howled in pain.

"Need a tissue?" Eliot taunted.

He moved in for the takedown, but before he could finish Carl off, a stray zombie ambled between them. A bloodshot rubber eye dangled from one socket. He had on a chef's hat and a bloody apron. He leered at Eliot, pleased to find a living victim among the undead. He licked his lips.

"Fresh meat!" he croaked. "I've got my eye on you!"

I don't have time for this, Eliot thought.

He decked the annoying zombie with one punch.

"Sorry, dude."

Stepping over the poleaxed zombie, Eliot looked for Carl. He spotted the injured thug rooting among the headstones for his lost gun. Shadows and fog made this a long shot, but not one Eliot was willing to risk. The last thing they needed was shots being fired in the middle of this mob.

He tackled Carl, knocking him over a solid stone sarcophagus. The thug tumbled over the tomb onto the frozen ground beyond. Eliot leaped onto the lid of the sarcophagus and used its height to kick Cark in the chest. The blond gorilla careened into a pack of college-age zombies who swore in a very human fashion.

"Not cool, douche bag!"

The fight finally caught the notice of the nearest zombies. Several panicked and tried to get away, impeded by the crowd, while a few others dove into the fracas. Somebody threw a punch at Carl, only to get a hammer fist to the face. Angry yells and curses joined the ravenous moans of the living dead. A brawl broke out in this corner of the churchyard, possibly for the first time in three hundred years. Grappling bodies bumped against trees and tombstones.

"Okay, this is getting seriously out of hand," Hardison admitted. *"Maybe you* can *have too many zombies."*

"You think?" Eliot said.

As if things weren't bad enough, a random zombie tripped on something among the headstones. He crouched and groped through the fog before he stood up with Carl's missing Glock in his mottled gray hand.

"Hey, look what I found!" he called out to his undead brethren. "Somebody lose a toy gun?"

Carl's eyes lit up. He bulldozed through the crowd toward the unsuspecting zombie with the weapon. Eliot headed the same way, hoping to get there first, but the curious zombie was already fumbling with his prize. Eliot hoped to God he knew what he was doing.

He didn't.

The Glock discharged into the air. The sharp report of the gunshot cut through the general clamor. The shooter dropped the gun like it was red-hot. Startled zombies froze in their tracks.

"Gun!" somebody shouted.

Panic broke out. The zombie herd turned into a stampede. Hordes of frightened zombies rushed for the exits, discarding their severed limbs and shambling gaits. Blood streaming from his nose, Carl called it quits as well. He disappeared into the spreading pandemonium.

"Damn it," Eliot said.

"Don't blame me," Hardison said. "I'm not the one who brought a damn gun to a zombie walk!"

Any hope Sophie had of catching up with Parker and Brad vanished when the gunshot threw the mob into a panic. Already separated from her teammates, she found herself caught up in a crush of frightened zombies, all rushing for the gates. She went with the flow, but it was hardly an orderly exodus. Unsure which way the danger was, members of the fear-stricken crowd shoved against each other in every direction, obstructing progress. Discarded rubber arms and legs and heads littered the ground. Granite headstones, sarcophagi, and monuments blocked the escape routes. A fight had broken out, adding to the confusion. "Watch out!" someone shrieked. "She's got a Taser!"

Parker, Sophie realized. *It has to be.*

Sophie searched the crowd, trying to locate her compatriots, but it was no use. Dim lighting, fog, and what seemed like hundreds of frightened people in zombie makeup made joining up with the others problematic in the extreme. It was like Frankfurt all over again, but darker and decomposing.

"Sophie?" Nate whispered electronically in her ear. *"We've lost you in the mob. Where are you?"*

"Stuck in an amateur remake of *Dawn of the Dead*," she said. "Trying to make my exit, preferably in one piece." Frantic zombies bumped and jostled her. A ghoulish mime, in a shredded black leotard, stepped on her foot. "Easier said than done, by the way."

"So I gather."

She struggled to get her bearings and determine the quickest route out of the churchyard, only to lock gazes with the last person she wanted to see right now.

Beria.

Their eyes met through the fog and confusion. His thin lips twisted in a snarl and he began shoving his way toward her. He lashed out with his cane, attempting (with mixed results) to drive the interfering zombies out of his way, while hanging on to the briefcase containing the book. Clearly, he had not given up on capturing Tarantula as well.

Lucky me, she thought. *I'm in demand.*

She spun around and pressed forward in the opposite direction. Unarmed and on her own, she wasn't eager to confront an irate assassin who was having a very bad night. Alas, she didn't have a cane or a Taser or an Eliot to help her get through the mob, which stubbornly refused to part before her. Glancing back, she saw Beria slowly gaining on her. Malevolence shone in his eyes. His urbane hauteur had given way to a genuinely angry expression. Evidently he didn't appreciate having his well-laid plans compromised by an unexpected influx of walking corpses.

To be fair, who did?

"Beria's after me," she reported, "and he doesn't look happy."

"Can you get away from him in the crowd?" Nate asked.

Sophie watched Beria get closer. "I don't know."

Yet more zombies were invading the churchyard, oblivious to the panic stampeding the early arrivals toward the gates. Possibly the stragglers thought the screams and shouting were all part of the show. In the dark, it was no doubt hard to distinguish genuine terror from Romero-inspired fun and games. Squeezing between the zombies, Sophie realized that her best option was to try to blend in with the mob.

"Time to switch roles."

Fortunately, quick changes were an essential part of her repertoire. She hastily mussed her hair, abandoning her stylish coif for a wilder, more unruly look more befitting a mindless zombie. She smeared lipstick over her face to create a bloodthirsty impression and applied powder to her hair to make it grayer and more corpselike. Despite the late-night chill, she ditched the trench coat, hoping that Beria wouldn't be looking for the practical gray top and slacks she was wearing underneath. Slumping her shoulders and twisting her face into a hideous grimace, she kept her head down as she joined the ranks of the walking dead. With any luck, Beria would see merely another make-believe zombie, not the glamorous and elusive Tarantula.

It was a good plan, and, she liked to think, an inspired bit of improvisation. It might even have worked if not for the fact that the foggy, murky, overcrowded cemetery was a veritable obstacle course. Stumbling in the dark, she tripped over a jutting grave marker and toppled forward onto the ground. A gasp escaped her lips and she barely threw out her hands in time to break her fall. Sprawled upon the cold, hard earth, she found herself in danger of being trampled by the undead masses. Pounding feet stomped over and around her. Still dazed by her tumble, she lunged to her feet, even as fleeing zombies smacked into her, threatening to knock her down again. Her clothes got roughed up, improving her zombie act, but it was a battle to stay upright.

"Sophie!"

A voice, calling out for her, caught her by surprise.

Who?

"Sophie! Over here!"

To her dismay, she saw Larry Meeker, her number one fan, jumping up and down by the gate. He waved his arms in the air, trying to get her attention. Concern for her safety was written all over his face.

Oh, no, she thought. *What's he doing here?*

In retrospect, it was obvious, of course. Clearly, her obsessive fan/stalker had been unable to resist trailing her to the "movie shoot," and was now intent on rescuing her from the stampede, although all he was really doing was blowing her cover.

So much for my attempt at camouflage . . .

"Hang on!" he shouted. "I'm coming for you!"

But his would-be heroics attracted Beria's attention as

well. Seizing the opportunity, the spymaster came up behind Larry. A six-inch blade slid from the tip of his cane, which he pressed against Larry's throat.

"Don't move," he advised.

Larry froze in terror. "Is . . . is this part of the movie?"

"Quiet." Beria called to Sophie. "A friend of yours, I take it?"

Not exactly, Sophie thought.

Keeping his blade at Larry's throat, Beria steered the hapless fan into the panicky throng pouring out through the gate. By now, police sirens and helicopters could be heard converging on the churchyard. Carl, having somehow gotten away from Eliot, rejoined his boss and began hurling zombies out of the kidnappers' way. Fresh cuts and bruises marred the thug's already vandalized features; Eliot had obviously done what he did best. Beria beckoned for Sophie to follow them—or else. His blade pricked Larry's neck for emphasis. A drop of real blood, as opposed to the stage variety, glistened upon the point of the blade.

Marvelous, Sophie thought. *We've just exchanged one hostage for another.*

Sighing, she joined the procession toward the exit, where the black limousine was still waiting at the curb. Carl shoved Larry into the back of the limo even as the fleeing mob disgorged Sophie onto the sidewalk outside the churchyard. She reluctantly climbed into the limo, wishing she had kept her trench coat at least. The night was getting colder by the moment.

"*Sophie, wait!*" Nate called. "*What's happening? What are you doing?*"

His obvious alarm warmed her heart.

"I'm sorry, Nate. I don't have any choice."

She couldn't let Larry get hurt.

He was her biggest fan after all.

"Damn it."

Eliot watched helplessly as the limo peeled away from the curb, beating the oncoming police cars and news copters by mere moments. Camera crews, arriving on the scene, hastily shot footage of the departing zombies, who were now making themselves scarce. Eliot guessed that the zombie flash mob would be all over the morning news.

As opposed to Sophie's abduction.

"They got her, Nate," he reported. "And that stalker dude, too."

He seethed at the way Larry Meeker had screwed up their plans, and put Sophie in jeopardy. *I should have decked him when I had the chance.*

"I was too far away," he explained. "I couldn't get to the limo in time."

"Understood," Nate said grimly. *"Head back to Lucille and we'll take it from there."*

Eliot didn't know whether to be impressed or appalled at the way Nate kept his cool, and never stopped planning, even when Sophie was in danger. The hitter wasn't sure he could stay so calm if, say, Denise had been carried off by a ruthless black-ops team. Sometimes it seemed like Nate had ice in his veins, to go with the high blood alcohol content.

"Roger that."

Not wanting to answer any awkward questions from the

police or reporters, Eliot cleared out of the churchyard, along with the horde of zombies dispersing back into the city streets and subways. Less conspicuous than the assorted blood-spattered ghouls, he managed to take his leave without incident. He wondered what the police would make of the two stunned goons Parker had left behind in the cemetery. He imagined the thugs would clam up and keep quiet until Beria pulled strings to get them released.

"Eliot!"

Parker caught up with him on the sidewalk, around the corner from the churchyard. Still done up as a zombie nurse, she was dragging Brad by the wrist. Gavin's worthless brother looked like he was in a state of shock. Eliot could hardly blame him, what with the kidnapping, death threats, double crosses, and zombies.

"Officer Kolchak!" Brad blurted. Shaking like a leaf, and paler than most of the zombies, he staggered toward Eliot. "Oh God, I can't take any more of this." Parker let go of his hand and he collapsed against a streetlamp, as though his legs were too rubbery to hold him up any longer. His face was slick with sweat despite the chill in the air. His bloodshot eyes darted from Eliot to Parker and back again as he visibly struggled to make sense of the night's bizarre twists and turns. "I don't get it. What are you two doing here, working together?"

"Denise sent us," Eliot said bluntly.

"Well, tell her she can have those damn books!" Brad blurted. "I don't want anything to do with any of this anymore! Let her deal with assassins and tarantulas and all that crap." He shoved off from the lamp pole and headed for the subway. "I'm through—for good!"

Eliot let him go. He figured Beria and Co. were long gone by now, and they already had what they wanted most: the sequel and Tarantula.

"So much for Brad," Nate said. *"I suppose that counts as a silver lining."*

"Yeah," Eliot said. "But what about Sophie?"

|||||| THIRTEEN ||||||

MANHATTAN

"I'm not certain how you managed that stunt with the zombies," Beria said, "but I'll give you points for imagination."

Sophie and Larry faced their abductors in the back of the limo, which raced away from the churchyard as fast as city speed limits would allow. The hostages shared one set of opposing seats, while Beria and Carl sat across from them. The gunman had replaced his firearm with a brand-new Glock. An open partition revealed a thirtyish Hispanic woman, with bobbed pink hair and multiple piercings, at the wheel. Seat belts and handcuffs ensured that Sophie and her fan stayed put. Their captors had not bothered to blindfold them or place hoods over their heads. Apparently, Beria didn't care if Sophie saw where she was going.

That did not bode well.

"I don't suppose you'd believe that all this was just a

stunning coincidence." Lipstick was still smeared like blood over Sophie's face. Her hair was a fright. "That the living dead just happened to choose tonight to go for a stroll?"

"Hardly." Beria's cool, condescending manner had returned now that things were going his way again. He no longer looked as coldly furious as he had been when pursuing Sophie through the flash mob. The blade of his sword cane had been retracted. He handed Sophie a handkerchief so she could wipe the garish makeup from her face. She dabbed at the lipstick.

"Please," Larry said, visibly distraught. He was even paler and twitchier than usual. "Somebody tell me what's happening." He gaped at Beria, who was obviously in charge. "What do you want with Ms. Devereaux?"

Sophie cringed. Larry had already said too much.

Beria arched an eyebrow. "Ms. Devereaux, is it?" He shifted his gaze from Larry to Sophie. "How interesting."

"Is this about that restraining order?" Larry asked. "Because that was totally a misunderstanding . . ."

"Just sit back, Larry," Sophie said, although the damage was probably done. She took his hand to comfort him. It was cold and clammy to the touch. "Let me handle this."

Larry nodded and shut up, at least for the moment.

"He has nothing to do with any of this," Sophie tried to explain to Beria. "That's the absolute truth. He's just a . . . ardent admirer . . . who was in the wrong place at the wrong time. He doesn't know a thing about Gavin or the books or your dubious past. He's completely innocent."

Aside from that business with the stalking, she thought.

"How unfortunate for him, then," Beria said, unmoved.

Larry gulped.

"Hey, chief," Carl interrupted. He held a bloody Kleenex over his nose. "What about Drake and McCullough?"

Sophie assumed these were the henchmen Parker had dropped with her stun gun. They had been left behind at Trinity.

"They know better than to say anything," Beria said, "even in the unlikely instance that they are picked up by the authorities." The spymaster appeared unconcerned about the missing men. He made Nate seem warm and fuzzy. "Chances are, the local constabulary will simply assume that our comrades got caught up in the commotion at the churchyard. At worst, they will be charged with trespassing and/or disturbing the peace."

Carl still looked worried. "Yeah, but—"

"I will handle matters if necessary," Beria said curtly, annoyed by Carl's persistence. "I have the connections to protect them. You know that. But at the moment I am more concerned with our new guests." He regarded the hostages warily. "Scan them."

Carl got the message. "Yes, sir."

Rummaging beneath his seat, Carl produced an electronic wand of the sort employed by airport security personnel. This wand proved to be somewhat more sophisticated, however; within moments, an electronic beep betrayed the presence of Sophie's hidden earbud.

"Ah," Beria said. "It appears we did not search you quite thoroughly enough before."

Bollocks, she thought. *I was afraid of this.*

"Fine." She cast a warning glance at Carl. "You can keep your grubby paws to yourself." Letting go of Larry's hand, she extracted the comm from her ear and handed it over to Beria. "There. Satisfied?"

"Tsk, tsk," he said. "Such subterfuge could be seen as a violation of our agreement."

You're one to talk. She shrugged. "You never said I couldn't accessorize."

"I suppose not," he conceded. "Still . . ."

He rolled down the window, letting in a gust of cold air, and tossed the bud out of the limo. Sophie imagined it being run over by the next passing vehicle. Hardison and the others were likely to get a burst of static in their ears.

I'm a one-woman show again, she realized. *At least for the time being.*

Carl scanned Larry next. No beeps resulted. "He's clean."

"I told you so," Sophie said.

"You'll forgive me if I doubt your word," Beria said. "My world is not a trusting one."

Larry couldn't keep quiet any longer. "This really isn't a movie, is it?"

"I'm afraid not," Sophie told him.

The limo headed southwest on Broadway, toward the Brooklyn–Battery Tunnel. The tunnel entrance swallowed the vehicle, which headed under the East River, leaving Manhattan behind. Carl peered out the back window.

"Nobody following us, chief."

"I would hope not," Beria said.

Carl confiscated Larry's wallet and handed it over to Beria for inspection. He then searched Larry's backpack. "Hey, chief, take a look at this."

He passed Larry's scrapbook to Beria, who switched on

an overhead light to examine it. Beria flipped through pages of photos and playbills documenting Sophie's on-again, off-again acting career. She found herself wishing that Larry had been a little less diligent in his devotion.

"'Sophie Devereaux,'" Beria read aloud. He lifted his eyes from the scrapbook to contemplate the woman sitting across from him. "An actress?"

"A great actress!" Larry insisted. "The best!"

"And yet I've never heard of you," Beria said.

No need to rub it in, she thought. "It's my cover story. One of many."

"So you say." He frowned, troubled by this latest revelation. "And yet I find myself with more complications . . . and questions."

"Take your time mulling them over," she stalled. "It's not as though I'm going anywhere . . . except our final destination, that is."

"Final?" Larry quailed at the word. "What exactly do you mean by that? Do you mean 'final' as in just the end of this trip, or . . ."

"Silence," Beria said. "I need to think."

He leafed through the scrapbook, a pensive expression on his face. Sophie was inclined not to disturb him. Although not part of the plan, Larry's scrapbook was proving useful in distracting Beria from the alleged sequel in the briefcase, and muddying the waters a bit. With luck, Beria was too busy trying to figure out where Sophie Devereaux came from, and how she fit into the picture, to take a closer look at *Assassins Remember.*

Good, Sophie thought. *We don't want him reading the whole book just yet.*

Traffic was light at this hour, so the limo made good time. Exiting the tunnel, they continued south along the expressway, hugging the western edge of Brooklyn. Before long, a metallic green exit sign pointed the way toward Coney Island. The limo took a left onto Shore Parkway.

Coney Island slumbered outside the van. The world-famous playground was only a shadow of its legendary glory, having been in a slow, steady decline for decades. The amusement area had shrunk to a few seedy blocks between Surf Avenue and the Boardwalk. The Cyclone roller coaster, having attained landmark status, had survived, but the towering Parachute Jump ride was now just a sky-high relic that had been out of commission for nearly half a century. The limo cruised down sleeping streets lined with shuttered flea markets, furniture stores, clam bars, and side-shows. Sophie caught an occasional glimpse of beach and ocean shore. Ugly high-rise apartment buildings loomed farther inland.

"Almost there," the driver announced. A Cuban accent betrayed her roots. She wore a chauffeur's livery, complete with cap. She seemed roughly the same age as Denise. A replacement or contemporary? Sophie thought she recognized her from *Assassins Never Forget.*

Right, Sophie thought. *"Marisol," the fiery Cuban refugee who was Yvette's colleague and rival.* Sophie had personally killed her off in the sequel.

"Thank you, Pilar," Beria said. "A smooth ride, as usual."

Unlike the one that ran down Gavin, Sophie thought. But, of course, Beria had been behind the wheel that time. Sophie wondered if "Pilar" had balked at doing the deed herself. Driving a getaway car was one thing; running down an innocent man was something else altogether.

I couldn't do it, Sophie thought. *Except to save someone I cared about.*

A bumpy side road brought them to the entrance of what appeared to be an abandoned amusement park. Not one of the famous ones from the turn of the previous century like Luna Park or Steeplechase; those had all been consumed by fires and financial reversals. This park appeared to be of more recent vintage, yet another failed attempt to recapture Coney's illustrious past. JOYLAND read the unlit neon sign above the front gate.

JunkLand was more like it.

A chain-link fence, topped with razor wire, surrounded a weed-infested ghost town composed of rotting booths, cracked concrete foundations, a few skeletal rides, and boarded-up games and concession stands. Graffiti defaced the weather-beaten structures. Broken glass, beer cans, and other refuse littered overgrown pedestrian pathways. Pools of stagnant water filled gaping potholes. A faded sign, posted at the front gate, announced the park's GRAND REOPENING IN 2007!

From the looks of things, that had been a tad optimistic.

Towering over the grounds was an old-fashioned wooden roller coaster at least eighty feet tall at its crest. Nature was in the process of reclaiming the dilapidated ride; brown vines and moss infested its undulating climbs and dips so that it resembled an ivy-covered trellis more than a thrill ride. Letters composed of busted neon lights spelled out the defunct coaster's name: LIGHTNING-BOLT.

Sophie thought it looked more like a firetrap.

The limo came to a halt outside the entrance. BEWARE OF DOGS! read another sign.

She hoped it was obsolete as well.

"End of the road," Pilar announced. She turned around in her seat and snapped photos of Sophie and Larry. "Say 'cheese!'"

The flash made Sophie's eyes water. She wondered why the driver had taken their pictures.

Nothing good, I'm sure.

Carl uncuffed Sophie and Larry from their seats before getting out of the limo to open the gate. He stood to one side as the vehicle drove a short ways into the park, passing a deserted ticket booth and heaps of frosty rubble. He yanked the side door open and ordered the hostages out. He waved his new gun.

"Hurry it up!"

Sophie helped Larry out of the limousine, instead of the other way around. They had barely set foot on the ground when a chorus of earsplitting barks and growls startled Sophie and caused Larry to jump in fright. A trio of vicious-looking Dobermans came dashing out of the ruins toward the new arrivals. Foam flew from their jaws. Sharp teeth gleamed in the night. Tapered ears stuck up like the horns. *Beware of Dogs,* Sophie remembered. She couldn't help visualizing those teeth tearing into her, but she stood her ground. Beria had not brought them all this way just to feed them to his pooches.

Presumably.

"Halt!" Carl barked at the guard dogs, who slowed to a stop. The ferocious barking quieted, although the Dobermans continued to eye Sophie and Larry warily, suspicious of the strangers. Carl smirked at Larry, enjoying the fan's obvious terror. He patted the lead Doberman on the head. "Good doggies."

"I'm more of a cat person myself," Sophie said.

"Not spiders?" Beria asked. He got out of the limo behind them. "I would have expected you to keep a pet tarantula . . . or perhaps not."

Was he implying that she wasn't really who she was claiming to be? Sophie chose to keep him guessing. "I'm seldom that obvious."

"You might reconsider your strategy," he said. "The time for evasion is rapidly coming to a close."

Leaving the limo behind, the party advanced toward the decrepit coaster. Carl and Pilar flanked the hostages while Beria, as ever, led the way. As they drew nearer to the coaster, more evidence of its obsolescence presented itself. Weeds sprouted through the lower tracks, while the motor and lift chain had practically rusted away. Birds and bees nested in the upper trusses. Derelict coaster cars were parked in the thick brown grass around the base of the tracks, their once-brilliant paint jobs scratched and faded. Horsehair sprouted from ripped leather seats. Despite her dire situation, Sophie couldn't help being struck by the decaying ruins. There was a certain melancholy beauty to the setting, as time slowly ate away at the bygone pleasures of summers past. If you listened closely, you could almost hear the ghostly screams and laughter of the coaster's long-departed joyriders.

Or maybe that was just the wind from the shore.

"Move it," Carl grunted, killing the mood. "We haven't got all night."

Larry gazed up at the creeper-covered coaster. He turned slightly green as well. "I'm not really into roller coasters. They make me nauseous."

"I wouldn't worry about that," Sophie said. The coaster had obviously been out of operation for years, maybe even decades. "I doubt we'll be taking a ride."

"Step lively," Beria said. "My home away from home is just ahead."

To Sophie's surprise, there was a house built under the far end of the coaster, nestled within the looming steel supports. Dingy white paint, mottled with greenish mold, peeled off the two-story building's timber walls. A rusty tin roof was impaled by one of the coaster's steel support beams. Clotted gutters dangled precariously from the eaves. A brick chimney was badly in need of repointing; it looked like it was on the verge of caving in on itself. The windows were boarded up with two-by-fours or else painted black. The weeds around the building were knee-high and growing out of control. At first glance, the house appeared to be just as forlorn and neglected as the coaster above it. Any casual observer would assume it hadn't been inhabited in years.

A closer inspection, however, offered hints that the house was not quite as vacant as it appeared. Sophie spotted security cameras discreetly mounted to the coaster's trusses and support beams, keeping the grounds under watch. A satellite dish, in excellent condition, connected the house to the wider world beyond. Rather than hanging on its hinges, the front door of the house appeared both solid and secure. A wasp's nest above the doorway, no doubt intended to discourage unwanted visitors, looked to be a well-crafted fake.

This is no squatter's dump, she deduced. *This is a going concern.*

An overgrown pedestrian pathway led to the front door. Carl undid the locks and hustled them toward the door. Larry balked at entering the crumbling house, but Sophie gave his hand an encouraging squeeze.

"It will be all right," she whispered. "Just let me do the talking."

Larry nodded and stepped inside. "No autograph is worth this," he murmured unhappily.

Sophie felt mildly betrayed.

Carl switched on the lights as they entered. In contrast to the house's ramshackle exterior, the interior had been fully restored and brought fully into the twenty-first century. The living room had been converted into a working command center, not unlike the one back at Nate's apartment. A state-of-the-art computer station was set up in a corner. Flat-screen monitors occupied one wall. Open doorways offered glimpses of a kitchen, bathroom, and living quarters. A stairway climbed to the second floor. A cherry-red coaster car, in much better condition than the derelict ones outdoors, had been transformed into a padded sofa. Logs were piled in a fireplace. A Persian carpet was spread upon the floor. Old carnival posters, mounted on the walls, paid tribute to the house's Coney Island roots. Sophie suspected that Hardison would feel quite at home.

"Love what you've done with the place," she said. "Most safe houses are so lacking in character."

Beria took off his coat and hat. The room was comfortably heated, compared to the cold night air outside. He wore a gray bespoke suit. He deposited the briefcase on top of an antique mahogany desk.

"This house has quite the colorful history," he informed her. "Built over a century ago, it has served, at various points, as a hotel, a brothel, a speakeasy, and even a private residence for the ride manager and his family. The coaster itself was built over the hotel back in the Roaring Twenties. I've read that the coaster cars racing overhead sounded like thunder to the residents of the house. But, of course, that was long before my associates and I took possession of the property. The coaster closed some thirty years ago and, as you saw, has since fallen into a state of disrepair."

"And now the house makes a nicely private, secure location for certain clandestine operations?" Sophie supplied.

"Precisely," Beria said. "I would offer you a tour, but we still have business to conduct." He nodded at Carl and gestured dismissively at Larry. "Secure our other guest. I wish to speak to Ms. Devereaux first." He chuckled wryly. "Or would you prefer I call you Tarantula?"

"Sophie will do," she said. "Since the object is to get to know each other."

"Indeed."

One of the coaster's vertical supports actually pierced the ceiling, rising up like a solid steel pillar from the center of the room. Carl handcuffed Larry to the beam so that the unlucky stalker was left standing on his feet. He didn't look particularly comfortable.

Sophie fared somewhat better. Pilar pulled out a stool for her to sit on while Beria sat down behind the desk. He opened the briefcase and took out both the electronic tablet and the bound manuscript, which he placed next to Larry's scrapbook. Pilar shed a few layers before seating herself at the computer station. Carl sought out a first-aid kit and began tending to his Eliot-inflicted injuries. He winced as he applied antiseptic to his cuts and scratches.

"Finally," Beria said to Sophie, "I can give you my full attention." He settled in for the interrogation. "Let me get straight to the point. Who are you, truly?"

She indicated the scrapbook. "You have my entire career in front of you, such as it is."

"Your obscure acting credits do not interest me." He poured himself a drink from a bottle of scotch on his desk. Yet another trait he shared with Nate. "Is Sophie Devereaux your real name?"

"No," she confessed. *When in doubt, tell a truth.*

"Very good," Beria said. "Now we are making progress. And what exactly is your real name?"

Sophie had no intention of answering this question. That particular bit of biography was something she shared only with her closest friends and lovers. She had even kept it from Nate for years.

"You really expect me to cough that up right away?" She looked pointedly at the bottle of whiskey. "At least fix me a drink first. All that running around in the cemetery has left me positively parched."

Beria's face hardened. He did not oblige her.

"Do not think that you can charm or distract me with your witty repartee. Such banter was amusing up to a point, but that time has passed. You are not performing before a besotted audience now. I expect answers, not evasions, and I am losing patience with your theatrics."

The story of my life, she thought. *Just ask the critics.*

"And here we were having such a good time," she quipped.

"Speak for yourself." He toyed ominously with a stainless-steel letter opener, letting its sharpened edge catch the glare from the fluorescent lights overhead. He scrutinized her features once more, perhaps looking for the telltale signs of plastic surgery. "Does the name Vicki Rhodes mean anything to you?"

Keep stalling, Sophie thought. "Should it?"

"Vicki Rhodes is a woman who is supposed to be dead, but would have known of the events alluded to in the first book. You do not resemble her, but you *are* the right age and gender . . ."

"Nice of you to notice," Sophie said. "If you don't mind, I'm going to choose to take that as a compliment . . ."

Beria contemplated the letter opener, holding it like a scalpel. "How long have you had that lovely face? I wonder."

"I may have had a little work done," she lied, stringing him along. "But what actress hasn't? It can be such a sexist industry sometimes . . ."

"But how does an actress, of no particular distinction, come to know about certain matters?" He flipped idly through Larry's scrapbook. "I cannot help wondering if I am attending your latest performance—in which you are simply playing the role of Tarantula."

Right on the money, Sophie thought. Beria was no dummy. He was zeroing in on the truth, which she had to steer him away from. "I told you before. The acting gigs are just a cover. The footloose, nomadic life of an actress is ideal for espionage. It allows me to travel, get invited to the right parties, mingle with smitten admirers." She smiled slyly. "Don't forget. Mata Hari started out in showbiz . . ."

"And wound up before a firing squad," Beria reminded her.

A few feet away, Carl made a point of working the slide on his Glock. Larry whimpered.

"Well, her exit left something to be desired," Sophie said. "I'll give you that. But my point stands. Acting and espionage often go hand in hand."

"Perhaps," Beria said. "But the thing is, I don't recall ever employing an actress—and your credits, as listed here, do not match up with various past operations. The chronology doesn't track."

Sophie was starting to wish that Larry had left that bloody scrapbook at home, or chosen to stalk another actress altogether. Maybe Lindsay Lohan?

"Or perhaps"—she vamped—"your secret operations weren't as secure as you thought. People talk, rumors and gossip get around, loose lips spill things that maybe they shouldn't have. As Tarantula, I heard all sorts of interesting shoptalk, some of which may have made it into Gavin's books."

Was he buying this? Sophie watched Beria closely, trying to read him.

"My people do not talk," he insisted, "and live."

"Are you sure about that?" She gestured at the manuscript before him. "Then why are we here?"

"That is what I mean to find out, one way or another." He turned toward his distaff accomplice at the computer station. "Pilar, what progress have you made verifying our guest's story?"

"Facial recognition is running now," she reported, "cross-referenced against the alias 'Sophie Devereaux.'"

The woman looked away from her monitor, where a snap-shot of Sophie was being compared to a rapid-fire stream of flickering close-ups. Female faces, young and old, flashed by faster than human eyes could process. "In a pinch, we can run her fingerprints and DNA, too."

"Maybe later," Beria said.

Sophie understood now why Pilar had taken her picture. She watched anxiously as the computer worked its magic. Sophie had often seen Hardison employ the same tactics to identify unknown parties, including Beria himself; she didn't like being on the receiving end. Hardison had done an expert job of scrubbing their pasts, so her criminal record wasn't likely to show up in any of the usual databases, but Beria had high-powered connections to the intelligence community. Who knew what resources he had access to? It wasn't all that long ago that the Leverage crew had landed on the CIA's radar, after that business with the illegal experiments on homeless veterans . . .

Sophie tried to conceal her apprehension as she perched uncomfortably upon the stool. Beria let her sweat, choosing to delve into *Assassins Remember* while they waited for the computer to yield the answers he wanted. Putting Larry's scrapbook aside, he picked up the bound manuscript.

"The dead-tree version?" Pilar mocked him. "Really?"

Shades of Hardison, Sophie thought. In her experience, ebook enthusiasts could be a bit evangelical at times, like they couldn't wait for the rest of the world to get with the program. Pilar struck her as an early adopter.

Beria plucked a fountain pen from his vest pocket. "I prefer taking notes on paper," he explained.

"Dinosaur," Pilar said, shaking her head. An electronic chirp interrupted their debate. "Hang on, we have a winner!"

"Put it on the screen," Beria said.

Oh hell, Sophie thought as her face and file took over the video wall. The dossier was distressingly complete, listing a large variety of her aliases as well as her recent involvement with Leverage Consulting & Associates. Sophie felt uncomfortably exposed. She had often imagined her face on the big screen, but this wasn't exactly what she'd had in mind. At least her real name was still listed as "Unknown," she noted. *That's something, I suppose.*

Beria scanned the data on the screens. "Actress, con woman, occasional thief. Known associates include . . ." He followed a link to a photo of Eliot. The hitter glowered at the camera. "Eliot Spencer, ex–Special Forces, mercenary, and retrieval specialist. Formerly employed by the likes of Damien Moreau?" The latter was a ruthless crime financier whom Eliot had long regretted working for; the Leverage crew had put finally put Moreau behind bars a few years back. It was not surprising that Beria recognized his name. "Curiouser and curiouser."

Files on Nate, Hardison, Parker, and even Tara Cole flashed across the monitors. Beria took it all in.

"You keep fascinating company, I must say," he said eventually. "And judging from the most recent reports, you and your friends have acquired a definite reputation for inserting yourselves into matters that do not concern you."

Sophie did not deny it. "We like to think we make a difference."

"But as a grifter and occasional Robin Hood," he observed. "Not an assassin or black-ops veteran."

"A girl can't change careers?"

"Your career, according to this, is pretending to be what you're not." Beria seemed to have made up his mind. "Such as Tarantula?"

"You can't be sure of that," she said, making a last-ditch attempt to salvage her cover. "All that 'Robin Hood' business with my new crew? Simply my own way of atoning for my guilty past, just like in the books."

"A valiant effort to maintain your role," he said, "but you are wasting your breath. I am sure enough." He put down the letter opener. "You are *not* Tarantula, but I suspect you know who is. And you are going to tell me that . . . without further delay."

I don't think so, Sophie thought. She wasn't about to rat out Denise. "What if I have no idea? What if my crew and I were simply trying to con Brad Lee out of the rights to the sequel?"

"Then 'Larry' here has a very short life expectancy."

"Hey . . . what?" Larry didn't miss the not-so-veiled threat. He rattled his cuffs, tugging uselessly on his restraints. "Why me? What have I got to do with this?"

"It's very simple," Beria said to Sophie. "If you don't tell me who Tarantula is, in the next few minutes, Carl is going to shoot your friend Larry in the head."

"What?" Larry yelped. "You can't."

Carl pressed the business end of the Glock against Larry's temple. He didn't look like he was bluffing.

"No more games," Beria said. "No more acting. You remember what happened to Gavin. Tell me the name now . . . or Larry will be just as dead."

"Sophie!" Larry entreated her desperately. His Adam's apple bobbed up and down. "Please! You can't let them do this!"

No, she realized. *I can't.*

"All right. Let's put all our cards on the table." She hopped off the stool, seizing the spotlight. "You want to know who the real traitor is? Read Chapter Thirteen of the new book. It's all there." She made eye contact with both Carl and Pilar. "In fact, you should *all* read it . . . if you want to find out what kind of man you're really working for. And just how far you can trust him."

"Chief?" Carl asked. "What's she talking about?"

"Anton?" Pilar said.

Beria scowled at Sophie. "I'm not sure what sort of game you're trying to play here . . ."

"No games," Sophie said. "Just the truth, at last." She nodded at the manuscript and tablet on the desk. "Chapter Thirteen. It's a must-read. Trust me."

Beria snatched up the bound manuscript and leafed hastily through its pages, searching for Chapter Thirteen. Pilar darted across the room to reach for the tablet containing the electronic version. Beria grabbed her wrist.

"What's the matter, Anton?" Sophie asked. "Don't you want her to read it? Afraid of what she might learn?"

His eyes shot poisoned daggers at her. He let go of Pilar's wrist. "This is a trick," he growled. "Don't forget that."

Pilar claimed the tablet and returned to her computer nook. Carl craned his head, trying to see what was on the screen. His gun remained pressed against Larry's skull. "What's it say?"

"Give me a minute! I'm reading!"

Anton raced through the pages of the manuscript, trying to stay ahead of his accomplices. His face darkened.

"What the devil? This never happened!"

Clearly, he had reached the part where "Darius Anton," a cagey, manipulative spymaster who bore a not entirely coincidental resemblance to Beria himself, had betrayed Yvette and her handler. Seems that Anton had been playing both sides for years, providing terrorist groups with arms, tactics, and the occasional tip-off. Yvette had grown suspicious of his double-dealing, so Anton had been forced to eliminate both her and her handler, "David Honda." He had personally killed Honda, framing Yvette, then arranged for Yvette to perish in a fiery plane crash. But she survived to tell the tale . . .

Nate had personally plotted Chapter Thirteen himself, although Sophie liked to think that she had polished the dialogue and character motivations somewhat. She braced herself for the fireworks.

Over by her computer, Pilar gasped aloud. She stared in shock at Beria.

"Anton? Is this true?"

"What?" Carl asked, still in the dark. "What does it say?"

"Lies!" Beria slammed the manuscript down onto the desk. "This is a total fabrication—and a blatant attempt at slander!"

"Is it?" Sophie didn't back down. "You know what they say. The truth is stranger than fiction . . . and often more incriminating."

Carl swung his gun away from Larry. He waved it angrily. "Somebody tell me what's in the friggin' book!"

Sophie was happy to oblige. "The CliffsNotes version? Your boss is a double-dealing turncoat with plenty to hide and no loyalty to anyone but himself. But, of course, you knew that already. Just ask Drake and McCullough. Beria wasn't too concerned about leaving them behind, was he?"

"I don't know . . ." Carl's brow furrowed.

"This is ridiculous!" Beria said. "Don't you see what she's trying to do here? This is obviously a setup."

"Really?" Sophie scoffed. "Then why did you return from the dead to deal with Gavin's books, even going so far as to see to Gavin's murder personally? Why go to such lengths to find out what was in the sequel? Unless you were afraid of the ugly truths contained in these so-called novels." She segued smoothly from prisoner to prosecutor, putting Beria on the hot seat. "You weren't worried about Gavin—or Tarantula—shining a bright light on the dirty little world of black ops. You were scared that your current associates would find out that you had betrayed and murdered your own people because they had figured out what kind of man you truly were."

"Nonsense," he insisted. "This is a transparent ruse."

"But you were never supposed to get your hands on the sequel in the first place," Sophie pointed out. "You wouldn't even be reading it right now if you hadn't kidnapped Brad and held him for ransom. What are you suggesting, that Gavin—whom you killed—wrote an entirely new book in the last forty-eight hours?"

"That does seem like a bit of a stretch, chief," Carl said.

"How did she know we were going to force her to give us the book?"

"I couldn't, and neither could Denise. We could only give you the book Gavin had already written, complete with the truth about Beria." She turned toward Carl and Pilar. "Of course, now he's going to have to dispose of you two at some point. Sorry about that."

Carl swung his gun toward Beria. "Is this true, chief? There anything to this?"

Pilar stared at Beria. "You killed Okata?"

"Don't be absurd!" Beria snapped. "Carl, Pilar, don't tell me you're falling for this libelous tripe. Just look at her record again. Who are you going to believe, me or a career con artist who lies as easily as she breathes?"

No need to get nasty about this, Sophie thought. "As opposed to a spymaster who sells out his own people?"

"*¡Carajo!*" Pilar exclaimed, continuing to scroll through *Assassins Remember.* "It says here that Anton—I mean, 'Anton'—sold out an operative who had infiltrated al-Qaeda. And ratted on his own agents in exchange for immunity from prosecution."

"Oh, right. I forgot about that part." Sophie gave Beria a withering look. "For shame."

"You duplicitous bitch!" Beria snarled. His elegant diction and manners evaporated once more, exposing the murderous fury Sophie had glimpsed in the cemetery. "I should have cut out your tongue back in that wretched graveyard!"

"Before I could spill the beans about your treachery?" she challenged him, playing to her audience, which now consisted of Carl and Pilar. "See! He wants to silence me now, just like he did with Gavin!"

"Who is Gavin?" Larry asked frantically. "I don't understand what's happening! Are you still going to shoot me?"

Shut up, Larry, Sophie thought. *You're not helping.*

"Don't listen to her!" Beria ordered. He lunged across the room and snatched the tablet from Pilar's grip. "And stop reading that garbage!"

Sophie smirked. Beria was playing right into her hands.

"You can't stop the truth from coming out, Beria. No matter how many of us you kill . . ."

"Everybody freeze!" Carl shouted. "I'm not going to—"

Frenzied barking, coming from outside, cut off whatever he was about to say. All eyes turned toward the blackened windows, which offered no glimpse of what had upset the Dobermans.

"The dogs!" Carl said, stating the obvious. "Something's got them riled up!"

The Dobermans raised a racket, then abruptly fell silent.

"What the—" Carl glanced about in confusion. He even looked sincerely worried about the suddenly incommunicado canines. "What happened to them?"

Beria had other priorities. "Pilar!" he ordered. "Check the cameras!"

"Like I couldn't figure that out on my own." She worked her keyboard, momentarily putting aside her doubts about Beria, although she sounded more than a little on edge. Multiple windows opened up on her monitor, which just as quickly went black. "No!" she exclaimed. "No, no, no . . ."

"What is it?" Beria demanded. "What's wrong?"

The video wall dissolved into a cascade of visual static.

Pilar stabbed at her keyboard, but to no avail. Her windows to the world had closed. The cameras on the coaster had gone blind—or perhaps been appropriated by another user.

"We've been hacked," she said, "by a wizard." She struggled to reboot the cameras. "Whoever this is, they're good."

Explosions went off outside, the blinding flashes visible even through the painted windows. Deafening blasts shook the house. Gunshots were fired in the air. Choppers could be heard approaching from above. The noises seemed to be coming from all sides. Carl spun in circles, not sure where to point his gun.

"Chief?"

Pilar stared up at the ceiling, hearing the choppers draw nearer. She had to shout to be heard about the tumult. "*¡Mierda!* It's a full-fledged assault!"

It certainly sounds like it, Sophie thought.

"What's happening?" Larry looked like he wasn't sure if he should be relieved or terrified, and was somehow managing generous portions of both. "Are we being rescued?"

A loudspeaker boomed overhead:

"Attention! We have you surrounded. Throw down your weapons and surrender, or face severe consequences!"

Sophie suppressed a smile. She recognized the voice, despite an affected southern twang, which, frankly, was a little over-the-top.

"Oh, thank God!" Larry exclaimed. He shouted up at the ceiling. "Help us, please! They have Sophie Devereaux! She's in danger!"

"Shut your trap!" Carl stepped back and opened fire at the ceiling, as though trying to bring down the copters single-handedly. The sharp report of the Glock added to the din. Sophie covered her ears as Carl emptied his gun, then paused to reload. "I don't get it! How did they find us?"

Pilar had her own questions. "Who is it? FBI? Homeland Security? Seal Team Six?" She wheeled about, turning on Beria. "What happened to your vaunted connections? I thought we were protected, unless . . ." A sudden suspicion dawned behind her eyes. "Did you arrange this? Are you throwing us under the bus?"

"Sounds like him," Sophie said. "Bastard."

"Are you insane?" Beria's thin face was livid. An angry vein pulsed at his temple. "You think I had something to do with this?"

"If the shoe fits . . ." Sophie said airily. She calmly inspected her nails. "Remember Chapter Thirteen?"

Concussions rattled the tin roof one story up. A bomb tumbled down the ceiling into the fireplace, exploding as it struck the hearth. Clouds of thick white smoke spewed from the bomb, filling up the command center. The billowing fumes had a distinctly chemical odor. Sophie placed a hand over her mouth and nose. It helped a little.

"Oh God," Larry moaned. "I think I'm going to throw up . . ."

Lovely, Sophie thought. *I really do have the best fans.*

By now, the oppressive *whump-whump-whump* of the choppers was threatening to drown out everything else. It sounded like an entire fleet of helicopters was circling above. All that was missing was "The Ride of the Valkyries."

The loudspeaker's stentorian tones descended from the heavens:

"Attention, all suspects! Repeat: Attention, all suspects!

Exit the building with your hands up! This is your final warning!"

"Er, maybe you ought to listen to him," Larry said. "Just a suggestion."

Carl ignored him. "That's it! I'm getting out of here." He yanked the carpet up to reveal a trapdoor built into the floor. He tugged it open, exposing the mouth of an escape tunnel. The spies had obviously planned ahead. "Let's go!"

Beria glared at Sophie. "Not without her. She has much to answer for."

"Forget it," Carl said, more interested in his own survival. "You're not calling the shots anymore, not until we figure things out!"

"Oh, for God's sake!" Beria looked like he wanted to throttle the other man. "Don't you realize she's responsible for all of this? I don't know how, but she brought this all down on our heads!"

"Moi?" Sophie said. "But I thought I was just an actress, 'of no particular distinction.' How could I manage all this—unless, perhaps, I'm really Tarantula?"

"Why, you lying witch!"

Beria lunged at her, murder in his eyes.

"Time's up!" the loudspeaker boomed.

A shot rang out, shattering the blackened window behind her. Sophie stiffened in shock, then staggered forward, clutching her back. Her eyes were wide with horror. A trickle of blood escaped her lips. She groped for the light.

"The rest is silence," she whispered, before toppling over into the converted red coaster car. The dense smoke shrouded her still and silent form.

"Dear Lord, no!" Larry stared aghast at his martyred idol, concern for his own safety shredded by the sheer enormity of the tragedy. He yanked on his cuffs, trying to get to Beria. Righteous fury shone behind his glasses. Spittle sprayed from his lips. "You got her killed, you fiend! Sophie Devereaux is dead!"

He collapsed into sobs, sagging against the steel pillar.

"Good riddance," Beria said. "I hope."

Keeping his head down, in case another shot came through the window, he moved to check on Sophie's body.

"Leave her!" Carl said, blocking him. "We don't have time for this."

Another smoke bomb fell down the chimney. It was getting hard to breathe, let alone see. The choppers sounded like they were descending.

"Perhaps you're right." Beria turned away from Sophie's supine form, choosing the better part of valor. He reached for his sword cane.

"I don't think so." Pilar beat him to the cane. She had wrapped a scarf around the bottom half of her face, so that she looked like a Wild West train robber, albeit one with a pierced eyebrow and bubble-gum-pink hair. "I believe I'll be handling this for the time being."

She prodded Beria toward the tunnel entrance. "You go first. No way am I turning my back on you." She shook her head. "I still can't believe you killed Okata."

"But . . . I didn't . . ."

"Step on it!" she hissed. "We'll deal with you later!"

This time Beria went first, under duress. He disappeared into the tunnel, followed closely by his onetime accomplices, who were possibly rethinking their loyalties.

Only Larry was left standing in the smoke-filled house. Outside, bangs and flashes made it sound like the Fourth of July. The whumping of the helicopters competed with his heaving sobs. The grief-stricken fan gazed forlornly at the body lying motionlessly in the coaster car. Tears of sorrow streamed down his face.

"I'll never forget you, Sophie Devereaux. You were taken from us far too soon. But your talent will live forever, like a star in the celestial firmament . . ."

"You really think so?" she said, sitting up in the car. "That's so sweet."

This was hardly the first time she had heard herself eulogized, but she never got tired of it. It was possibly the best part of being killed.

That and getting to perform a nice, juicy death scene.

"Aaagh!" Larry let out a strangled cry. His jaw dropped. All the blood drained from his face. "You . . . you . . ."

He fainted dead away. He went limp against the pillar, held up by his restraints.

Sophie sighed.

"Not exactly a standing ovation," she murmured, "but close enough."

She stood up and looked around. Beria and his disenchanted colleagues appeared to be long gone. She doubted they would be coming back.

She closed and locked the trapdoor anyway.

FOURTEEN

BROOKLYN

"Smoke and mirrors," Nate said. "That's all it was."

The crew, plus Larry and Denise, was crowded into the back of Lucille, which was speeding away from the decaying amusement park. Police cars and fire engines blared past them on their way to investigate the pyrotechnics at JoyLand. Parker drove the van while Hardison monitored the police and emergency radio bands. Nate was relieved to hear that nobody had reported a suspicious van before or after all the fireworks. It looked as though they had made a clean escape.

"But it all seemed so real," Larry said. A blanket was draped over his skinny shoulders. His hands trembled as he took some restorative sips from a flask, which Nate just happened to have on him. Smelling salts had been required to rouse Larry after Sophie's miraculous resurrection. His precious scrapbook rested on a counter nearby; Sophie had taken care to rescue it from captivity as well. "It sounded like we were under attack by a small army."

Nate grinned. "That was the idea."

EARLIER:

"Three dogs. Two guns," Eliot said. "How you want to divvy this up?"

He and Denise were lying side by side atop Lucille, belly down and equipped with matching tranquilizer rifles and night-vision sights. They took aim at the fenced-in amusement park before them. JoyLand appeared to be completely deserted, but they knew better.

Denise grinned at him. Black camouflage grease blended her face into the night. A dark wool cap, similar to Eliot's, hid her henna-colored hair. She was decked out in matte-black commando gear that fit her to a tee. The innocuous author and temp had taken a backseat tonight, letting an old friend out of the closet. Tarantula had returned for one last mission.

"Race you to the third shot," she said.

"You're on."

He thumped on the roof of the van to get Hardison's attention. The hacker was ensconced within Lucille as usual.

"Hey," Hardison protested via the comms. "Don't you go beating on my girl."

"I thought I was your girl," Parker piped up. "Or pretzel."

"Pretzel?" Denise gave Eliot a quizzical look.

"*Don't ask.*" He thumped the van again. "*Damn it, Hardison. Fire it up.*"

"*I hear you,*" *Hardison said.* "Just respect the van. That's all I'm saying."

"*Hardison!*"

Lucille's high beams switched on, targeting the park beyond the fence. The glare of the beams illuminated the ominous sign affixed to the fence.

BEWARE OF DOGS!

Sure enough, a trio of snarling Dobermans came racing toward the fence, enraged by the intrusive beams and Lucille's infuriating proximity to their territory. The team had taken a head count of the watchdogs earlier, after Hardison had hacked into the park's security cameras. Now the animals were barking up a storm, jumping up onto their hind legs against the fence. Froth flew from their snapping jaws.

"I've got the left," *Eliot said, bracing the stock of the rifle against his shoulder as he peered through the sight. The dog's eyes glowed demonically in the green phosphor view of the night-vision scope. Hardison had insisted on stocking Lucille with tranq darts after his run-in with some aggressive watchdogs in a police impound yard one time. Not a bad precaution, Eliot had to admit. You never knew when an unfriendly canine might object to a little friendly trespassing.*

And then, there was that time with the panther . . .

Eliot got the left-hand dog in his sights. He didn't like guns, but he knew how to use them. His finger tightened on the trigger and a burst of compressed gas shot a tranq dart at his target. The dart struck the frenzied Doberman in the neck. It yelped once before crumpling to the ground. The steady rise and fall of its chest confirmed that the dog was only knocked out. That was how Eliot liked it; he had enough blood on his hands.

Denise's gun went off beside him.

The blowback from his first shot loaded the next round. He swung his rifle to the right, hoping to sight the last dog before Denise did, but he'd underestimated her speed and accuracy. The other two Dobermans were already down for the count, snoozing along with the one he had sent to slumberland. All three dogs were now out of commission.

"Whoa," he said, impressed. He turned to look at Denise. "Damn, you're good."

"Don't mess with Tarantula," she said with a rueful smile. Her long hair was tucked under the cap, exposing the cobweb tattooed at the nape of her neck. "I was good at my job, back in the day. Too good."

"That's almost over," he promised her. He laid a gentle hand on her neck, hiding the tattoo. The chilly night had cooled her smooth skin, raising goose bumps. He started to thump the roof again, then decided to go easy on Hardison for once. They were depending on him now. "Hardison, you knock out the cameras yet?"

"They're blind as Matt Murdock," *the hacker replied,* "minus the radioactive radar sense."

Eliot took that as a yes.

"Parker?" Nate chimed in over the comms. "You good to go?"

"Go?" she echoed. "I'm already gone."

The first explosions went off.

Whoo-hoo! *Parker thought.* Now we're talking!

She ran along the top of the roller coaster, gleefully hurling miniature flash-bang grenades all around the house below. The rickety wooden tracks had seen better days, but that only made this nocturnal workout more exhilarating. A wolfish grin spread across her face. After being cooped up in the hotel suite for what felt like forever, slaving away on some boring book, this was just what she needed.

Too bad the coaster was only *eighty feet tall.*

Granted, the chain-link fence around the park had been something of a letdown. Just razor wire? Really? Getting over the barrier had been a breeze; she hadn't even snagged her working clothes and pack on the barbs. Beria was obviously a cheapskate where security was concerned.

What? *she thought.* He couldn't spring for lasers?

She scampered across the rotting tracks and trusses as fearlessly as if she was jogging along a well-paved path. A generous supply of minigrenades was clipped to her climbing harness and belt. Gaping cavities, created by missing tracks, threatened to send her plunging to the earth, but she bounded over them without hesitation, flinging the grenades all around the park below. The devices, which Hardison had procured by redirecting a delivery meant for some wacky right-wing militia, produced an impressive amount of light and noise, but that was all. She didn't want to actually blow up the coaster house, at least not while Sophie and her stalker were still trapped inside.

Maybe later, *she thought, although Nate and the others didn't really approve of recreational arson.* Party poopers.

"Parker," *Nate said in her ear.* "The sound equipment?"

"*Oh, right.*" *She had been so caught up in the thrill of running the rails that she had almost forgotten. Reaching into her pack, she extracted the first of several compact microspeaker/amplifiers, which she clamped to a relatively sturdy timber high atop the coaster.* "*Okay. Ready to go.*"

"That's my girl," *Hardison said.* "You wearing your ear protection?"

Parker scowled. She didn't like being babied. She hoped this wasn't going to become a thing.

"'Cause I'm being serious here," *he persisted.* "We're talking serious decibels, above and beyond the flash-bangs. Dolby Stereo meets Sensurround by way of rock concert volume. And I'd kind of like you to be able to hear me the next time I drop some pithy words of wisdom. You get what I'm saying, girl? I'm just looking out for those sharp little ears of yours. You know, the ones you use to crack all those safes?"

"*I get it.*" *She double-checked the fit of her industrial-strength muffs, which fit snugly over her ears. The sophisticated sonic filters protected her hearing while not interfering with the comm device deeper inside her ear.* "*I'm covered. Can we get on with it?*"

"You bet," *he said.* "Let's rock-and-roll, baby!"

Gunfire and helicopter noises blared from the miniature speaker, which Hardison had designed himself. Parker could even hear the thunderous sound effects through the heavy-duty muffs. Invisible rotors rattled JoyLand. She had to hand it to Hardison. For a dinky little gizmo, his mi-

crospeaker packed a lot of punch. The sound effects themselves had been sampled from a variety of news clips and action movies. Parker recognized a burst of automatic gunfire from Die Hard 5. If she didn't know better, she'd think a heavily armed assault team really was closing in on the coaster.

Nate's amplified voice issued from the speaker, joining the show:

"Attention! We have you surrounded. Throw down your weapons and surrender, or face severe consequences!"

Parker wondered why he'd gone with the southern accent. Were there no hard-ass military guys from Boston?

Real gunfire, shooting blindly from inside the house below, blasted through the tin roof dozens of feet beneath her. Bullets splintered the wooden rails not far from where she was standing. Springing from the curve at the top of the upper track, she dived for a horizontal support beam farther within the coaster. Momentum, competing with gravity, carried her across the empty space until her outstretched fingers caught on to the rickety beam, which tore loose beneath her weight. It swung sideways like a pendulum, out over one of the lower slopes of the coaster. Parker let go and fell toward the track below. She hit the track, rolling to absorb the impact, and tumbled through an open gap. At the last minute, she grabbed on to a rail and swung herself back up onto the track, nailing the landing like a gold-medal gymnast. She took a second to catch her breath.

"Parker? What's happening?" Hardison asked urgently. "You okay, girl?"

"Oh, yeah!" she exclaimed, grinning broadly. "Never better!"

Sure, the odds had been against the wild gunshots actually hitting her, but she couldn't afford to take a bullet right now. She still had work to do. Dashing up the nearest hill, she attached a second microspeaker to a support beam. She raced from one end of the coaster to another, tracing its steep slopes and curves. Despite a serious sleep deficit, she wasn't even breathing hard. Blood coursed through her veins, energizing her. She felt more like herself than she had in days.

This was what she lived for.

Or at least it used to be. Since she'd joined Nate's crew, her priorities had changed in ways she didn't entirely understand. The last few years had taught her that, bizarrely, there might be more to life than money, heists, and adrenaline. A crazy idea, no kidding, and she wasn't entirely convinced yet, but maybe, just maybe, she could be something more than a thief?

Still, that didn't mean that she couldn't let loose once in a while.

Flash-bangs flew from her fingers, keeping the "assault" going. The gunfire from indoors died off, so she clambered up to one of the elevated tracks running directly over the house and anchored one end of a carbon-fiber jump line to a flattened steel rail. The other end was attached to her customized climbing harness. She tugged once, to make certain both the line and the rail were secure, then threw herself off the track.

The cold air rushed past her face as she plunged toward the house below. Parker savored the sensation; diving off buildings was high on the list of her favorite things, along with theft and Tasers. The rush of free-falling ended too *soon, however, as the jump line's autobraking mechanism slowed her to a halt about ten feet above the coaster house. She dangled upside down.*

There was no time to bask in the afterglow. A brick chimney jutted up from the roof. Quite at ease hanging in the air, she unclipped a different kind of grenade from her belt and lobbed it into the chimney. The bomb disappeared down the shaft.

"Look out below!"

Seconds later, puffs of white smoke escaped the chimney. The chemical smoke was harmless enough, but would surely add to the confusion and chaos. By now, Beria and his flunkies had to be thinking that they were under attack by a full paramilitary strike force—and not just one fast-moving thief.

"Attention, all suspects!" Nate threatened at top volume. "Repeat, attention all suspects! Exit the building with your hands up! This is your final warning!"

Parker hit the retractor on the cord, which ratcheted her back up to the top of the coaster, before the idiots inside could open fire once more. She readied another smoke bomb and peered speculatively at the narrow opening of the chimney below.

Wonder if I could sink a bomb from here?

From her lofty vantage point, she could see Lucille parked on the other side of the fence. The front gate had been pried open and a pair of tiny figures, the size of dolls, scurried across the ruins of JoyLand. Everybody was moving into position, right according to the plan.

"So far, so good," she muttered.

It was almost time to kill Sophie.

—————

"You have this?" Eliot asked.

"Absolutely," Denise said. She had traded the tranquilizer gun for an M24 sniper rifle and enhanced thermal-imaging goggles. "I think we've already established that I'm the best sniper here."

"Says who?" Eliot said.

"Just the facts. You're a hitter. I'm a shooter."

They had taken up a position atop a boarded-up concession stand that offered a clear view of the house beneath the coaster. She got in place, belly down upon the roof of the stand, and took aim at a blacked-out window. The window interfered with the goggles to a degree, but she managed to make out five heat signatures inside the house. Beria, two flunkies, Larry . . . and Sophie.

Eliot crouched beside her. She knew he had to be worried about Sophie. "Try not to miss."

"I'm Tarantula, remember? I don't miss."

Her confident words belied a bad case of nerves. Her palms sweated inside leather gloves. It had been a long time since she had done this kind of thing—and seldom for such a good reason. The inked webbing on her neck itched even though she knew that had to be psychosomatic. Painful memories, that she had tried to trap between the pages of her book, threatened to overwhelm her.

Okata crumpled against the ventilation fan, his life leaking from his chest. He had saved her life on more than one occasion, but now he was dying on a Paris rooftop. A smoking rifle weighed down her hands. He coughed up blood.

"Assassins never forget . . ."

She shoved the distracting flashback aside.

Save it for the next book, *she thought. If there is one.*

Seen through the goggles, living targets inside the house showed up as glowing red silhouettes. The window blurred the images, and Parker's flash-bangs weren't helping, but Denise could still make out enough to shoot by. She assumed the female figure standing calmly in the middle of the chaos, surrounded by the bad guys, was Sophie, keeping her back to a window as planned. Denise tried to tune out the distracting flashes from Parker's grenades.

"Any time now," *Nate prompted. It felt strange hearing his voice in her ear. Hardison's clever little buds were certainly state-of-the-art. It sounded like Nate was right there with them, urging her on.* "We're on the clock."

"Tick, tock," she whispered.

She squeezed the trigger, firing in the space between her heartbeats, just like she had been trained to do. A single bullet shattered the distant window, missing Sophie by less than an inch, before slamming harmlessly into the fireplace. Given the clamor and smoke, there was a good chance that nobody would see where the bullet had really hit, what with Eliot's team staging their mock attack at the same time. Denise watched from afar as Parker dropped a second smoke bomb down the house's chimney in order to keep the bad guys off balance.

"It done?" Eliot asked.

Denise nodded and put down the rifle. She had done her part, just as Nate had requested.

Now it was all up to Sophie.

The shot blew out the window behind her.

That's my cue, _Sophie realized._

Nate always drew up multiple contingency plans, anticipating every possibility. Plan A had not involved Sophie being captured at all; the idea had been to liberate Brad, get the incriminating sequel (including Chapter Thirteen) into the hands of Beria and his associates, and then slip away under the cover of the zombie mob. In theory, no one would have been taken hostage and they would have planted the seeds of Beria's downfall. But then Larry had stuck his nose into things and Plan A had gone into the rubbish bin, as it usually did.

Time for Plan B, _she thought._ Or was it Plan C . . . ?

Gasping, she acted as though she had just been shot in the back. She clutched the fictitious wound and staggered forward like a woman on the verge of extinction. Trembling fingers groped poignantly for the fading light, a bit of business she borrowed from her classic performance as Cleopatra, post-asp. To truly sell the scene, she bit down hard on the inside of her mouth, drawing blood. It hurt like the dickens, naturally, but she wasn't the first actress to suffer for her art. The blood dribbled dramatically out of the corner of her mouth.

Beria, who had been lunging at her only a moment before, froze in surprise. His eyes bulged. His jaw dropped. He definitely hadn't seen this twist coming.

And so perishes Tarantula, _she thought._ Rest in peace.

Only then did she realize that she had neglected to craft some memorable last words for this death scene. Bugger, *she thought.* How did I forget that? *She couldn't meet her end without some choice dialogue. That was how a spear-carrier died, not a star. With no time to think of anything new, she did the next best thing.*

"The rest is silence," she moaned, cribbing from the Bard.

You really couldn't go wrong with the classics.

She collapsed into the convenient red coaster car, figuring it might provide a little extra cover if the bullets started flying for real. The swirling smoke enveloped her and she struggled not to cough or choke on the fumes. Playing dead was always harder than it looked.

"Dear Lord, no!" Larry blurted, sounding suitably horrified. "You got her killed, you fiend! Sophie Devereaux is dead!"

Sophie was touched by his outburst. It was good to know that her tragic demise had affected someone, even if it was only her stalker.

"Good riddance," Beria snarled.

Staying limp and seemingly lifeless, she listened as Beria's unhappy minions dragged their boss away. From the sound of things, the framed spymaster had plenty of explaining to do to his disgruntled accomplices.

Good luck with that, *she thought.*

"It was all faked?" Larry asked.

"All of it," Nate assured him. The van rolled toward Manhattan, leaving Brooklyn and Coney Island behind. "It's amazing what you can do with sound effects and fireworks these days."

"I guess," the shell-shocked fan said uncertainly. You could practically see him trying to make sense of everything that had happened to him since the ambush in the cemetery. He scratched his head in confusion. "But, wait, how did you find us anyway? How did you know where they were holding us?"

"Oh, that," Nate said.

EVEN EARLIER:

Parker wasn't the only team member taking part in the zombie walk. Nate shambled toward the churchyard, blending in with the other make-believe monsters. His disheveled hair was even more unruly than usual. His haggard face was gray and spotted with patches of fresh decomp. False teeth, fitting over his real ones, were jagged and clotted with gore. Like Parker, he had eschewed red or yellow contact lenses in favor of actually being able to see. The trick lenses hadn't been necessary either; after staying up two days straight to edit Assassins Remember, *his eyes were already bloodshot enough.*

Playing a zombie was easy; at this point, he felt like the living dead. He staggered down the crowded sidewalk like a drunk on a bender. Bristling whiskers cried out for a razor. His grimy, ill-fitting suit had seen better days. A blood-spotted tie hung askew around his neck. Scuffed shoes, splitting at the seams, dragged across the pavement. If not for the Halloween makeup and the accompanying mob, he could have easily been mistaken for a wino—and not for the first time.

Hardison had been disappointed by how generic Nate's zombie getup was. He had pressed Nate to go with something with more flair, like maybe a zombie ringmaster or rabbi, but Nate had not wanted to stand out in the crowd. The whole idea was to go unnoticed.

The mob carried him toward the black limousine idling outside the churchyard. Nate's eyes narrowed as he recognized the vehicle. A slow-burning sense of injustice, never terribly far away, flared up deep inside him. The limo was more than just a pricey means of transportation.

It was a murder weapon.

Moving anonymously within the throng, just another nameless nightwalker, he deftly slapped a magnetic tracking device beneath the limo's bumper.

"You reading that?" he asked.

"Like it's one of Oprah's picks," *Hardison replied.* "From now on, that bad boy's not going anywhere without us knowing."

Nate planted another bug on the limo just to be safe.

He glanced around. As expected, nobody seemed to have noticed his sleight of hand. He shambled past the limo into the churchyard, where Beria's inevitable double cross had succumbed to some well-orchestrated zombie bedlam. Nate tried to pinpoint the rest of his crew, but it was a lost cause. It was a mob scene, literally.

"Nate!" Parker said. "I lost Sophie . . . I think."

Nate's mouth went dry. He had been worried about something like that happening. There was no way around it; passing Sophie off as Tarantula was a risky play. For a moment his own complicated feelings for Sophie threatened to cloud his thinking, but he shoved that part of him-

271

self back into a box. Losing his head wasn't going to help anybody, let alone Sophie.

"Stick to the plan," *he said brusquely.* "No matter what."

"But . . ."

"Keep moving, Parker."

Following his own advice, he focused on his next objective: Anton Beria. The frustrated spymaster was caught up in the middle of the flash mob, trying to cope with the chaos. Nate was pleased to see that Beria had managed to hang on to the briefcase in the confusion. Never underestimate a spook's grip on his secrets, *Nate thought.* They don't surrender them readily.

He was also pleased to observe that Beria was on his own for the moment, having been temporarily deprived of his goon squad.

Thank you, Parker and Eliot, *Nate thought.*

Moaning hungrily, Nate maneuvered through the mob, charting an intercept course with Beria. The same horde that sheltered Nate also slowed him down, but he eventually managed to get within arm's reach of the other man. Nate's questing fingers brushed against the back of Beria's coat, leaving a bug behind.

Got you, *Nate thought smugly.*

Even if Beria managed to recapture Sophie, and located her earbud, it was unlikely that he would think to search himself. Or the murder car.

They had him tagged, redundantly.

Nate smirked behind his greasy gray makeup. He slipped back into the zombie horde, which was growing larger and more out of control by the second. Wannabe monsters bumped and jostled him. An undead beauty queen, complete with a tiara and a sash, wailed shrilly in his ear.

Forget brains, *he thought.* I need a drink.

The bugs had led them straight to Coney Island and the "abandoned" amusement park, but, of course, Nate couldn't tell Larry that. He needed to come up with a different story for Sophie's stalker, one that left the crew and its operations less exposed.

"Why wouldn't we know where you were?" Nate said. "It was all part of the movie."

"Movie?" Larry could not have looked more baffled. Too many twists in too short an interval had his head spinning. "What movie?"

"*The* movie." Nate looked over at Sophie, who was brushing her frazzled hair back into something less horrific. "You did tell him you were going to a movie shoot, right?"

"Well, I wasn't really at liberty to discuss it," she said, playing along. Her dark eyes gleamed with amusement. She smiled mischievously. "Perhaps it would be better if you explained . . ."

He accepted the challenge.

"See, it's your basic *Candid Camera*/cinema vérité/ found footage kind of thing, shot in real time with hidden cameras and spontaneous, unscripted reactions. Like *Blair Witch* meets *Borat.*"

"Very cutting edge," Sophie insisted, "blurring the lines between reality and artifice." She effortlessly slipped into the role of an enthusiastic leading lady. "I'm quite excited to be a part of it."

Larry looked at Nate. "And you're . . . the director?"

"Always," Sophie said drily.

"But . . ." Larry took another swig from the flask to steady his nerves. He struggled visibly to reconcile his memories with Nate's explanation. He questioned Sophie with his eyes. "But you said it wasn't a movie."

"Of course I was going to say that," she explained, as though it was patently obvious. "I was *in character* at that point. And the cameras were rolling."

"What cameras?" Larry blurted. "I didn't see any cameras!"

"Naturally," Nate said. "That was the point." He beckoned to Hardison, who was seated a few feet away at his computer terminal. "Show him."

Hardison caught on right away. "Come on, man," he scoffed to Larry. "You don't think we still use those big cumbersome cameras and lighting setups anymore? That's so old-school."

He scooted across the back of the van and plucked the miniature spy cam from Eliot's cap. "Hey!" the hitter barked. "Keep your hands to yourself!"

"Don't mind him," Hardison said. "You know how testy stuntmen can be. Comes from being dropped on their heads so many times."

Eliot glared at Hardison. "I'll drop you—"

"See, this here's what I'm talking about," Hardison said, ignoring Eliot. He held out his hand, displaying the captured spy cam on his palm. "Full audio and visual pickup, from a state-of-the-art microcamera less than the size of a malted milk ball. Plant a few of these beauties around your locations, to get plenty of coverage, and you could shoot an entire trilogy downtown right under everybody's noses. Edit the raw footage into shape, add some CGI and whatnot in post, redub any lost dialogue, and . . . bingo, you got yourself a movie!"

He made it sound convincing, Nate thought. But would Larry buy it?

"So all of that was being filmed?" Larry asked. "Even the part where I fainted?"

"After valiantly confronting the bad guys after my death," Sophie stressed, "which I was deeply touched by, incidentally. As a matter of fact, I was wearing one of those hidden cameras myself, as were the very talented actors playing the villains."

She was lying, of course. Beria's scanner would have detected any hidden scanner on her person. But Larry didn't need to know it. Just as long as it sounded plausible, and there was actual physical hardware to back it up.

"But I really thought you had died!" Larry protested. His voice quavered as he relived the horror of her shooting. He shook with emotion. "I thought *I* was going to die!"

"Which only made your unscripted reactions all the more intense and dramatic," Nate said. "You really sold the senseless tragedy of Sophie's death. It was a lucky break having you there. Better than anything we could have planned."

"It gave me chills, brother," Hardison said. "Sincerely."

"I understand that it was hard on you at times," Sophie said, taking his hand. "But what were we to do when you unexpectedly inserted yourself into the zombie scene? It was vital that we stayed in the moment; the very conception of the project demanded that we keep on filming. And in the end, I think we captured something very real and powerful." She gazed at him fondly. "Thank you so much for bringing the truth of your own personal experience to our artistic endeavor."

"Of course, you're going to need to sign a release," Nate said. He snapped his fingers and looked around. "Who's got the releases?"

Hardison and Sophie exchanged embarrassed looks. Eliot and Denise shrewdly kept out of the conversation. "Don't look at me," Parker called out from the driver's seat. She still had a few leftover grenades clipped to her belt. "Talk to legal."

"Er, I think we forgot the releases," Hardison confessed.

Nate feigned exasperation. "Christ on a crutch, people! Do I have to do everything around here?" He gave Larry an apologetic look. "Guess we'll just have to e-mail it to you later. And a comprehensive nondisclosure agreement, you understand."

"Nondisclosure?"

"Just the usual boilerplate, nothing to worry about," Nate said. "After all, we can't have you giving away the plot of our movie before it's ready to be released. We just need you to swear that you won't tell anybody what you saw— until the film opens, that is."

Not that there was ever going to be a film.

"Spoilers suck, man." Hardison grimaced in disgust. "Gotta hate the spoilers."

"Larry understands about all that," Sophie said, batting

her lashes. "I'm sure he wouldn't want to do anything to ruin my big break. Would you, Larry?"

"No, of course not," Larry said quickly. "But I'm still not sure how—"

"Great!" Nate slapped Larry on the back. "We'll just send those forms along, then. Make sure we've dotted all our *i*'s and crossed our *t*'s."

"Don't forget the restraining order," Eliot muttered.

Sophie shut him up with a look. "He's just joking. I don't need to worry about you, do I? After all, you're my biggest fan."

"Er, about that," Larry said sheepishly. He slid his sweaty hand out of hers. "I'm glad, really truly, that you're not actually dead and all, and that you've got this big new movie in the works, but I'm thinking, now that I've finally got your autograph, that maybe I should branch out a little. Broaden my horizons, you know?"

Sophie was taken aback. Her hand went to her heart.

"You don't want to stal—I mean, follow my career anymore?"

He tried to break it to her gently. "No offense, but this new direction of yours, it's a bit . . . too intense . . . for my tastes. Maybe it's time I move on and give another actress a chance?"

"Such as?"

"I'm thinking maybe Lindsay Lohan," he said.

"Oh."

Nate winced in sympathy. It was never easy getting dumped by your own stalker.

"In fact, if you could drop me off somewhere, anywhere,

that would be great." He stared longingly at the door, as though he couldn't wait to put the van—and this whole nightmarish experience—behind him. "Like now, maybe?"

"But we're crossing the Brooklyn Bridge," Nate pointed out.

Larry didn't care. "I'm good."

Five minutes later, they had left Larry on a high pedestrian walkway, clutching his scrapbook and Nate's flask. Sophie had needed to remind him to take the former, which he had almost left behind in his haste to get away.

"How sharper than a serpent's tooth," she murmured as they drove away.

"Don't let it get to you," Nate consoled her. "The public is fickle, you know that. You'll have other stalkers."

"You really think so?"

"I know it," he assured her. "Comes with being the world's greatest actress."

She sighed. "It *is* my cross to bear . . ."

He wasn't lying when he told her that she was the greatest actress he knew. It was just that her finest performances were seen only by their targets.

"Besides, Larry was never your number one fan, not really." Nate smiled warmly at her, unlocking that box just a crack. "That position is taken."

She glowed. "You know, that may just be the sweetest thing you've ever said to me."

He shrugged. "Once in a while, I get lucky."

"No, that comes later," she teased him. "Back at the hotel."

Nate was momentarily at a loss for words.

"Ahem," Eliot said, clearing his throat. "We got company, remember?"

"How could I forget?" Nate shared a brief, private look with Sophie before turning his attention to their client. Denise looked up as he approached. "Thanks again for your assistance," he said. "To be honest, I don't ordinarily approve of clients taking part in the proceedings, but rules are made to be broken, I guess, especially when dealing with a trained professional such as yourself."

"But I'm not a professional," Denise said firmly. She took off her wool cap, letting her red hair tumble down. She had already washed the camouflage paint from her face. "Not anymore."

Good for you, Nate thought. Everybody deserved a second chance.

"But what about Beria?" Eliot asked. "We still going after him?"

Nate shook his head. "I think we can count on his own people to take care of that for us."

LATER:

The old man trudged along the beach at Coney Island, taking his usual early morning stroll. The tide was out and Lily, his Jack Russell terrier, tugged eagerly at her leash. In the summer, when the picnickers and sunbathers descended by the thousands, the beach could be too crowded to traverse, but on this cold October morning, the old man and his dog had the miles-long expanse of sand and surf all to themselves. A salty breeze blew off the ocean. To his right, the Boardwalk ran parallel to the shore, beneath the shadow of the slumbering Wonder Wheel. Gulls cawed overhead. Rush-hour traffic sounded more than a mere block away.

A damp chill began to settle into the man's bones. Hot coffee and a microwaved bowl of leftover clam chowder called to him. He pulled on Lily's leash.

"C'mon, girl. Let's head back. Breakfast's waiting."

Lily perked up her ears at the b-word.

Before they could turn back toward the Boardwalk, however, the terrier lifted her nose to sniff the air. Her head turned toward the shore.

"What is it, girl? You smell something?"

All at once the dog raced toward the waves, nearly yanking the old man's arm from his socket. Lily dragged him across the beach.

"Whoa there! Not so fast!"

He let go of the leash, figuring there was no harm in letting her run free. It wasn't like she was going to get hit by a car on the beach. There was nothing around but sand and ocean. He could always call her back if she went too far.

Lily ran toward the edge of the water, yapping furiously. The old man followed to investigate. He wondered what had the dog so worked up.

Probably a dead fish or crab, *he guessed.* Or some smelly flotsam.

But as he got closer, he saw a body lying in the surf. Seaweed was tangled around the motionless figure. Waves lapped over the body, which was facedown in the sand.

"Oh, crap," the old man said. He had grown up along the ocean and he knew a floater when he saw one. His mind ran through the usual possibilities: suicide, accident, the mob.

Lily yapped excitedly. Reclaiming her leash, the man pulled her away from the body. "C'mon, girl. Leave it alone."

Curiosity compelled him to check out the body, which belonged to a lean, middle-aged gentleman in what had once been an expensive suit. Duct tape clung to his wrists. A single gunshot wound, to the back of his head, made it clear that he had been dispatched execution-style.

So much for suicide, *the old man thought.*

Lily tugged a stick from the sand nearby, then trotted over to show it to her human. At first, the man thought it was just a piece of driftwood, but then he realized that it was actually part of a broken ebony cane, which must have washed up along with the stiff. The old man shook his head. It looked like it had been a nice cane.

He fished out his cell phone. Shaking fingers dialed 911. "Hello, police? I'd like to report a body."

LOS ANGELES

WORLD PREMIERE proclaimed the lighted marquee of Grauman's Chinese Theatre, which was lit up like a Christmas ornament in brilliant hues of red and green. The world-famous movie palace was a vision of Oriental splendor, its ornate exterior embodying Hollywood's idea of a traditional Chinese pagoda. Towering coral-red columns, adorned with elaborate wrought-iron masks, flanked the entrance, which was guarded by a pair of imported stone Heaven Dogs. A thirty-foot-high stone dragon coiled above the front entrance. Copper-topped turrets rose from the jade-green roof. Dramatic lighting added to the effect as the landmark theater played host to the gala premiere of *Assassins Never Forget,* now a major motion picture.

A parade of stretch limousines disgorged well-dressed celebrities, who posed on the red carpet for the fans and paparazzi swarming Hollywood's Walk of Fame. A barrage of camera flashes strobed the scene. Massive floodlights projected wheeling beams of light high into the darkening sky. It was a beautiful summer evening, and everybody who was anybody had turned out for the premiere, as had a few very special guests.

"Admit it," Sophie said, resplendent in a red satin gown. Standing off to one side, away from the red carpet, she basked in the old-time Tinsel Town glamour. You could practically smell the showbiz in the air. "Wasn't this worth making a special trip for?"

"I'm glad you're enjoying yourself," said Nate, her escort for the evening. He had cleaned up nicely for the occasion, looking positively dapper in a tailored Armani suit that, for once, didn't look slept in. He had even gotten a decent haircut. "Hold on for just a moment," he said, consulting his smartphone with a distracted air. "There's this slumlord in Chicago I've got my eye on . . ."

"Oh, no you don't," she said firmly, confiscating the phone. "You can put the job on hold for one night. For my sake, if not for yours."

"But you don't understand. This guy is trying to drive out his tenants by . . ." He started to protest, but relented. "All right. I guess he can wait." He took her arm and watched the glitzy spectacle with her. "I'm sorry you didn't get a chance to walk the red carpet yourself, but that might be a bit too conspicuous. There's something to be said for keeping a low profile, considering."

"I know." She couldn't deny that the spotlight called out to her, especially given how dazzling she looked tonight, but he was right. It wouldn't do for their faces to be plastered all over *People* magazine and glimpsed on *Entertainment Tonight,* not if she needed to impersonate a real estate agent or nuclear physicist next week. "Besides, it's not as though I haven't crashed plenty of red-carpet events in the past. This is just the first time I've never had to con my way in."

"Feel free to pose as a countess if it will make you feel more comfortable," Nate said. "I can always be your oily European gigolo."

"Thanks for the offer, but tonight I'm happy to be myself." She glanced across the courtyard at another couple attending the premiere. "Parker and Hardison look like they're having a good time."

"I see," Nate said. "Should we be worried?"

"C-3PO has tiny feet," Parker observed.

She and Hardison were checking out the famous Forecourt of the Stars, where generations of Hollywood legends had left impressions of their hands, feet, and miscellaneous body parts in the cement courtyard in front of the theater. More than two hundred colored concrete blocks, bearing the imprints of everyone from the Marx Brothers to Trigger, surrounded the pair. Hardison literally stood in Darth Vader's footprints.

"The magic of the movies," he said, decked out in a powder-blue tuxedo and shades. "Makes even an ordinary protocol droid seem larger than life." Like millions of starstruck visitors before him, he placed his own hand within Vader's glove print, seeing how they compared. He couldn't help wondering if it would be possible to lift a human star's fingerprints from one of the other blocks. It was something to think about, for future reference.

"Feel the power of the Dark Side," he murmured.

"Always," Parker said. Contemplating the robot footprints before her, she kicked off her shoes.

"Hold on there," he said, restraining her. "Not sure you want to be doing that. This is a formal event, you know. Shoes and shirts strictly required."

"Seriously?" Parker said, disappointed. She wiggled back into her shoes. Her embroidered black jumpsuit had been picked out by Sophie, who had also personally taken charge of Parker's hair and makeup. The blond thief had already pocketed her earrings and necklace.

Hardison thought she looked like a movie star.

Taking her hand, he dragged her across the sprawling forecourt, in search of his ultimate goal. A daunting collection of concrete signatures stretched before them. You needed a map to find the block you were looking for.

Fortunately, there was an app for that.

"Full impulse ahead!" he said eagerly, quickening his pace. He consulted the interactive map on his phone. "Sensors indicated that we are coming within visual range of . . . oh my."

His voice grew hushed as he gazed upon the holy of holies: a concrete block bearing the handprints and signatures of Gene Roddenberry, William Shatner, Leonard Nimoy, and the entire cast of *Star Trek*. A bronze plaque in the center of the square bore an embossed image of the starship *Enterprise*.

"O, Great Bird of the Galaxy," Hardison whispered,

choking up. His eyes watered. "Excuse me, I need a moment . . ."

Parker was somewhat less awestruck. "Which was the one with the ears?"

She stepped forward for a closer look, about to set foot on George Takei's splayed handprints.

"Red alert!" Hardison blurted in alarm. "Reverse all thrusters!" He yanked on her arm, pulling her back before she could plant her heels in the final frontier. "What in the name of the United Federation of Planets are you thinking, girl? You don't go stomping over sacred ground like that. You just don't." He formed the Vulcan salute with his fingers. "Respect the five-year mission. Live long and prosper."

Parker tried to make the sign back, with mixed results. She cocked her head and examined him like she would a tricky combination lock, making an effort to understand. "This means a lot to you, doesn't it?"

"Girl, you have no idea. This here, it's a geek relic. A genuine slab of sci-fi history."

"Oh," she said. "You want me to steal it for you?"

The suggestion caught him by surprise, like a Klingon battle cruiser decloaking.

"No! I mean, you can't be serious. That would be wrong, so wrong." He hesitated, imagining how the block would look on display in his apartment, next to his collection of vintage Mego action figures. "Wouldn't it?"

Parker grinned evilly.

Going inside the theater, Sophie and Nate met up with Eliot and Denise in the opulent lobby. Gleaming red-and-gold columns supported the lofty ceiling. Colorful murals captured exotic scenes from the Far East. A vast chandelier, far more impressive than the one that had once graced Brad Lee's tacky Long Island mansion, glittered overhead. The hubbub of excited voices echoed off the walls.

"Good to see you again," Sophie greeted their former client. Several months had passed since the Leverage crew had straightened out Denise's problems, and since Beria's body had washed up on the beach. "Thanks so much for inviting us to the premiere."

"Are you kidding?" Denise replied. She looked much happier and healthier than she had when they had first met back in Boston. Shadows no longer haunted her eyes, and a weight seemed to have lifted from her shoulders now that Gavin's death had finally been avenged. A metallic copper gown matched the brass compass she still wore. She gave Sophie an enthusiastic hug. "It was the absolute least I can do. You folks put everything right . . . and made all of this possible."

Nate grudgingly accepted a hug as well. "We're looking forward to seeing the movie," he said, although Sophie knew that he would rather be running down a slumlord, crooked tycoon, or war profiteer. She couldn't remember the last time he'd simply gone out to a movie.

Baby steps, she thought.

"Speaking of which," Denise said, turning back to Sophie, "I'm sorry nothing came of that audition. I put in a good word for you, but you know how it goes. Since when does Hollywood listen to the author . . . or the executor of the author's estate? The book is all mine these days, but I'm afraid I didn't have much say over the casting of the movie."

"I'm sure you did your best," Sophie said graciously. She was disappointed not to have landed a part in the film, after killing the audition, but apparently it was not meant to be. "I can't complain, really. After all, I've already played the starring role . . ."

"Until I killed you," Denise said.

"That was a pretty good shot," Eliot recalled. "Not sure I could have pulled it off."

That was high praise coming from him. He and Denise made a nice couple, Sophie thought, seeing them together for the first time since they'd wrapped up the sequel scam. Eliot never talked about it, of course, but Sophie wondered what exactly had happened between Denise and him.

Not that it was any of her business.

EARLIER:

"You look great," Eliot said, admiring Denise, who was stunning. "More than great, actually."

"You, too," she replied. There was an awkward pause before she came forward and gave him a peck on the check. He didn't know what to do with his hands. "It's been too long."

They disengaged in a less than strategic manner.

"Who's counting?" he lied.

Things had been hot and heavy for a while, but then, after laying Gavin's ghost to rest, they had eventually drifted back to their own lives. Calls and visits had grown less fre-

quent, *increasingly preempted by one crisis or another. Their last real rendezvous had been months ago.*

"*I'm sorry I haven't called or e-mailed more,*" *she apologized,* "*but what with taking charge of Gavin's estate, finding an actual agent I can trust, a new apartment in a new city . . .*"

"*You're moving on,*" *he translated.* "*I get it.*"

Despite what had gone down between them in New York, he suspected that Denise was ready for a new life now, one that didn't involve a hitter with a guilty past— and an old friend of Gavin's. All of that was behind her now, or it ought to be.

"*Do you?*" *she asked.* "*Really?*"

He let her off the hook.

"*I'm fine,*" *he said.* "*Don't worry about me.*"

In retrospect, he should have seen this coming. Women came and went in his life, which was probably just as well. His life didn't lend itself to white picket fences and anniversaries, at least not anymore. Permanent attachments were not in the cards. It was better that way.

Or so he kept telling himself.

"*I'm happy for you,*" *he said.*

The A-list crowd was beginning to make its way toward the auditorium. Palatial staircases led to the upper balconies. Hardison and Parker joined the others in the lobby, but there was no need to rush. Their seats were reserved.

"So things are going well?" Nate asked Denise.

"It's been a like a dream," she said. "The hype over the movie has shot *Assassins* back onto the bestseller list, which means more royalties that I can donate to human rights groups throughout the world. And, maybe I'm being naive, but I like to think that all this attention might lead to increased public awareness of what people like Beria are up to. There have already been plenty of feature stories asking how real the world depicted in *Assassins* is."

"I saw the piece on *60 Minutes*," Nate said. "Strong stuff. I hear there's even talk of a congressional investigation."

A wistful look came over Denise's face. "I just wish Gavin could see all this."

"How do you know he can't?" Nate said.

Sophie recalled that Nate was a former altar boy, who had once contemplated going into the priesthood and even attended seminary. Lucky for her, he had reconsidered.

Nowadays he preferred to play God instead.

"I'd like to think so," Denise admitted. "Things are going so well, in fact, that I might even write a sequel . . . for real this time."

"Just keep us out of it," Nate said.

ACKNOWLEDGMENTS

On *Leverage*, the crew's grateful clients always thank Nate and Eliot and Sophie and Hardison and Parker for everything they've done. Books are the same way. I could not have written this novel without the help and support of several key individuals, all of who deserve my gratitude.

First off, I want to thank my talented editor, Ginjer Buchanan, for thinking of me in the first place. And my agent, Russ Galen, for making sure the deal happened.

And I'm grateful to the real-life *Leverage* crew, including John Rogers, who carefully reviewed my outlines and manuscript and offered many valuable suggestions, and Geoffrey Thorne, who allowed me to pick his brains on matters *Leverage*-related—during the San Diego Comic-Con, no less! And to my friend Rob Brubaker for suggesting one particular bit on business.

Finally, none of this would have been possible without my girlfriend, Karen Palinko, who let me take over our air-conditioned kitchen so that I could keep on writing even during a brutal heat wave, and who provided generous amounts of emotional and logistical support throughout. And, of course, I have to mention our four-legged distractions—Henry, Sophie, and Lyla—who kept me sane by occasionally dragging me away from the keyboard for walks and games of fetch.

Oddly, it's the cat who wants to play fetch. . . .